ALL GONE

AN IRELAND & CARTER THRILLER

A NOVEL BY
JOEL GOLDMAN
&
LISA KLINK

Published by Character Flaw Press, LLC

ISBN-13: 9780990868729
ISBN-10: 0990868729

Published in the United States of America

Books by Joel Goldman

Motion to Kill
The Last Witness
Cold Truth
Deadlocked
Final Judgment
Shakedown
The Dead Man
No Way Out
Stone Cold
Chasing The Dead
Freaks Must Die

Books by Lisa Klink

Slaves to Evil
Evil to Burn

Reborn

Books by Joel Goldman & Lisa Klink
All In
All Gone

For Greyson & Asher —
The Next Generation

ONE

In a northern suburb of London, Sarah St. James lay in her dark bedroom, tossing side-to-side. Wide awake, she let out a sigh and sat up. The clock on the nightstand next to her bed read *Monday 3:48 a.m.*

Her husband Michael stirred. "What is it now, luv?"

"You'll think I'm crazy."

Michael propped himself on his elbow. "Already do, that's why I married you."

After twelve years of curating medieval manuscripts for the British Library, Sarah had been assigned to curate the Unification exhibit displaying the four remaining original copies of the Magna Cartas together for the first time in eight hundred years. At thirty-four years old, it was her first major exhibit and would be a career make or break moment. She'd devoted the past year and a half to perfecting every detail, promising Michael, that when it was over, they would start the family that he'd pressed for every time she told him she wouldn't be home for dinner.

"It's the little details that are driving me mad," she said. "I can't remember if I told the maintenance crew to fix the wobbly sign under the portrait of King John."

Michael peered at the clock. The exhibit opened in six hours. "I can live with a crazy wife but not one that's stark raving mad so go have a look."

Sarah leaned over and kissed him. She took a quick shower and put on the dark green, scholarly-yet-stylish dress she'd purchased for the grand opening. She applied make-up to soften her cheekbone's sharp angles and tried fixing her thick, sandy brown hair in various styles before pulling it back into its usual, functional knot, reminding herself this was a museum exhibit opening, not a red-carpet affair.

As she drove to the Library, the list of details to check and double-check grew, making her more anxious. Once she reached the parking lot, she began to feel better because she was doing something instead of just worrying. She dashed through the rain to the staff entrance and pressed the intercom button, then dug her ID badge out of her purse and held it up to the camera. At that hour, it was the only way into the Library.

"Hi, Dr. St. James. Back again, eh." said Colin Saunders, one of the guards manning the security control room. It was her third pre-dawn appearance this week.

"Hi, Colin. I'm going to the Magna Carta exhibit, so could you…"

"Turn off the motion detectors?" He hit a control at his workstation. "Already done. I'll let the other guards know that you're here so they don't get excited if they see you roaming the halls."

"You're an angel," she said.

Colin buzzed her into the building. The exhibit was in the PAC-CAR gallery, named in appreciation for a generous contribution by PACCAR, Inc. A steel gate that descended from the ceiling closed the gallery off from the rest of the Library.

The gallery began with a long, wide entry hall. *Magna Carta 1215-2015* was written in large Gothic script on one wall. Surveillance cameras and infra-red motion detectors were mounted throughout.

Down a short flight of stairs, the gallery spread out into an open, two-story space with freshly painted white walls and new gray carpet. Temporary interior walls created a path through a series of exhibits describing the history and politics of 13th century England, setting the stage for the world-changing documents visitors would line up around the block to see.

The Magna Cartas were kept in custom-built display cases lined up side by side in an alcove against a dramatic red wall. Each stood forty inches tall, with wide pedestal bases covered in oak veneer. Beneath the veneer were removable panels that provided access to the Magna Cartas. Like the rest of the security for the exhibit, the cases had been designed by Titan Security Solutions.

The Magna Cartas were encased under impregnable glass hoods, each framed copy sealed in protective acrylic. The frames rested on motion sensors that would sound an alarm if they were moved. All four documents rested on plush red velvet, angled upward to offer visitors the best view, illuminated by floodlights in the ceiling.

Sarah swiped her badge through the card reader next to the steel gate, tapping her foot as it slowly rose. She was pleased to see that the sign beneath the portrait of King John had been put straight. Everything was ready. The grand opening just might be a success and she just might keep her job and make her husband a father.

She was about to chide herself for needlessly worrying when she saw a sheet of oak veneer lying on the gray carpet just inside the archway leading to the room where the Magna Cartas were displayed. Puzzled, she continued into the room and saw that the veneer had been stripped from each display case, the access panels were lying on the floor and the glass hoods were open. Suddenly unsteady, she ventured a few steps closer until she saw that the cases were empty.

"Noooo."

Staggered, she grabbed hold of an open case, then looked around the room, blinking, not wanting to believe what she was seeing. Her gaze stopped on a folded piece of paper lying inside one of the cases. She picked it up, wishing it contained a reprieve, the message printed in bold font crushing her faint hope.

One hundred million pounds for the safe return of the Magna Cartas. No police or they go in the shredder. You've got five days. Wait for instructions.

To make the point, a thin strip of torn parchment was taped to the page. She couldn't tell if it had been ripped from one of the Magna Cartas but it was enough to send a chill through her.

Her initial shock gave way to her curator's training. Mounting an exhibit was all about the details. Every object, every display case, every sign, light and rope line had to be exactly right. And the exhibit had to be secure.

Only three people had ID cards that would open the steel gate that protected the gallery - Malcolm Bridges, who'd designed the security for the display, Ian Thorpe, the Library's Director of Security, and her. Motion detectors should have sounded an alarm the instant the thieves crossed the threshold and video cameras should have recorded their every movement.

Even if they'd gotten past all that, they should never have been able to break into display cases Bridges had assured were fail safe. And, if they'd somehow done that, the motion sensors inside the cases should have triggered alarms the instant they touched the Magna Cartas.

She looked at a camera mounted in the corner of the ceiling, waving her arms and jumping up and down. Yet Colin didn't call on the public address to ask her what was wrong. He must have seen the wreckage, if not the actual robbery. But how could he have and not summoned Ian Thorpe and the police.

She stuffed the ransom note in her dress pocket and turned her attention to the empty frames in each case, wondering about the duct tape stretched across the frames. Kneeling for a closer look, she saw thin cuts around the edge of the acrylic sheets. She dug her thumbnail under the corner and lifted the loose panel. So that was how they had removed the Magna Cartas. And, they'd used the duct tape to hold the frames in place to avoid setting off the pressure sensors. Clever.

Sarah knew nothing about criminal investigations but she'd read enough about museum robberies to know they were often inside jobs. She couldn't imagine Colin being part of it. He was too dim for that. And if he were, she doubted he would have hung around to finish his shift.

Before she called Ian Thorpe, she wanted to see the video footage of the gallery. It would soften the blow if she could tell him that they had the thieves on tape. She took the stairs to Basement Level One and knocked on the door to the security control room.

Another guard, Paulie Reed, opened the door and she brushed past him. "Colin, let's have a look at the Magna Carta exhibit."

"Sure thing, Dr. St. James."

Sarah was stunned for a second time when the images from the gallery showed the display cases intact and the Magna Cartas resting safely inside.

"That can't be right," she managed.

"That's the live feed from the gallery," Colin assured her.

"Run the tape back to yesterday's closing and then fast forward it."

He pointed at one of the other monitors. "I'll pull it up on number 12."

Sarah stared spellbound as the rewound tape ran forward at high speed. No one entered the gallery. No one broke into the display cases and no one stole the Magna Cartas. She wanted to believe that she'd lost her mind and imagined the whole thing but she knew better. The thieves had opened the gate, disabled the motion detectors and blinded the cameras. More than clever, it was bloody brilliant. But that only happened in the movies, not in her library. How could it?

"Where are the other guards?"

"Patrolling, I expect, ma'am," Paulie said. He pronounced it 'mum', making her feel ancient. "Three inside and two outside."

"Have any of them reported anything unusual?"

"Like what?" Colin asked.

"Anything!" She heard herself shouting and calmed her voice. "Strange noises? An object out of place?"

Paulie shook his head. "It's been quiet as an empty church."

Sarah stepped away from the monitors and leaned against a wall. Incredible as it seemed, she was the only one, besides the thieves, who knew that the Magna Cartas had been stolen. But that was going to change as soon as she called Ian Thorpe. She checked her watch. In five hours, forty-one minutes, the rest of the world would know when the exhibit was canceled. And Thorpe would convince the board it was her fault so they would sack her.

Worse, even if Thorpe and the board didn't go to the police, it would be impossible to keep the theft quiet even if the exhibit was sealed off. There were no secrets in this building. Once the news broke, Scotland Yard would swarm the library. She closed her eyes, shuddering as she imagined the thieves feeding the Magna Cartas into a shredder. Eight hundred years after King John signed the Magna Carta, the four remaining original copies would be destroyed.

The media would blister the Library for failing to protect the priceless historical treasures in its care. Which would drive away donors, and discourage patrons from loaning their collections to the

Library, which would then attract fewer visitors, and the downward spiral would go on. She'd seen it happen to other institutions before. It would be calamity piled upon catastrophe. For now, the situation was contained. Maybe she could keep it that way.

"Dr. St. James?" Colin's voice startled her. She'd forgotten the young men were even there. She turned to see them staring at her like she'd gone off her nut.

"Sorry to disturb," she muttered, and left the control room.

The idea taking shape in her mind was utter lunacy, she told herself as she headed to the second floor, keeping watch for security guards. As if she were one of the thieves.

She let herself into the Conservation Centre. She'd spent hours there, supervising the conservators as they painstakingly cleaned and repaired her precious manuscripts. The Digital Preservation team took it a step further. They were in the process of digitizing the Library's entire collection, using a high-resolution scanner to create image files of every document and every book that would far outlast the originals.

She logged into the computer next to the scanner. She knew that the team had scanned in the London and Canterbury Magna Cartas the Library owned and desperately hoped that they had also scanned the visiting documents from the Salisbury and Lincoln Cathedrals.

"Oh, thank you, Lord," she said, letting out a breath and leaning back in her chair when she found digital files for all the Magna Cartas.

She stared at the images, running through her impossibly crazy plan. Each step took her closer to the point of no return. If she failed, Thorpe would probably accuse her of being an accomplice despite her good intentions but the alternative was equally terrible. Carry on, she told herself.

She needed parchment to print the Magna Cartas. Unfortunately, the Library didn't keep a stock of blank, eight hundred-year old parchment on hand. She would have to use the fake stuff. As part of the Unification event, the Library was offering classes and activities for visitors of all ages, including a hands-on workshop where students used medieval bookbinding techniques to make their own authentic-looking replicas.

She slipped down the hall to the Learning Centre and collected sheets of imitation parchment, regular paper which had been aged by crumpling it up in a ball, soaking it in tea and fraying the edges. To her expert eye, it was clearly phony, but it would have to do. Back in the Conservation Centre, she printed a copy of the London Magna Carta on the imitation parchment. Then she took an empty frame from the storage cabinet and slid the document inside.

For the first time since she discovered the theft, she started to smile. The fake looked good enough. In the proper frame, behind a thick glass hood, it could pass for the real thing until they could recover the originals. At least, to an untrained observer. If a Magna Carta scholar or documents expert examined it too closely, they would recognize a tell-tale difference in the fiber content of the paper, or the reflective quality of the ink. She'd have to put up velvet ropes to keep people a safe distance away.

Sarah printed the other three Magna Cartas and hurried to the entrance to PACCAR gallery, watching for security guards and re-hearsing what she'd say if she ran into someone. But luck was on her side and she didn't see a soul.

Back inside the gallery, she stopped for a moment to consider the cameras. Whatever the thieves had done to disable them had better keep working long enough for her to commit her own crime. That's what she was about to do, she realized. Presenting forgeries as authen-tic historic documents was fraud. Career ending, prison risking fraud.

The hell with that. This was her exhibit. She would make the deci-sions and face the consequences. She could and would make this work. She slid the Salisbury copy under the acrylic in its frame and removed the duct tape. Then she eased the hood down into its slot around the base.

Sarah stood back a few feet and regarded the display. The phony Magna Carta looked like the real thing, even to someone who knew better. From here, she couldn't see the cuts in the acrylic. This was going to work.

She still had to replace the access panels and the wood veneers. She retrieved a toolbox from a utility closet and got to work. When she finished, she placed a set of brass posts and velvet ropes several feet from the cases to keep people from looking too closely at the fakes. That was the best she could do. She had either saved the exhibit or destroyed her life. Only time would tell.

More importantly, she had to get the Magna Cartas back safely. To do that, she had to come up with a hundred million pounds in five days. The Library certainly didn't have that kind of money to spare. But the Magna Carta Trust might. The Trustees were some of the wealthiest people in England and had been appointed to protect the Magna Carta and preserve its principles. They'd provided much of the funding for the preservation of the original documents and for the Unification exhibit.

She was grateful for the financial support. But the Trustees, led by Sir Robert Howell, had been a constant distraction throughout the planning and construction of the exhibit, offering opinions and suggestions that she didn't need but couldn't afford to dismiss. Now she'd find out how dedicated to their mission they were.

She found Sir Robert's private number in her list of contacts and called. It was 4:52 a.m., but Sarah didn't care about waking him. She'd go over there and drag him out of bed by his ankles if she had to.

TWO

assie Ireland spent Sunday afternoon strolling the 16th Arrondissement in Paris. She walked past a two-story mansion several times, lingering to aim her cellphone at it as the owner, Jason Seabolt, came and went. She'd downloaded software to her phone enabling it to receive and transmit wireless radio signals, including the unencrypted signals from the home's alarm system so that she could identify and store the code to disarm it.

The house was surrounded by a wall that came up to her chin. On one of her passes, she peeked over it, drawing the attention of two Doberman Pinschers that raced toward her, barking, lips curled back and fangs exposed. They threw themselves against the wall, sticking their noses close enough to hers that she could smell what they'd had for breakfast.

"See you soon, boys," she said.

Seabolt was a wealthy, ex-pat African American. He lived there with his wife and six-year old daughter, Ameila and a caretaker for the estate. A month ago, he put the house on the market for 12.5-million euros. Cassie had studied the photographs of the exterior and interior and a drawing of the floor plan the realtor had uploaded to its website.

There were nine rooms on the first floor, including a ballroom, study and music room, plus five second-floor bedrooms. On the lower level, there was a 1000-bottle wine cellar, state-of-the art fitness center and cinema. French doors opened to the back of the house from the lower level onto a large flagstone patio where there was a fountain with jets of water spouting from a statue of Poseidon. The grounds were landscaped with mature oaks and shrubs manicured into the shapes of monkeys, giraffes and other zoo animals. The dogs had what the realtor described as their own mini-mansion near the back wall, a hundred square-foot heated and air-conditioned pitched-roof shelter with front and side entrances.

Relying on aerial photographs of the neighborhood she found on Google Maps, Cassie scouted the route she would take to and from the house, practicing it with Google's street view feature. Her Sunday afternoon walk was a dry run.

The house was filled with valuable works of art and museum quality collectibles but she'd been hired to recover only one of them. A human skull, cast in platinum and encrusted with ten-thousand flawless diamonds with a pear-shaped pink diamond mounted in the forehead. The mouth was open in a silent grin, the original teeth, dull with age, in sharp contrast to the skull's glittering afterlife glow. The diamonds alone were worth more than twenty-million dollars. Some critics derided it as kitsch. Others called it genius, appraising it for five times that.

Seabolt had acquired the skull by persuading its owner, an elderly man too incompetent to know better, to change his will, giving the skull to him rather than to his daughter. After her father's death, the daughter hired Cassie's employer, Prometheus, to recover the skull. She was happy to pay his million-dollar fee, twenty-five percent of which was Cassie's share.

Cassie returned to Seabolt's house after midnight dressed in skin-tight black running pants and a matching top under a black zippered waist-cut jacket and wearing a black watch cap and thin, black leather gloves. She strapped a black fanny pack around her waist. Her ebony skin blended with the clothes.

The house was dark. She walked around to the side, clambered up onto the wall and whistled for the Dobermans. They bolted from their doghouse and jumped at her, snarling. It took a second for them to recognize the raw steaks she was holding in each hand. She let them get a good sniff, then threw one to her right and the other to her left. The dogs didn't hesitate, splitting up to claim their prize. She waited for them to chew the meat and for the sedative she'd laced it with to take effect. If that didn't work, she'd use her tranquilizer dart gun. Five minutes later, they were asleep.

Cassie stood in front of the French doors to the lower level and sent a signal from her cellphone transmitting the code to turn off the alarm system. The lock was a simple deadbolt that she picked in less than a minute. When she opened the doors, the alarm remained silent.

The client had assured Prometheus that the skull was in Seabolt's house but said she didn't know where. Cassie had a lot of ground to cover and knew that the longer she stayed, the more likely something would go wrong. If things went her way, the skull would be displayed on a table or shelf rather than locked in a safe.

The skull wasn't on the lower level. She checked her watch as she searched the first floor. Fifteen minutes had passed. Too long. She stood at the foot of the spiral, marble staircase in the entry hall, listening for any hint that someone on the second floor was awake. Hearing nothing, she moved on.

The study was paneled in honey-colored wood. The parquet floor was partly covered by a Persian rug. Cassie surveyed the bookshelves covering two of the walls. They were filled with first editions and rare manuscripts. A desk faced a wall of glass with a sliding door leading to a side yard. An overstuffed easy chair was in one corner. The skull sat on a gold stand in the center of an end table next to the chair. Cassie admired it for a moment, then slipped it into a cushioned velvet bag from her fanny pack.

The lights came on and a gruff voice from behind her said, "Don't move. I have a gun and I'm not afraid to use it. Turn around and keep your hands where I can see them."

Cassie eased her dart gun out of the fanny pack. "Okay, take it easy. I'm not armed."

She turned toward him, dropped to a knee and fired a dart before he realized what was happening, hitting him in the shoulder. He let loose his gun and tried to move his mouth but no sound came out. A quizzical look came over his face as he sank to the floor. It was the caretaker, a short, middle-aged, skinny Frenchman wearing boxers and a t-shirt. Cassie picked up his gun. It wasn't loaded. She pulled the dart from his shoulder and dragged him to the easy chair, placing his gun under the cushion. Then she lifted him off the floor and sat him in the chair, letting his chin rest on his chest.

Cassie put the dart gun back in the fanny pack and latched the velvet bag to her belt with a carabiner. When she turned around, Amelia was standing in the doorway to the study, her natural hair coils hanging over her eyes and past her ears, wearing a nightgown that hid her feet. Cassie towered over her. For an instant, she thought she was looking back in time at herself at that age. Same dark skin, same hair style. But there was something else familiar in the wide-eyed expression on the child's round face. She was more curious than afraid.

"What's the matter with Francois?" she asked.

Cassie crouched in front of the girl. "Nothing. He's just sleeping. Why aren't you in bed?"

"I had a bad dream. Francois always tells me a story after I have a bad dream. I went to his room and he wasn't there."

"So, you came looking for him."

Amelia nodded. "Who are you?"

"I'm a night watcher."

"What's a night watcher?"

"I watch over little girls when they're sleeping to keep them safe."

The girl looked at the table where the skull had been, then at Cassie. "What happened to the skull?"

Cassie said, "I took it."

"Why?"

"It belongs to someone else. I'm going to return it to her. Is that okay with you?"

Amelia thought for a moment, then nodded. "I'm glad because I don't like it."

"You don't? Why not?"

"It's scary."

"Well, I won't let it scare you anymore." Cassie walked to the sliding door. She stepped outside and looked back at the girl. "Go back to bed, mon Cheri, and dream sweet dreams."

The girl waved as Cassie closed the door behind her.

She walked toward the wall, stopping when she heard growling coming from either side of her. She had been inside too long. The Dobermans were awake. She broke into a run as they charged after her. Leaping onto the statue of Poseidon, she held onto its neck as she spun around, letting the dogs pass beneath her. She jumped to the ground and ran toward the doghouse. The Dobermans were closing fast. She scrambled onto the roof, grabbed an overhanging branch on a nearby oak tree and swung over the wall. Hitting the ground, she kept running until she couldn't hear the dogs barking.

THREE

Sir Robert Howell studied one of the fake Magna Cartas, leaning over the display case until his nose was inches from the surface. He was tall enough that he had to bend his knees and fold him forearms on top of the case to get a good look without losing his balance. He drew an ivory handkerchief from the front pocket of his tweed jacket and wiped away the fog his breath had left on the glass, then straightened and returned the handkerchief without uttering a word. He repeated the routine for each of the fakes, keeping his thoughts to himself.

Sarah St. James stood a few paces behind him, digging her fingernails into her palms as she waited for him to say something, anything. When she explained to Sir Robert over the phone what had happened, he said he'd be there straightaway and hung up without asking for details or raising his voice. He was so calm she wondered if he'd understood what she'd said. And he was just as calm now, betraying none of the anxiety that threatened to reduce her to a puddle.

She backed up as he stepped behind the rope line, eyeing the exhibit from the same distance as the visitors who would fill the gallery in a few hours. He tugged on his mustache, an abundant, iron gray shock of hair that dominated his thin face, and tilted his head to one side, muttering as he walked back and forth.

"Hmmm…quite right….indeed."

"I did the best I could…"

Sir Robert turned to her and raised his hand to cut her off. "You're quite the clever girl, aren't you?" She didn't know what to say. He let her suffer for another long moment. "From behind the rope, these reproductions look entirely authentic and would certainly satisfy all but the most discerning eyes."

Sarah exhaled a long, shaky breath. "Then we'll proceed with the opening."

"I believe that's our best option."

"Brilliant. If we're lucky, no one else will ever have to know what happened."

"Unless we fail to recover the originals, which is frankly the more pressing matter. I'll have to alert the other Trustees, of course. I rather think they'll want an explanation before they part with a hundred million pounds."

Sarah tried not to sound too desperate as she asked the crucial question. "Do you think they'll pay the ransom?"

He shook his head, again playing with his mustache. In his early sixties, his bony frame, complimented his oblong head and gray eyes. Take away his money and station in life and he'd pass as an ordinary commoner. Dressed and rich, his piercing gaze and cool, detached manner warned others to tread lightly.

"We shall see, my dear. None of us want the Magna Cartas lost on our watch but, shared among the nine of us, the ransom comes to a bit more than eleven million pounds each, a not inconsiderable sum even for the Trustees. I've called an emergency meeting for later today. I will urge them to be prepared to pay but it might be well to consider other options."

"You can't mean the police. The ransom note said…"

"Yes, yes, I've learned from hard experience that it would do more harm than good to involve them, especially Commissioner Wilkinson. He'd like nothing more than to strut before the cameras and tell all of England that he recovered the Magna Cartas notwithstanding our collective incompetence."

Sarah looked at him, surprised. "I thought… Didn't he rescue your grandson a few years ago?"

His eyes creased with a flash of pain at the memory of the boy's kidnapping. "That was the official story. The truth is that he nearly got Lawrence killed. The Commissioner insisted on taking charge of the case himself since it was such a high-profile affair. He took a hard line with the kidnappers because he said that if we showed any sign of weakness, they would demand more for Lawrence's release."

"And I take it that didn't work out."

"They sent my daughter two of her son's toes in a gift-wrapped box. We managed to keep that out of the news but I'd had enough. My solicitor suggested I engage a firm called Global Security."

"What do they do?"

"They specialize in recovering lost assets, anything of exceptional value."

"An asset recovery firm for a kidnapping?"

"Yes, it sounded unorthodox, and Global Security's methods are just that, but I had lost faith in the police and was willing to try anything." Sir Robert fixed his eyes on hers. "That's who really saved Lawrence. Within forty-eight hours, they rescued my grandson and told the police where to find the kidnappers all trussed up like a flock of Christmas geese awaiting the butcher."

"The newspapers didn't say anything about…"

He cut her off again. "Global Security wanted it that way so I let Commissioner Wilkinson take all the credit which he was happy to do. I didn't trust him then and I won't trust him now. I've already reached out to them. Their operative will be at the Library today. Give them your full cooperation. Until then, you are to say nothing to anyone about this matter. Is that understood?"

"Of course, Sir Robert, but aren't you worried the thieves will consider Global Security the same as the police and destroy the Magna Cartas?".

He waved his hand dismissively. "My experience is that the thieves won't know about Global Security until after the Magna Cartas are recovered."

"Still, in all, it's quite a risk, isn't it?"

He smiled. "This from the woman who mounted such a remarkable cover up in the blink of an eye?" He patted her cheek. "Chin up. Now be a good girl and get yourself cleaned up for the opening." He tapped his watch. "Tick tock."

Sir Robert took the stairs from the gallery at a brisk clip, leaving Sarah alone. The mild relief she'd felt after calling him had vanished, replaced by a sickening certainty that the world as she knew it was about to end. An asset recovery firm? What could they possibly do? Then again, what could anyone do but pay the ransom and hope the thieves were honorable men.

FOUR

An hour later, Cassie weaved her way through a crowded private poker club in Montmarte until she reached the VIP room. The paneled walls were painted a creamy shade. Impressionist prints hung on the walls. The plush carpet was a muted tan. Amber light fixtures mounted on the walls kept the light soft. Servers waited nearby, pouring wine, whiskey and beer without waiting to be asked. Jake Carter sat with seven others at the only table. She stood next to a server, watching him.

Jake pursed his lips, then turned the corners of his mouth up in a wry smile as the dealer turned over the final card in the middle of the table. When the bet came to him, he tossed five thousand euros into the pot. Four other players were still in the hand. Three folded leaving only a stocky German named Gunther. He studied Jake for a moment.

"You're bluffing."

Cassie couldn't tell. He'd taught her that there were all kinds of poker faces from idiot grins to disgusted frowns. Only amateurs tried to maintain a perpetual, imperturbable flat expression. It was like trying not to blink. You could do it for a while, but not all night. For a professional like Jake, the trick was to be both natural and inscrutable. His handsome, boyish features and native charm were his secret weapons.

Jake cocked his head to one side, stretching his smile by a fraction. "Then call."

"You're bluffing, I know it!"

"Gunther," one of his friends who'd folded said, "you can't let him steal the pot. You've got to call."

"No, you don't," Jake said. "You should fold."

"Listen to you," said Gunther. "Giving me advice like you're my friend."

"I'm not your friend. I'm the guy who's going to take your money."

"This is supposed to be a friendly game and now you threaten me?"

"I'm doing you a favor." Jake was matter of fact, making his prediction a certainty.

"Look at the table," Gunther's friend said. "There's no way the last card could have helped him. I'm telling you, he's got nothing. You're a fool if you don't call him."

Gunther stiffened his spine, set his jaw and matched Jake's bet along with another wad of Euros. "Ha! I call and raise you five thousand."

"You really shouldn't have done that. I'm all in," Jake said and pushed twenty-five thousand euros into the center of the table.

A red flush rose from the German's neck and crept across his face. Sweat popped along his upper lip as his hand hovered over the last of his cash, his fingers trembling. He looked at his cards, then at Jake, then back at his cards. Grimacing, he gave his cards a final look before slamming them down on the table.

"Fold, gottverdammt!"

Jake placed his cards face down on the table and mixed them with the rest of the deck, making certain no one would ever know if he had been bluffing. As he gathered his winnings, he flashed Cassie a grin that made his blue eyes dance and her heart skip a beat. She gestured to the door and left.

"That's it for me," Jake said as he passed five hundred euros to the dealer.

Outside, Cassie looped her arm around his.

"Back there," Cassie said, "were you bluffing?" He didn't answer. "I know. You never bet and tell. But, if I can't tell when you're bluffing, how can I ever trust you?"

"You're asking me about trust? You're a thief. A brilliant, beautiful, sexy thief, but still a thief."

"That's not the way I see it. I'm more of a twenty-first century

Robin Hood."

"Except you don't rob the rich and give to the poor. You rob the rich and give the stuff back to some other rich guy."

"Who happens to be the rightful owner," Cassie said.

"According to Prometheus. Who has a name like that? I might like him if he had a last name, maybe Jones or Smith or Goldfarb, or if he didn't sit on his ass all day on his secret island hideaway sipping drinks with floating umbrellas while you did all the dirty work."

"You wouldn't like him no matter what his name was or where he lived or what he drank."

"Because I don't like the hold he has on you. When I invited you to spend the weekend with me in Paris, I didn't think you'd spend it working."

"I owe Prometheus everything I have. That doesn't mean he has a hold on me. It means that I'm loyal. I told you I had a job to do here. And now that it's finished, we have the rest of the weekend."

Jake laughed. "It's Monday morning, or did you forget. We spent a weekend together in Paris with our clothes on. Tragic."

She punched him in the arm and then took him by the hand. "Come on. Let's go to the Pont Neuf and watch the sun rise over the Seine."

They passed a bakery that was just stirring to life, the employees inside preparing to open for early morning customers. The eastern sky was beginning to lighten.

They were almost there when Cassie's cell phone rang. As soon as she saw the caller ID, her smile faded and her brow tensed. "Sorry," she said. "Give me a minute."

She dropped Jake's hand and moved a few steps away to take the call. She had her back to him and didn't see him move close enough to overhear her side of the conversation.

"When?" she asked. "All four of them? Yes. As quick as I can."

She ended the call and turned around, frowning when she saw how near he was. "Were you eavesdropping?"

Jake shrugged. "Maybe. A little. Was that Prometheus?"

She glared at him. "Yes. And, haven't you ever heard of boundaries? Never mind. Of course, you haven't. I have to go."

"Boundaries. Right. I'm all about that. So, where are you off to?"

She planted her hands on her hips. "London."

"As in you're really going to Bangkok but want me to think you're going to London or are you really going to London?"

He grinned and she bit her cheek until she couldn't help herself and laughed.

"You are the most impossible man I've ever met."

"You left out irresistible."

She sighed and the tension in her face evaporated. "We'll see about that. And, yes, I'm really going to London."

"Need some help? I'm supposed to get a haircut this week but I can reschedule. You have to admit, we made a great team the last time."

"Great teams don't get thrown overboard during a storm in the middle of the Mediterranean."

"Great teams don't drown. Neither of us would have survived without the other."

"Jake…"

"We go after the same kind of people. They're rich and arrogant and think they're invulnerable. We come at them in different ways but together we'd be unstoppable."

"And you're ready to walk away from poker to be my sidekick? I don't think so."

"I said partner, not sidekick. And, who said anything about walking away from poker. That's my ticket to the circles you run in. And, it's the perfect cover." Jake hesitated, realizing he was re-opening a wound. "If it's because of what happened to Gabriel Degrande…"

Cassie crossed her arms over her chest. "Don't even…"

"I'm sorry. I know he was your partner and you blame yourself for his death, but…"

She raised her palm, stopping him. "It's not going to happen. Deal with it."

***

JAKE WATCHED UNTIL Cassie turned a corner and was out of sight, then walked to the Pont Neuf. Standing on the bridge, watching the sun burn the rims off slate gray clouds and listening to the city come to life all around him, he thought about her. They'd had their meet-cute moment and they'd gone through their pretend-to-be-annoyed with each other phase. He'd invited her to join him in Paris to put an end to their will-they-or-won't they phase. Then Prometheus called, leaving him in the what-the-fuck phase.

She hadn't lied to him about London. At least he didn't think so. He liked that it was hard to tell. He spent the rest of the morning mulling her latest refusal to let them work together until he came up with a plan to change her mind. Deal with it, she'd told him. Fair enough. He would. An hour later, he was at the train station holding a ticket to London, not worried that Cassie had a six-hour head start.

FIVE

Cassie took the Eurostar to London via the Channel tunnel. She made quick work of the bland breakfast that came with her first-class ticket, reminding herself that it was fuel, not food.

She imagined Jake sitting next to her. She would explain all the ways the thieves could have stolen the Magna Cartas while he calculated the risk and reward of each scenario, narrowing it down to the most likely. Together, they would've shortened the odds and solved the case. It was the together part that frightened her enough to turn Jake down each time he brought it up. He was right that she had to move on from the past. She just wished she knew how.

She shook her head and spent the rest of the two hour and fifteen-minute trip on her laptop learning all she could about the British Library and the Magna Carta exhibit. The Library's design drawings were public records. She studied them closely.

There was only one way in and out of the PACCAR Gallery where the exhibit was located. A retractable steel gate that descended from the ceiling at the entrance to the Gallery was the only security measure shown on the plans. From there, a broad corridor led to stairs that took visitors down to the display cases.

She knew that security guards and an array of cameras and motion detectors would also protect the Gallery and that the display cases would be equipped with separate alarms. It would take a team of three or four to overcome those complex and sophisticated defenses and the thieves wouldn't have taken on the job unless they knew what they were up against.

They could have obtained that information by hacking into the Library's network. But more and more institutions like the British

Library were keeping such information on a secure standalone computer not connected to the network to make it more difficult to hack.

Or, they could have stolen a hard copy of the plans if they knew where to find them. Most likely, they bribed or blackmailed someone on the inside with access to the information if that person wasn't the mastermind behind the entire operation.

Standard practice would limit the number of people that could open the retractable steel gate, giving her a starting point for a list of suspects. She guessed that at least two people had that authority. One was the Director of Security, whom the Library's website identified as Ian Thorpe. Normally, Thorpe would have been her contact but Prometheus told her it was Sarah St. James, the exhibit curator and the second person on Cassie's short list.

Thorpe would be able to recite the security measures – and how to defeat them - in his sleep. St. James would trust him to keep her exhibit safe while she focused on other details. Prometheus' choice of St. James as her contact combined with Thorpe's superior knowledge was enough to move him to the top of her list until she knew more.

She emailed Gunnar Agnarsson, Prometheus' tech wizard, and asked him to run full background checks, including financials, on both Thorpe and St. James. Gunnar shot back a reply, promising to get the information to her by day's end.

Cassie stepped off the train at the St. Pancras station, glad that it was only half a block from the British Library. She stowed her suitcase at the Excess Baggage Company on the station's main concourse.

It was ten a.m. when she arrived at the Library. A twenty-foot banner hung on an exterior wall trumpeting the Magna Carta exhibit. The line of people waiting to get inside snaked from the entrance across a brick-lined plaza, down the sidewalk along Euston Road and around the corner.

She stared at the crowd wondering what they would see when they reached the exhibit. If the hundreds of people waiting to get in was any indication, perhaps the story about the theft had been a false alarm or a hoax. If so, she'd be back in Paris – and with Jake – by dinner.

Just then, she received a text from Prometheus attaching a VIP e-ticket to the exhibit that allowed her to skip the line. She wouldn't need it if all were well. She showed her e-ticket to the security guard. He scanned it and waved her through.

Cassie joined the throng that had made it through security. She wanted to see the exhibit, or what was left of it, before she sought out Sarah St. James.

Half an hour later, she stopped in front of the display cases, shoulder to shoulder with a dozen others. Kept several feet away by a velvet rope, she could see the Magna Cartas, each elevated slightly to make them more visible. Except she knew they couldn't be the originals. Otherwise, Prometheus would have sent her back to Paris.

A plaque on the wall above the cases explained that the Magna Carta contained 3500 words and 62 clauses and that the four remaining originals ranged from 17 to 20 inches in length and 13 to 17 inches in width and that the text was written in Latin. The plaque failed to mention that when viewed from behind the rope, the writing was so small and so illegible that it could just have easily passed for Elven runes from *The Lord of the Rings* or tracks left by worms crawling across the parchment.

Someone had gone to a great deal of trouble in a short period of time to make certain that news of the theft hadn't been made public and that the exhibit opened as scheduled. Otherwise, the only people at the exhibit would be detectives from Scotland Yard.

Cassie drifted away from the display cases and started up the stairs that would take her back to the gallery entrance. A young woman wearing a knee-length green dress with a torn hem was standing at the top of the stairs. Cassie recognized Sarah St. James from the videos on the Library's website she had watched on the train. Though poised and animated on the videos, she had a wan complexion and her eyes flicked like jitterbugs from the Magna Cartas to the people behind the velvet rope. She tugged and toyed with the collar of her dress with one hand and clutched a tissue with the other.

Cassie walked up the stairs and stopped next to Sarah who didn't appear to notice her until Cassie spoke.

"It's a lovely exhibit."

Sarah gave her a quick glance and a tight smile. "It is, isn't it?"

"Too bad they're fakes." Sarah's eyes widened. Her face flushed and her shoulders slumped. Cassie cupped Sarah's elbow to keep her steady. "It's alright. I'm Cassie Ireland. I work for Global Security. Is there somewhere private we can talk?"

"Oh, thank heavens. Of course."

Cassie glanced down the stairs and saw an older man staring at them. She wanted to dismiss his interest but couldn't, not when he didn't look away when their eyes met. Fair enough, she thought. More players on the board. She took Sarah by the arm.

"Let's get out of here."

SIX

Sarah led Cassie to her office on the second floor. It was a utilitarian space with a desk, two visitor chairs and walls lined with crammed bookshelves that blocked the only window. She closed the door behind them and leaned against it, her words coming out in a rush.

"I don't know how this sort of thing normally works, but let's get something clear. No one else can know what happened. Not the staff or the public or, God forbid, the press. If the police get involved, the thieves will find out and the Magna Cartas will be destroyed. So, we must keep it quiet. All right?"

"Understood."

"Good." Sarah gave her a quick nod. "The most important thing… the *only* important thing is getting the documents back safely. Even if that means paying the ransom."

"The Magna Cartas are eight hundred years old. Are they likely to be damaged?"

"Not if handled properly."

"How would you do it?"

Sarah thought for a moment. "I'd keep them flat, in some kind of protective polyester sleeve so there won't be any chemical reactions. Keep them in a cool place. Never above room temperature and no exposure to direct or intense light. Oh, and, nowhere near heat, like a radiator, or blowing air, like from a vent. They're small enough to fit into an attaché case. I'd use a skinny one with a hard shell, the kind a barrister takes to court. And, I'd pad the interior with foam to cushion the documents."

"How likely is it that the thieves knew how to protect the Magna Cartas?"

"Easy enough to Google the bit about the sleeves. The attaché case is typical for transporting fragile documents of this size, though the case would be packed inside a secure shipping crate."

Cassie nodded. "Did you steal the Magna Cartas?"

"Did I steal the Magna Cartas? Are you daft?"

Cassie was more interested in Sarah's reaction to the question than her answer. Her surprise was instantaneous and her shocked facial reaction was involuntary. Both gave her reply the ring of truth.

"How many people can open the steel gate at the entrance to the PACCAR Gallery?"

"Three, including me. We have to swipe our ID badges through a card reader."

"Which means you could have opened the gate for the thieves. Did you?"

Sarah's voice raised an indignant octave. "No!"

"Can you prove that?"

Sarah ran her fingers through her hair, then folded her arms across her middle and paced across her office, head down.

"Yes. Yes, of course I can." She sat at her desk and opened the Library's internal network on her desktop computer, clicking through a series of screens. "There. You can see for yourself. Every time one of us swipes our card, it's recorded on this access log and…oh, my God. That's impossible. I don't believe it. It was Malcolm."

Cassie looked over her shoulder. "Malcolm who?"

"Malcolm Bridges. He works for Titan Security Solutions. He designed the display cases and the whole security system."

Cassie pointed to the screen. "And it looks like he opened the gate at 12:47 this morning."

Sarah sagged into her chair. "I can't believe it. It must be a mistake. Malcolm would never… I mean he couldn't have done it. He just couldn't."

"Is Ian Thorpe the third person that can open the gate?"

"Yes. My, you've done your homework. Most impressive."

Cassie studied the screen. "His name doesn't show up on the log. Just Bridges and you."

Sarah moved the cursor across the log to the entry next to her name. "But you can see for yourself that I didn't get here until after four this morning. I couldn't sleep so I came in early to make certain everything was ready to go. The gate was down when I got here. I opened it and when I came down the stairs, the Magna Cartas were gone and the gallery was a mess."

"Call Malcolm Bridges."

"Call him? What would I say? Morning, Malcolm. Would you mind bringing back the Magna Cartas you stole?"

Cassie smiled and handed her the phone. "Invite him to dinner to celebrate the opening of the exhibit."

Sarah inhaled deeply, her eyebrows arching, put the phone on speaker and dialed Bridges' direct line.

A woman answered. "Margaret Jameson speaking. May I help you?"

Sarah scratched a note for Cassie – *M's secretary*. "Hello, Margaret. It's Sarah St. James from the British Library. I'm calling for Malcolm. Is he available?"

"No. I'm afraid Mr. Bridges resigned two days ago."

"Resigned? Why? Where did he go?"

"I'm afraid you'll have to ask Mr. Bridges. It was very sudden. We're all at loose ends here."

Cassie signaled to Sarah to end the call. She'd track Bridges down on her own.

"Thank you, Margaret. If you hear from him, please ask him to give me a ring." Sarah hung up and looked at Cassie, bewildered. "How could he? Why would he?"

"I'll ask him when I find him. In the meantime, I need to see the videos recorded by the security cameras in the gallery."

"They won't help. As soon as I realized what happened, I ran to have a look at them. When I did, the cameras showed that everything was fine. How could they do that? And how did they get past the motion detectors to even get close to the display cases."

"It's easier than it sounds. They hacked into the Library's network and set up a video loop showing the same scene over and over. The motion detectors were easy. All they had to do was hit them with infrared light and the sensors inside the detectors would burn up. Did the guards say whether they noticed anything unusual?"

"No. That's when I decided to substitute the fakes until we could sort this out." Sarah explained how she put the exhibit back together. "Then, I called Sir Robert Howell because he's the chair of the Magna Carta Trust, and told him everything. He came to the Library and looked at the fakes and decided we should go ahead with the exhibit and hire your company to get the originals back."

Cassie thought for a moment. "The exhibit has been open for a couple of hours. If the thieves left the video loop running, the guards on the day shift in the security center must have realized something was wrong when they didn't see anyone in the gallery."

"I thought of that too. Practically had a panic attack until I went back there just after the exhibit opened and checked the monitors. Everything was back to normal. I could see people from every camera angle. How did they do that?"

"My guess is that they had the loop on a timer so they could be long gone before anyone noticed something was wrong. You were able to put the exhibit back together before the timer went off and the regular feed came back on."

"But what about the sensors inside the cases. Malcolm Bridges said that it was impossible to break into them."

"Well, he was wrong. The sensors were probably Piezo electric. They're porcelain and if the porcelain gets hot enough, the heat kills the sensor. If it were me, I'd use a laser or maybe a cordless soldering iron. Aim it at each sensor."

"You make it sound so easy."

"It's not. One wrong move and the whole thing is blown. Malcolm could have told the thieves everything they needed to know. Why didn't you notify Ian Thorpe?"

Sarah hesitated, staring at her hands. "I don't trust him."

"Why not?"

She rose from her chair and turned her back to Cassie. "He's not an honorable man."

"How so?"

Sarah spun around, her eyes aflame, and gripped the back of her desk chair. "The man's a stalker and a deviant. He pursued me from the first day I was here. I'm married. Happily, so. And even if I weren't, Thorpe is repulsive. He wouldn't leave me alone. One day, he cornered me in his office and put his hands on me."

"What did you do?"

"I pushed him off and went straight to the Executive Director and filed a complaint but Thorpe denied everything and I had no proof so nothing happened except that the Executive Director asked me if it was my time of the month. At least Thorpe's left me alone ever since."

Cassie studied her. "This job must mean a lot to you to put up with that."

"Ask my husband. Michael says he thinks I love it more than I love him and some days, like today…or what today was supposed to have been…I think he's right. That's why you've got to get the originals back. If you don't, everything I've worked for will be lost. I'll be lost."

"Well, we can't have that, can we? You did a great job putting the exhibit back together but the longer this goes on, the better the chances someone will figure out what you've done. We need to make it harder for that to happen."

"How?"

"Thorpe won't be happy when he finds out I'm here. He might decide to double-check the security for the exhibit just to cover his ass. So, tonight, we make repairs. I'll replace the sensors in the motion detectors and inside the display cases. You'll replace the acrylic sheets covering the Magna Cartas. That's the most we can control. After that, we'll hope no one takes too close a look at the documents."

Sarah raised her eyebrows. "Where are you going to find all that equipment?"

"At your neighborhood Maplin's. Best electronic stores in London."

"But the guys in the security center will see us on the video cameras."

Cassie gave her a sly smile. "If the thieves could hijack the cameras, so can we."

SEVEN

The nine members of the Magna Carta Trust sat around a sleek ebony table in the executive conference room on the sixth floor of the British Library, listening in dumbstruck silence as Sir Robert Howell told them about the theft of the Magna Cartas, the ransom note and the forged documents on display. They were a cross-section of the British elite, some living off inherited wealth; some having earned theirs in ways that might cause them to admire the thieves' brazenness. Two were politicians, acutely attuned to the impact on their futures if the Magna Cartas were lost – or successfully ransomed.

Lord Sommerton, whose ancestors had assured he would never work a day in his life, broke the silence. "We must close the exhibit immediately. I won't be a party to this grotesque lie." His normally ruddy face had turned crimson.

Dame Elizabeth Rowland, patted her perfectly coiffed silvery hair. She was a second-generation trustee, replacing her father who had been one of the original members.

"If we close it now, that will only draw attention, which is the last thing we want."

"No," Alexander Crossley, MP and Chairman of the Foreign Affairs committee, said, "No. The last thing we want is for the original Magna Cartas to be destroyed."

Sir Philip Blackburn, a self-described 'country squire' who owned most of Dorset and Hampshire counties, shook his head. "A hundred million pounds. That's… outrageous!"

Lord Sommerton pounded his fist on the table. "I won't pay. I refuse to be blackmailed. Let Scotland Yard track these bastards down and put them away."

"We must take the thieves at their word concerning the police and pay the ransom," insisted Crossley. "It's our sworn duty to protect those documents."

"Perhaps you have a few extra million in the bank…" Sommerton began, but stopped when Lady Liliane Tresch interrupted.

Lady Tresch was a striking woman with dark hair and darker eyes against alabaster skin. She was in her first term as a trustee and had made her fortune in real estate and the stock market. At fifty, she was the youngest trustee and had the self-confidence and presence to command any room she was in.

"Mr. Crossley is correct about our sworn duty. However, we must not, under any circumstance, pay a ransom."

"Of course, we'll do everything possible to avoid paying the ransom," Sir Robert said, "but you can't seriously suggest that we not pay it if that's the only way to assure the safe return of the Magna Cartas."

"I am most assuredly serious. The moment we pay that ransom, we set a precedent that will haunt us forever. How much will the next thief demand? Five-hundred million pounds? A billion? There will be no end to it."

"And what do you think the thieves will do if we refuse to pay?"

Lady Tresch folded her hands on the table. "Nothing, except return the Magna Cartas unharmed. Oh, they'll make a show of threatening us but in the end, they'll call in an anonymous tip telling us where to find them."

"Why on earth would they do such a thing," Lord Summerton asked, "after going to the trouble of stealing them?"

"Because once we refuse to pay, they're worthless. No collector in the world would take the chance of being caught with them. Pay them, and we'll rue the day. Patience, gentlemen. Patience is our greatest weapon."

"I quite agree with Lady Tresch that it would be most unfortunate to pay the ransom," Sir Robert said. "However, I am not willing to risk the documents that embody our heritage on the chance that thieves this bold will lose their nerve. They might destroy the Magna

Cartas out of spite if we refuse to pay."

"Then what do you propose?" Lady Tresch asked.

"We do as the thieves instructed and leave Scotland Yard out of it. We prepare to pay the ransom as a last resort. We have five days to make that decision. If we decide to pay, we'll be ready. In the meantime, I've engaged a firm that is quite expert in these matters to recover the Magna Cartas, one I know to be highly effective from personal experience."

"What firm is that?" Crossley asked.

"I'd rather not say, if you don't mind. The fewer that know…"

His strategy didn't work on Lady Tresch. "The fewer can ask questions, such as why we weren't consulted on that decision," she said, fixing her penetrating eyes on his.

He met her gaze. "In five days, the Magna Cartas may be reduced to shreds. There was no time to waste. As Chairman of the Trust, I take full responsibility."

"But only one ninth of the financial risk," Lady Tresch said. "Perhaps if you had addressed my concerns about the security of the exhibit at the outset, we wouldn't be having this conversation."

The other Trustees knew not to get involved in a clash between Sir Robert and Lady Tresch. They sat silently as she went on, her voice like ice. "I told you that Ian Thorpe was incompetent, and that Titan Security Solutions would cut corners if we didn't stay on top of them. And you said I was… what was it?… an imperious nag."

Sir Robert surveyed the hostile faces around the table. He went to the window, stroking his mustache to collect himself before he spoke.

"It serves no purpose to fight old battles now. The important question is how to proceed. We must be prepared for any eventuality. The thieves may well have benefited from inside information so we've been advised to say nothing to Ian Thorpe or Titan. And I remind all of you that not one word leaves this room."

"I assure you we shall revisit old battles when this is over," Lady Tresh said, keeping her eyes locked on Sir Robert. "Now, if we must have the ransom money ready in case your people fail, that's eleven point one million pounds each. Assuming we can all contribute our share, even those of us that have experienced recent reversals."

Sir Robert flinched. He'd been victimized by a money manager's fraud and forced to go public when he filed suit to recover damages. "I'm quite up to the task as are we all."

The Trustees turned toward Lord Sommerton. "Is this what we've come to, then? Surrendering to the demands of common thieves?"

"Give over, Harold," said the Right Honourable David Asquith. At 77, he was the elder statesman of the Trust. "Sell one of your yachts and stump up."

Sommerton started to respond but changed his mind, and moved off to join Sir Robert by the window.

"Your people had better come through."

EIGHT

Ian Thorpe's secretary, Edna Norris, was chatting on the phone while scrolling through Facebook posts on her computer when Cassie walked past her desk and reached for the handle on the closed door to his office.

Edna, a plump, middle-aged woman, dropped her phone and came around her desk. "Who are you? Do you have an appointment with Mr. Thorpe?"

"No."

"Well, you can't just barge in here like that."

Cassie opened the door. "Apparently, I can."

Edna followed her into Thorpe's office.

"I'm so sorry, Mr. Thorpe. She doesn't have an appointment and she won't tell me who she is. Should I call security?"

"I am security, Edna," Thorpe said. He surveyed her figure from head to toe and waved his hand at Edna, shooing her back to her desk. "I think I can handle Miss…?"

"My name is Cassie Ireland."

Edna retreated and Cassie closed the door behind her. Thorpe rose from his desk chair. He was half a head shorter than Cassie. His face was full - his thick neck and thicker body borne of muscle gone to fat. His cauliflower ears and mashed nose spoke to long ago fights while the spider web of red veins spreading across his cheeks testified to his continuing decline. An odor of stale cigars surrounded him like an invisible cloud. Cassie put him in his mid-fifties, silently betting against him seeing his mid-sixties.

His office was twice the size of Sarah St. James.' It was furnished with a large, mahogany desk with a matching credenza behind it, a pair of guest chairs and a lumpy sofa. A window looked out on the brick plaza in front of the Library.

Thorpe gestured to the guest chairs in front of his desk. "What can I do for you, Ms. Ireland?

"Cooperate." Cassie ignored his invitation to sit and handed him a business card.

He lowered himself into his chair, examined her card and frowned. "With what?"

"My company, Global Security, has been hired to audit the Library's security."

He narrowed his eyes. "On whose authority? I've heard nothing about this."

"The trustees of the Magna Carta trust."

"Rubbish. Sir Robert and that bunch have no such authority."

"The trustees are responsible for the preservation of all four remaining originals of the Magna Carta and have generously underwritten the Unification exhibit. That's all the authority they need."

Thorpe planted his hands on the desk. "What possible reason would the trustees have for an audit? We've been over our security with them a dozen times since the Magna Carta exhibit was scheduled. Nothing has changed."

"And that's exactly why I'm here. As you well know, complacency is the biggest threat to security."

"We'll see about that. I'm going to call Sir Robert and get to the bottom of this."

"Please do because I need to get started."

Thorpe picked up his phone and punched in Sir Robert's number. Cassie could only hear Thorpe's side of the conversation but it was enough to confirm that Sir Robert was in control.

"Very well, sir. Yes. Complete cooperation. Of course. Thank you, sir." He ended the call and looked at Cassie, his jaw clenched. "What do you need from me?"

"I'd like to start with the personnel files for the security guards and a schedule of the shifts they work."

"The personnel records are confidential and…"

"And," Cassie said with a smile, "you're going to give them to me, aren't you, Mr. Thorpe? Unless you want to call Sir Robert back and ask him to define cooperation."

"That won't be necessary. You'll find everything on our network." He scribbled a note and handed it to her. "You can use these login credentials."

"Thank you. What's your background, Mr. Thorpe?"

"Twenty years in the army. MPs. Last nine years here in security. Director for the last three."

"Do you hire and train all of the guards yourself?"

"I do. They're generally military veterans like me. Most reliable men I know. And they can handle themselves if there's trouble." Thorpe caught himself. "Not that we've had any trouble since I've been in charge."

"Good to know. I have to start somewhere with the personnel records. Who was on duty last night?"

"Colin Saunders and Paulie Reed were assigned to the operations center to monitor the video cameras. Joseph Okafor and Stuart Davies were on exterior patrol. Poor blokes, it was a miserable rain. Tom Galloway, Lloyd Pugh and Jeremy Bristol-Clarke were walking the halls."

"Any reason to question the reliability of any of them?"

"None. Every man is first rate."

Cassie zeroed in on the guards assigned to patrol the interior of the library. They would have been the most likely to notice something unusual and they would have had the best opportunity to either help the thieves or pull the job themselves, especially if Thorpe lent a helping hand.

"Tell me about the last three, the ones walking the halls."

"Army vets, every one. Jeremy Bristol-Clarke was a communications and IT specialist. Lloyd Pugh put helicopters back together after they'd been shot to pieces. And Tom Galloway survived three tours with a bomb disposal unit in Afghanistan."

Cassie had doubted whether any of the security guards could have possessed the necessary skills to carry out such a sophisticated theft. But these men were soldiers, fully capable of hijacking the Library's security cameras, defeating the alarms, and breaking into the display cases.

"How long have they worked for you?"

"I brought them on about a year ago."

"All at the same time?"

"No. Over the course of a couple of months. We have a lot of turnover given how poorly the job pays."

"Men with their skills should have been able to get better jobs, don't you think?"

Thorpe bristled. "You would think, especially after what they sacrificed for their country. Companies should have been begging them to come to work but they didn't attend the right universities with the right people and get the right bloody degrees. Best they could do was work for me for shit pay on the graveyard shift. It'd be a shame if anyone cared enough to notice. "

"If it was me, I'd be pretty upset about that.'"

"Lucky it's not you, then, isn't it? I know these men. I'd trust any one of them with my life."

Cassie nodded. "When did they clock in last night?"

Thorpe pulled up their time records on his computer. "Around midnight. Right on time."

"And when did they clock out?"

Thorpe studied the screen, running the cursor up and down the page. "What the hell?"

"What is it?"

Thorpe looked up at her, his bravado gone. "They didn't. Must have forgot."

"All three?"

Thorpe cast his eyes at his desk. "It happens."

"Must have."

She opened his office door.

"You'll keep me informed," Thorpe said.

"Of course," she said and left without looking back.

NINE

Sarah St. James studied her computer screen and the library floor plans spread across her desk. She held a red marker in her right hand and a blue one in her left. Her green dress hung from her frame, slack, as if she'd somehow lost ten pounds in a single day. Her hair was askew and her face was drawn. Two empty cans of Red Bull lay at her feet.

Cassie rapped lightly on the door. "Anybody home?"

Sarah half-jumped and dropped both markers. "Oh, my gosh! I didn't see you there. I'm so caught up in all this, I completely lost track of time." She ran a hand through her hair. "What time is it anyway?"

Cassie set her bag from Malpin's Electronics on the floor and took the chair opposite Sarah's desk. "A bit past midnight. It's you, me and the mice. And, hopefully, the guards."

"Same crew as last night?"

"Not entirely," Cassie said. "The guards that were working inside have gone missing."

"Missing as in disappeared, vanished – that sort of missing?"

"Yes. Lloyd Pugh, Jeremy Bristol-Clarke and Tom Galloway didn't time out last night. I got their cellphone numbers from their personnel files and called them but they didn't answer. Looks like their phones have been turned off or trashed."

"How can you be certain?"

"I had a colleague of mine try to trace their phones."

"Is that legal?"

"More or less. He's also looking for Malcolm Bridges and doing a run-down on your and Thorpe's finances to see if either of you had a motive."

Sarah blushed. "My finances?"

"Sorry. It can't be helped. I asked him to do it before we met. I know you had nothing to do with the theft. I hope you're not too angry."

"More embarrassed. Michael teaches. We barely get by. I'm glad you told me though. I don't want any special treatment."

Cassie was relieved at her reaction. She needed Sarah to trust her. "Don't be embarrassed. That just means you and Michael are part of the 99% that work hard while running in place."

"It's a struggle but we both love what we do. What about the guards? What did you find out about them?"

"Nothing yet. But there are some things I know from their files. Thorpe is married, Galloway lives with his mother and Bristol-Clarke lives alone. I talked with the wife and mother. Thorpe and Galloway didn't come home after their shift. I'll have to check with Bristol-Clarke's neighbors but I'm betting he didn't either."

"How did the wife and mum sound?"

"About what you'd expect. Somewhere between annoyed and hysterical. I didn't get a sense that they knew what had happened."

"What about the other guards that were on duty?"

"I've spent the last six hours interviewing them. I told them we were conducting a routine security audit and randomly chose last night's shift for a closer look. They weren't happy about having to come into work early but they felt better after I told them they were getting overtime. Colin Saunders and Paulie Reed were no help. Joseph Okafor said he thought he heard something odd coming from the PACCAR gallery not long after midnight but Galloway sent him back outside to check for a leak coming into the building before he could do anything about it. Stuart Davies ran into Pugh, Bristol-Clarke and Galloway at the elevator. He said that Pugh was acting strange, like he didn't know a thing about football when they'd talked about it the week before. And, he said that one of them had a big duffle bag on his shoulder which could have been for their equipment if they stole the Magna Cartas."

"Do you think they did it?"

"Too soon to know for certain but from what I've learned, I

wouldn't bet against it."

Sarah fell back in her chair. "Well, that ties it all in a neat bow, doesn't it? The three of them must have been in it with Malcolm Bridges. Any word about him?"

"No. What's with the floor plans?"

"I pulled up the keycard access logs that show each time a door was opened after midnight and by whom and I've been tracking that information on the floor plans. Red is Tom Galloway, green is Pugh and blue is Bristol-Clarke. Davies is purple and Okafor is orange. Malcolm Bridges is yellow, which feels right. Do you think Malcolm was there?"

"Either that or they had his ID card or they could have cloned it."

"Cloned it? What do you mean?"

"Your ID card has an RFID chip."

"RFID?"

"Radio frequency identification chip. When you swipe the card, the chip unlocks the door. If they got their hands on Bridge's card, they could have scanned it and downloaded the data to another keycard."

Sarah's ID card hung from a lanyard around her neck. She held the card up, studying it like she'd never seen it before. "I thought these things were supposed to be safe."

"Nothing is safe anymore. Everything can be hacked." Cassie pointed to the floor plans. "Why did you do all this?"

"I told you this morning. This is my exhibit. The Magna Cartas are my responsibility. I had to do something."

Cassie leafed through the plans, stopping with the drawings for the PACCAR gallery. "This is great work. They opened the gallery at 12:47 a.m. Was that the only time they used Bridges' keycard?"

"Right. Didn't have to use it again. They could open everything else with their own badges." Sarah used a marker to trace the trails of the three missing guards on the map. "From the start of their shift at midnight, they followed their usual routes. Until 12:31." She pointed to the numbers in red. "When Galloway opened the door to room 106."

"Just down the hall from the security control room." Cassie nodded. "That's probably where they hacked into the video system."

"But look at this," said Sarah. "At the same time Galloway was going into 106, Bristol-Clarke used his ID to access the elevator, took it down to Basement Level Five, and opened the door to Manuscript Storage."

"Why? What's in there? Other than manuscripts, of course."

"Nothing, as far as I know. But I couldn't even guess at the last time someone took a complete inventory."

Cassie saw another time written in blue by the door to the storage room. "Wait a minute. Davies said he ran into these guys at the elevator around 2:20 a.m. According to this, Bristol-Clarke went back to Manuscript Storage at 2:27 a.m., after Davies saw them." She took a closer look at the plans for Basement Level Five. "There's no way to get out of the library on that level. It's too far below ground. What was he doing there?"

"All I can tell you is that was the last place any of their keycards were used. None of them show up in the access logs again."

"Which means that they didn't unlock any doors, or use the elevator, after 2:27 a.m.," Cassie paced, thinking out loud. "But they could have taken the stairs to the first floor and opened an exterior door from the inside without leaving a record in the log." She looked to the Sarah for confirmation.

"Yes. Of course."

"So why go down there at all after they had the Magna Cartas?"

Sarah considered this. "To steal something else?"

"Maybe. I'd like to see that storage room for myself."

"Easily done. Come with me. Hang on." Sarah took an ID card from a desk drawer and handed it to Cassie. "I keep a few spares. You may need one of these. It will get you in anywhere in the library."

Cassie grabbed her bag from Malpin's and they took the elevator down to Basement Level Five. As they walked along a narrow hallway, the floor began to vibrate and the walls echoed a low, deep rumble.

"Is that the Tube?"

Sarah nodded. "The Victoria Line runs about fifty meters behind the north wall. I spend so much time down here that I hardly notice it anymore. Michael says I should just set up a cot."

Sarah opened the door and Cassie stared at the rows of floor-to-ceiling shelves. "How big is this room?"

"Two-thousand square feet. What are we looking for?"

"A reason for them to be here after they stole the Magna Cartas. Is there anything in here about them?"

Sarah led the way through the maze of shelves as easily as if she was in her own living room, then stopped and indicated several rows.

"The Magna Cartas were signed in 1215. Everything we have concerning 13th century England is all through here."

"Can you tell if anything is missing, or has been disturbed?"

The curator peered at each of the shelves, crammed full of parchment documents and leather-bound books. Finally, she straightened and shook her head.

"I'm sorry. I don't see anything obvious. Perhaps in another section…"

"Forget it. If they stole something else, we'll deal with that after we get the Magna Cartas back. I'm going to take a walk around the room."

The exterior walls were smooth concrete without any hint of a hidden exit. She stopped when she came to the door for a utility room. It was unlocked. Cassie looked inside. Tools and supplies filled shelves on two walls. The rest of the room was jammed with equipment, barely leaving space to turn around. She closed the door.

"I've seen enough." She shook her bag of electronics. "Time to get to work."

They began in room 106.

"Just as I thought," Cassie said, pointing to the hole in the wall and the exposed cables.

Sarah watched as Cassie attached a circuit board to the cables, grinning when the PACCAR Gallery appeared on the screen of Cassie's brand new laptop. Then they went to the gallery where Cassie repaired the motion detectors and the sensors in the display cases and Sarah replaced the acrylic covers over the fake Magna Cartas. Two hours later, they returned to room 106 so that Cassie could take down the circuit board.

Sarah shook her head. "I can't believe we just did that."

She tried to sound alert, but Cassie could see that the she was practically asleep on her feet.

"We're done for tonight," said Cassie. "Go home. Kiss your husband. Get some sleep."

"I'm all right…" she began to protest.

"You're wiped out, and I need you sharp. First thing tomorrow, I want to look at footage from the exterior security cameras. With a little luck, we'll see our boys coming out of the building."

TEN

Ten minutes later, Cassie left the Library through the main entrance. She stopped halfway across the plaza and took a moment to think about the thieves. If the three missing guards had stolen the Magna Cartas, they had gone about it like pros, minimizing the risk of getting caught wherever they could. Not what she would have expected if this was their first heist.

Collecting the ransom could prove riskier than the theft. They'd only given the Library five days to come up with the money. Had they allowed less time, the Library probably wouldn't have been able to assemble the cash by the deadline. Had they allowed more time, the odds increased that they would be caught. Five days was smart. High pressure but manageable.

What would the thieves do while they waited? They'd want to see what the Library did about the exhibit. No doubt they expected the Library to cancel it. When the exhibit opened as scheduled, they'd have to find out why. That meant sending someone inside. Someone who'd blend in and not attract attention. Someone like the man she'd seen staring at her and Sarah from the bottom of the stairs. She closed her eyes, summoning his image. He was average height. Older. Probably mid-fifties. Pudgy. Thinning hair. Dressed in a jacket and tie. But it was his eyes that she remembered the most. Dark, intense, penetrating. Unforgettable.

They'd consider the cover-up of the theft to be good news. Proof the library was keeping it quiet while they pulled the money together. And if the thieves believed that, they would have to keep the Magna Cartas close by, unless they had no intention of returning them.

She also expected the thieves to continue watching the Library for any signs that the police or someone like her had been brought in despite the warning in the ransom note. And, she expected them to pay special attention to Sarah St. James and Ian Thorpe to see if they did anything out of the ordinary.

If Thorpe was involved, he would be their eyes and ears. But if he were, why was the man at the bottom of the stairs so interested in Sarah and her?

And, if the thieves were as professional and thorough as she gave them credit for, they'd watch the library at night as well. Her senses sharpened, Cassie walked the rest of the way to the curb at Euston.

She caught the glow of a cellphone in a doorway across the street. It wasn't enough light to make out whoever was holding a phone pressed against an ear except she could tell it was a man. And, the light was enough to cast a shadow as he lifted something, probably a camera to his eye. Nothing she could do about him taking her picture. At the worst, whomever he worked for would identify her as an employee of Global Security, leaving her cover intact.

He was careless enough to let her to know he was there and what he was doing. Or he was too stupid to know that he'd been careless. That was a contrast to how skillful the robbery had been. A rookie mistake one of the missing guards might have made. Or maybe the man with the camera was as tired as she was.

She hoped he'd follow her so she could get a good look at him. Maybe he'd even try something so she'd have an excuse for a conversation she'd enjoy more than he would. And, if he didn't, she'd follow him.

She'd gone two blocks before she was certain that he wasn't tracking her but there was no trace of him after she circled back. He was sharper than she'd given him credit for. Good, she thought. More fun that way.

ELEVEN

J ake's plan was to figure out what Cassie was working on, then find her. That would, he hoped, prove to her that he had the skills to be a good partner. He had been to London often enough to know his way around but he'd never tried finding someone who didn't want to be found in a city of eight and half million people. The odds of being dealt two aces for his hole cards in a game of Texas Hold 'Em were one in two hundred twenty-one. Long odds, measurable odds but he liked them better.

He'd overheard Cassie say *all four of them* in her phone call with Prometheus. Easy enough. She was going after four items, though the number could refer to people or locations. Cassie only went after high value assets worth at least a million dollars, ensuring her minimum two-hundred fifty-thousand-dollar fee. Her clients had to be wealthy enough to both afford the assets and the fee. That didn't help much since London was home to more billionaires than any city in the world.

After checking into a suite at the Amba Charring Cross Hotel he surfed the net for news of any high-profile thefts or unexplained losses of valuable objects but found nothing that matched with the little he knew. He wasted the rest of the day and a good part of the evening wandering around London searching for clues as if one would suddenly appear out of nowhere. A good meal and a few drinks in the hotel bar didn't soften the harsh realization that he had no idea what he was doing.

Back in his suite, he took a shower, wrapped an oversized, soft white bath towel around his waist and flopped onto a plush easy chair, the cushions cocooning him. Everything about the suite, from the towels to the cushions was designed for comfort yet he was anything but comfortable. His day had been a total bust.

He shoved himself out of the chair and paced the length of the suite. If he couldn't find Cassie there was no chance he'd ever convince her that they should work together.

Stopping at the wall of windows twenty-five stories above the city, he stared out into the night. Bright yellow headlights blurred and blended with red taillights in a swirl of color snaking through the streets. Buildings glimmered and glowed as lights were turned on and off. Stars shown down from an ink black sky, the full moon shining its own glittering spotlight on the Thames. It was the kind of view that should have made him pause in appreciation but to his eye, it was a gigantic puzzle, a random maze that he couldn't navigate.

He slapped his hand against the glass and started pacing again, feeling like he was playing against the house in a rigged game. He could draw cards all night and still not have a chance. And that, he finally realized was his mistake. He had to think of this like it was a poker game and poker wasn't only about the cards - it was about the people playing them. He'd won more money by breaking the codes behind their expressions, body language and chatter than by hitting on the last card. He'd have to change the game to one in which he could talk to or, better yet, see Cassie.

The obvious solution was to call her but that was more problematic than it appeared. He needed to catch her off guard. Otherwise, she'd suspect that he was digging for information. If he called and she didn't answer, she'd have time to prepare before calling back. If she answered but didn't have the time or inclination to play his game, he'd have wasted what would probably be his only shot. Somehow, he had to make her call him when her case was the furthest thing from her mind.

Striding back and forth, he caught a glimpse of himself in the full-length mirror hanging on a wall between two four-drawer dressers, giving him an idea. Smartphone in hand, he stood in front of the mirror and loosened his towel, letting it drop to the floor. With one hand placed strategically over his groin, he smiled and snapped a selfie of his reflection. Chuckling, he texted the photo to Cassie, adding *what's up?* He put the towel back on and waited. Less than a minute later, his phone beeped with her invitation for a FaceTime call. He tapped a button on the phone and her face materialized.

"Oh, my god! You are totally insane!" She cackled and wiped tears from her eyes.

"Why? Was the lighting that bad?"

She sputtered and giggled, barely able to get the words out. "The lighting was fine but I didn't realize you had such small hands."

"You forget that the camera is like the side mirror on your car. Objects are much larger than they appear."

Cassie finally caught her breath. "No, dummy. They are closer than they appear. Seriously, though, you're out of you mind, you do know that? I can blackmail you for the rest of your life with this picture."

"You forget that I have no shame. I couldn't find a decent game and didn't have anything better to do so I thought I'd brighten both our days."

"Well, you succeeded."

He paused. "I miss you." He regretted the words as soon as they slipped out. Turning the call into a serious discussion of their relationship would end it before he got started.

Cassie dropped her eyes for a moment, then looked at him, her voice soft and low. "I know."

Jake wished she'd have reciprocated but shifted gears. "Hey, how about I send you another selfie. Just tell me where to put my hand."

Cassie couldn't help but laugh again. "No! No! No! Don't you dare! Wait! Forget the dare part. I know you can't resist that. Just, just – put some pants on."

"All I've got is a towel."

"Really?"

"Really. Ooops. It fell off," he said, letting it go. "I'll just bend over." He slowly aimed the camera toward his waist.

Cassie let out a scream mixed with laughter and turned her head away from the camera, giving Jake a view of papers spread across her desk. He snapped a picture and grabbed the towel.

"You can look now. I'm decent again."

She came back into view, still grinning. "I'm not sure that's possible."

"You know, you're probably right. I think I'll ditch the towel."

"That's my cue to say goodbye, but…."

"Yes…"

"This was fun…Let's do it again sometime."

He hadn't learned anything from Cassie that would help him find her. But, he'd taken a chance on a long shot with the photograph and opened it on his phone. Sheets of paper were layered one on top of the other face down except for the top inch of one sheet that was face up. There was handwriting on the paper but he couldn't make it out even after enlarging the image as much as the phone allowed. He emailed the photograph to himself, downloaded it and enlarged it on his laptop, zooming in and out until he could read Cassie's handwriting, saying the words out loud.

"4 MCs. What the hell does that mean?"

His Google search turned up entries about a musical group called Jazzy 4 MC's, the MCS 4-chip set in the Intel 4004 microprocessor and the role of mast cells in male infertility. Another dead-end. Feeling defeated again, he picked up the day's issue of the *Mirror* the hotel staff had delivered to his room.

Returning to his easy chair, he leafed through it, hoping the distraction would loosen some nugget hiding in his head. And there it was in a headline on the front page.

Historic Reunion Begins Today.

A grin spread across his face as he read the article. An exhibit at the British Library of the four remaining original Magna Cartas had opened that morning.

"4 MCs…four Magna Cartas." Jake let out a whistle. "Cassie," he said, wishing she could hear him. "What in the hell went wrong?"

TWELVE

Cassie's phone rang at 5:00 a.m. She rubbed the sleep from her eyes and saw that it was Gunnar. She cleared her throat and answered.

"And good morning to you."

"Did I wake you?" Gunnar asked.

"We're you hoping to?"

He huffed. "Of course."

"You poor thing. Do you want the truth or a lie?"

"With you the lie is always better."

"Okay," Cassie propped herself up in bed. The t-shirt she'd slept in was bunched below her neck, the rest of her bare. The sheets were tangled as if she'd spent the night wrestling. She thought about and was glad that Gunnar expected a lie because she couldn't possibly explain why she was telling the truth. "I was having a steamy, erotic dream verging on earthshattering heights of ecstasy when you called and ruined it for me."

"You left out moist and hard. Can't have an erotic dream without those adjectives."

"I'll let you write the script for my next one. What do you have for me?"

"Ian Thorpe and Sarah St. James are noble civil servants with no prospects of getting rich. While I was at it, I took a peak at Malcom Bridges. A million pounds was transferred to a Singapore bank account in his name ten days ago, the same day he opened the account."

"Transferred from where?"

He grunted, a sound Cassie only heard him make when he encountered a problem he couldn't solve. She didn't hear it often. "I haven't pinned down the source yet."

"Stay on that and check the finances of the three missing guards. I'll send you their information."

She ended the call, uploaded the guards' personnel files to Global's secure server and went for a run. It was still dark and the air was chilly and heavy with the scent of oncoming rain. Leaving the hotel, she turned right along the A4, scanning her surroundings as she built up to a steady, methodical pace. A morning run was her way of clearing her head but she had a different purpose today – to draw out anyone watching her.

Whoever had taken her photograph outside the Library had to have been involved in the theft. Why else would he have been hiding and so quick to disappear? Best to assume she'd been identified and traced to her hotel until proven otherwise.

A few pedestrians were hurrying down the sidewalk, but nobody lingered pretending to talk on the phone or read a newspaper. No cars slowed for a closer look as they passed.

She followed the curve of the road, then turned south toward the Thames on Savoy, a commercial street not yet busy. Three cars passed her. She glanced over her shoulder at a fourth, a white Ford Fiesta, creeping along a block behind her. It was the most popular car in the UK in the most popular color, a car so ubiquitous as to almost go un-noticed, which made it precisely the kind of surveillance she was ex-pecting.

Cassie stopped at the wrought iron gate into Victoria Embank-ment Gardens, a wedge-shaped pedestrians-only strip of green along the river. Rain began to fall. She turned and faced the car, now half a block away, locking on the driver, a burly man too big and broad to have been last night's photographer. His eyes widened, then narrowed to angry gashes as he stopped in the middle of the street, engine idling, his cover blown.

"All right, then," Cassie said. "Let's play."

Tugging the hood of her sweatshirt over her head, she bolted into the Gardens on the gravel footpath. She was alone, no other runners braving the weather. If her watcher wanted her, he'd have to come after her on foot or risk losing her when she slipped out another entrance. And, when he did, she'd have him on her ground. She liked nothing better than turning the tables.

The quarter-mile path ended at a band shell surrounded by a picnic area. Cassie hid behind a closed refreshment stand and waited.

The rain was pouring down in sheets moments later when the man trotted into view wearing jeans, a waist-cut jacket and black boots. His heavy brows and thick features didn't resemble any of the missing guards. Water ran off his uncovered head as he wiped his eyes. Smacking his fists against his sides, he studied the shell and refreshment stand before he went back the way he came.

Cassie waited a few minutes, then walked in the opposite direction, out of the Gardens onto Villiers Street where the shops and offices were still dark. The street was quiet. The rain had slowed. She'd lost him for now but knew he would be back.

She tightened the drawstring on her hood, tucked her hands in the pockets of her sweatshirt and headed for her hotel. She passed a shuttered convenience store called Cravings. The name was enough to stir her hunger. Just ahead, was Gordon's Wine Bar. She smiled to herself, now both hungry and thirsty. A gated wrought iron fence separated the two buildings, darkness filling the void.

She heard a rustle of movement and felt the brush of air an instant too late as someone reached out from the other side of the fence, grabbed her by the shoulder and threw her down a flight of stairs. Her back took the brunt of the fall leaving her sprawled on the ground, breathless.

Shaking her head, she stood and found herself on a concrete pedestrian path. The basement wall of the convenience store was to her left. The lower level of the wine bar was to her right. A dim light from inside the bar cast a faint glow across her surroundings. A pair of tables for Gordon's customers sat outside the bar. A large umbrella rose from the center of one of them. Another umbrella tied snugly around its middle lay across the second table.

Glancing behind her, she saw that the path continued in a straight line with small pockets of light above several doorways. And then she realized where she was. Watergate Walk ran along what used to be the banks of the Thames in the 1800s. It was where boatmen landed their ferryboats. Now a row of shops and restaurants lined the Walk and Victoria Embankment Gardens lay between it and the river. Her watcher had waited for her to leave and taken a short cut from the Gardens to the Walk to intercept her. She wouldn't underestimate him again.

The man stared down at her, framed by the open gate in the center of the fence, his shadow swallowing the light from the street, his gun aimed at her. Cassie had fought men bigger and stronger than herself, including some that were armed, and learned to take advantage of being underestimated because she was a woman. But this man wasn't just big. He was a predator. She saw it his conquering pose at the top of the stairs and in his unhurried swagger as he came toward her. She would have been a fool not to be frightened and she wasn't a fool.

"'Allo, Cassie. Lovely to make your acquaintance."

THIRTEEN

Cassie took a calming breath and staggered her feet slightly wider than her hips and angled to the side, her knees facing the same direction. She tightened her core enough to take a punch. It wasn't a fighting-ready stance but it was a start. Remaining flat-footed with her arms loose at her sides made her more vulnerable but she counted on that to draw him close enough that she might be able to disarm him.

The man reached the bottom of the stairs, stopping out of her reach, holding his gun at his side. He ran his eyes up and down her, a small smile at the corners of his mouth like she was a special treat he was savoring before devouring her.

Cassie kept her face slack, her breathing even. Owning the ground wasn't always about who held the gun. It was also about keeping control of herself while rattling her opponent. She brushed off her sleeves, nonchalant.

"So, you know my name. Who are you?"

"I'm the man with the gun."

Cassie sighed and shook her head. "Didn't your mother teach you any manners? You should always introduce yourself when you attack an unarmed woman. Unless, of course, you're too shy to talk to girls. Or maybe you're just embarrassed because your parents gave you a sissy name."

"You're a snarky one, aren't you? I like that in a woman…to a point. You can call me Aramis, not that the name will do you any good."

She pulled her phone from her sweatshirt, hoping he didn't notice when she snapped a picture of him. "I'll just call 911 and let you tell the first cop that shows up your real name."

He raised his gun toward her. "Do that and your precious Magna

Cartas will end up confetti tossed about like it was New Year's Eve. Tell that to your friends at Global Security and make 'em believe it."

Though Cassie's picture had been taken barely six hours earlier, both she and her employer had been identified. They might know about Global Security but she was certain they knew nothing about Prometheus. Still, their sophistication and resources were impressive. She decided to reinforce what she hoped Aramis thought he knew about her.

She lifted her hands in mock surrender. "Well, I'm glad we're past the I-don't-know-what-you're-talking-about bullshit because that makes my job a lot easier. The British Library's insurance company hired Global Security to investigate their loss and you've got to admit this is one seriously big-assed claim. If you destroy the Magna Cartas, it will cost them a fortune and I'll lose my job. All we care about is getting them back so we don't have to write a huge check. Help me out with that and I'll tell anyone that asks I tripped and fell down those stairs."

He cocked his head to one side. "Insurance, eh? How much?"

Cassie paused, letting the hook sink in a bit deeper, hoping this was the turning point. "Ah…I'm sorry, but…ah…that's confidential information." He took a menacing step toward her and she put up her hands again. "Okay, okay. It's a lot, a hundred million pounds." She took a chance. "I probably shouldn't tell you this, but there's also a reward for anyone providing information leading to the recovery of the Magna Cartas."

"A reward, now. You don't say. How much are we talkin' about?"

"It's negotiable, depending on the information and how helpful it is but it's enough that you could stop throwing women down the stairs for a living."

"Ah, but I like throwing women down the stairs and I don't like ratting out my friends. Now, I'll have that phone."

"What phone?"

"The one in your hand you just took me picture with, you stupid twit."

"This phone? Sorry. It was a gift and I'm kind of attached to it."

"Maybe I'll just shoot you and take the phone."

"You're not going to shoot me."

He aimed the gun at her heart. "And why not?"

Cassie put her hands on her hips and smiled. "Because as soon as you do, you're going to walk out of here and be picked up by one of the ten million cameras that record every ass scratch in London. You'll be arrested before you can figure out that you're too stupid to unlock my phone. So, that's why you aren't going to shoot me."

Aramis nodded and tucked his gun behind his back in his waistband. He stroked his chin and folded his massive arms across his chest. "You make a good point. I'll just take it from you then and pardon me if I break a few bones."

Cassie raised her back heel, keeping her right elbow and forearm close to her body, her left arm slightly in front. "Pardon me if they're yours."

Aramis' eyes flashed as he charged her. Cassie launched a kick to his solar plexus but he grabbed her foot in midair, twisted it in the opposite direction and sent her tumbling toward the wine barrel tables. Crouching, she grabbed the umbrella lying on one of the tables and sprang at Aramis as he closed in. She speared him in the belly but he brushed the umbrella aside as if it was a feather. And then he was on her, arms wrapped around her middle, lifting her off the ground and squeezing her in a bear hug.

Cassie dug her hands in his hair and yanked his head back and smashed her forehead into his nose. The cartilage crumbled and his blood washed over her cheeks. Aramis yowled, released his grip and backhanded her across the face, knocking her to the ground. Dazed, she looked up at him, scooting backward at the sight of his gun pointed at her head. Blood ran from his ruined nose. He pinched his nostrils, staunching the flow and wiped his face with his sleeve.

"You don't know who you're fuckin' with you manky bitch but you're sure as hell gonna find out. Now give me your goddamn phone or decide that it's worth dyin' for."

Cassie handed him the phone. "You won't get away with this," feeling foolish for trotting out the cliché but unable to think of anything better.

"That's where you're wrong, Missy. We've got all the bases covered. You tell that to the gaffers at the Library and Global fucking Security and tell them if they even think about doin' anythin' but payin' the money, they'll never see the Magna Cartas again in this life or the next."

FOURTEEN

ooking in the bathroom mirror in her hotel room, Cassie studied the dark welt blossoming on her cheek and began to tremble. It was an involuntary reaction stirred by fear and anger. She hated it but accepted it, grateful that there were no witnesses to her moment of weakness.

The shaking passed. She examined her bruised face again. Makeup might cover it but if that didn't work, she'd blame it on walking into the bathroom door in the middle of the night. She pulled off her top and looked over her shoulder at the reflection of her back in the mirror. Splotches of black and blue were puddling from her shoulders to her waist.

She put her top back on and called Gunnar from her laptop using the secure videoconference network he and Prometheus had designed.

"Va! What happened to your face?"

"I had a chat with one of the gang that stole the Magna Cartas. He's a real charmer. Calls himself Aramis. He admitted that he's part of the gang that stole the Magna Cartas. And he knew my name and that I work for Global Security. What's worse is that he took my phone. How big of a problem is that?"

"No problem at all. I can track the GPS chip in the phone and I can save whatever is on the sim card to our cloud server and then erase the card remotely. But the phone has to be turned on. Let me check." He paused for a moment. "And yours is still on. Give me a second." Cassie heard him humming in the background. "Done. I've sent a kill signal making it useless. Do you have another one of our phones?"

"Yes."

"Try not to lose it."

Cassie considered whether to ask her next question but couldn't think of any way to avoid it. "When you said you backed up my phone did you mean that everything that was on it is now on Prometheus' server?"

"Is that a problem?"

Cassie crunched her eyes. Her body flushed and her cheeks burned. She hadn't felt so foolish since her mother read her diary out loud when she was ten years old. "Maybe…sort of."

"Maybe, sort of what?"

She took a deep breath. "A friend of mine sent me a picture that I'd really rather no one else saw, especially Prometheus. Can you delete it?"

"Not without looking at it."

"Oh, come on, Gunnar! Give me a break!"

He laughed. "Hey, I have to know which one to delete. Hang on. I'll have a look…Va! That Jake Carter knows how to wear a towel."

"I know. He must have been drunk." Cassie chewed her lip, hoping Gunnar would buy her excuse.

"Very drunk. You're right. You don't want Prometheus seeing this. I'll wipe it off the server."

"Yeah, about that…"

"Don't worry," he said, laughing again. "I'll send it to your new phone but you owe me."

"When have I not?"

FIFTEEN

It was just after 8 a.m. when Cassie found Sarah St. James in her office glued to her computer with a second monitor connected to it. Sarah took one look at her, gasped and covered her mouth.

"Good God, Cassie. What happened?"

Cassie grimaced. "I ran into the bathroom door in the middle of the night."

Sarah stood and came around her desk for a closer look. "That's what my mum used to tell me when my dad slapped her around. I didn't believe her then and I don't believe you now." Cassie turned her head away. "You were in a fight, weren't you? Was it about the Magna Cartas? Please tell me you're alright and that you didn't call the police."

Cassie stepped past her. "I'm fine. It's nothing for you to be concerned about and I didn't call the police."

Sarah folded her arms over her chest. "Don't treat me like a child, Cassie. There's too much at stake."

Cassie studied Sarah. Her jaw was set, her shoulders were square and the determined look in her eyes said she was anything but a child.

"I had a not very polite chat with one of the gang of thieves when he caught up with me on my morning run. I broke his nose and he gave me my new look. He calls himself Aramis. He's not one of the guards. I don't know where he fits in but he let me know they're serious about destroying the Magna Cartas if we don't pay the ransom."

"How'd he know about you? I thought your firm was supposed to be experts at this sort of thing."

Cassie didn't deny Sarah's criticism. "We are but these guys are good. They had someone watching the Library when I left last night and he took my picture. They knew who I was, where I worked and where I was staying before dawn this morning."

Sarah thought for a moment. "No comfort in that, is there." She paused. "You broke his nose? How?"

"I head-butted him."

"What is that?"

"I smashed my forehead into his nose."

Sarah covered her mouth. "Oh, dear God. That sounds awful."

"Worse for him than me. Don't worry. I handled him."

Sarah tilted her chin up, surveying Cassie's face again. "So far, I'd say it's the other way around. Maybe we need more help, maybe a…"

Cassie bristled. "Man? A big, strong man to scare the other big, strong man? I've fought that battle too many times with men who thought I couldn't do the job because I was a girl. And they all underestimated me."

Sarah blushed. "I'm so sorry. You're right of course. It's the same for women here." She clenched her jaw. "I wish I'd have taken a swing at that pig Ian Thorpe when he tried to grope me. I took a self-defense course a few years ago but in that moment, I forgot everything I'd learned."

"Don't feel bad. There's a big difference between the classroom and the alley."

"Or the library. Maybe you can give me a quick refresher just in case Aramis the Ape returns to the scene of the crime."

"Sure, if we get a chance but I doubt you'll need it. First rule – keep your client out of the fight. As for guys like Thorpe, it's the same everywhere. There's no getting used to it or getting over it but you should never have to put up with it. We just have to keep proving we can do the job. I know I can do mine and I know you can do yours so let's do them. What are you working on?"

Cassie followed Sarah to the other side of her desk to look at the computer. The main monitor was divided into four quadrants, each displaying a frozen frame from a camera feed.

"These are the feeds from four exterior cameras, one on each side of the building, and they cover every possible exit." She pointed out two doors and two windows visible in the frames. "I've paused each feed at midnight on the morning of the robbery. We can fast forward through them until we see someone."

"How many more cameras are there?"

"There's four hundred twenty-five in all."

Cassie winced at the prospect. If the exterior cameras didn't pick up the thieves, they'd have to review all the videos to try and trace their movements inside the library. She looked at the second monitor, which displayed a live feed from inside the Magna Carta exhibit.

"What's this for?"

"Peace of mind. There was an incident yesterday with one of the visitors jumping the barrier, getting right up to the display case. If someone who knew what they were looking at were to examine those documents too closely…" She shook her head at the very idea.

"The reproductions look great," Cassie said, knowing that she'd feel the same way in Sarah's place. She pulled up a chair and they settled in to watch the long hours of security footage, hoping to catch a break.

SIXTEEN

J ake arrived at the British Library as soon as it opened. The long line of people waiting to get into the exhibit made him question whether he'd guessed wrong about Cassie's case. Either she wasn't trying to recover the Magna Cartas or the ones on display were fakes.

Though he liked the binary outcomes, he realized there were other possibilities. Someone could have threatened to disrupt the exhibit or vandalize the Magna Cartas. But he doubted Prometheus would have sent Cassie to London on such short notice for something like that, not because it was too mundane but because it didn't require Cassie's special skill set as an asset recovery specialist. And those possibilities didn't fit with the question he'd heard Cassie ask Prometheus over the phone – *All four of them?*

When Jake reached the PACCAR Gallery, he wasn't surprised that the display cases held Magna Cartas, whether they were originals or replicas. He scanned the gallery, doing the same kind of analysis he did in a poker game, studying the cards on the table, watching the players, predicting the odds each had a better or worse hand than his own. Instead of a felt-covered table, he was reading the room.

He noted the security cameras, motion detectors and the two guards, one at the top of the stairs and the other near the display cases. If the Library was worried about an attack on the exhibit, there would have been much more security. The guards looked bored. The Magna Cartas appeared legitimate but he wouldn't have known if they weren't.

Poker players had tells that gave away their secrets. Jake wondered if a museum exhibit did as well.

He took his time, making his way slowly around the gallery until he was back at the display cases. The guards hadn't moved, even to listen or speak to the radios pinned to their shoulders. None of the conversations he overheard included mention of any problems with the exhibit or concerns about security.

He climbed the stairs, stopping to talk to a short, squat, pasty-faced guard rocking back and forth on his heels. His nametag said he was Lyman Bransford. His eyes were puffy and red, the way Jake's looked after an all-night game.

"Big crowd," Jake said.

Bransford looked at him. "Aye."

"Must keep you on your toes."

"Aye."

"Must get tiring standing here all day. You look like you could use a day off. Get some sleep, if you don't mind my saying so."

"A day off?" Bransford scoffed. "Not likely since today's my first day and it's been a long one. Came on at midnight and I'm pulling a double. Not that I mind, seeing as how I've been on the dole for two months and the missus was driving me bonkers about it."

"A double shift, huh. That's tough duty especially with an exhibit like this. I imagine somebody's head would be on the block if anything happened to the Magna Cartas."

Bransford gaped at Jake. "Who said anything about that? It all looks tight and tidy."

Jake shook his head. "Not me. But the Magna Cartas must be worth a fortune. Hell, they're priceless. I mean where are you going to get another one, right? The security has got to be airtight." Bransford nodded. "I mean, if it wasn't, if there was any kind of problem, there'd be a lot more of you guys keeping an eye on things. Am I right?"

"Don't ask me, mate. This is my first go at security guarding since I got out of the army. I just go where they tell me."

"Boy, I know what that's like. It's crazy, though, for you to have to pull a double on your first day. How does that happen?"

Bransford rolled his eyes. "It happens when three blokes walk off the job and never come back. At least that was the talk when I clocked in."

"Ouch. When did that happen?"

"Night before last, right before the exhibit opened."

"And you got stuck picking up the slack. That sucks."

Bransford shrugged. "Not for me, mate. Gets me out of the house and puts a few quid in my pocket so I can pay my tab at the pub and answer silly questions from the likes of you."

SEVENTEEN

Cassie and Sarah fast-forwarded through as much of the video as they could, slowing to normal speed whenever someone appeared on the screen. They zoomed in on faces, frame by frame, identifying each guard and making notes of when they were seen at different locations in the library. They were slowly creating timelines for everyone that had been in the building the night of the robbery.

"Looks like all of them were doing their jobs, sticking to their assigned areas," Sarah said.

"Except we know that Pugh, Galloway and Bristol-Clarke didn't. None of them were assigned to the sub-basement levels but we know they were there."

"It's too bad there aren't any cameras on those levels. The only way we even know they were down there is because of the keycard records."

Cassie pushed her chair away from the monitor and ran her hands through her hair. "And that's the last sign of them. After that, they disappeared or put on their invisibility cloaks and walked out the front door."

"Makes no sense."

"Not yet, but it will."

Cassie glanced at the monitor showing the PACCAR Gallery and did a double take. She scooted forward and gripped the monitor with both hands.

"No..."

"What? What is it?"

"It can't be." Her jaw dropped as she watched Jake climb the stairs from the gallery floor and stop to talk to a guard. "How did he...how could he…" She stood and slapped her hand against the side of the monitor. "I'm gonna kill him…"

"Kill who?"

"Him," Cassie said, pointing at the monitor.

"Oh, my. He's too good looking to kill," Sarah said, turning her head toward Cassie only to realize she was out the door and down the hall.

Cassie found Jake strolling through the busy main hall of the Library. She watched him collide with a Korean tour group and apologize as he wedged his way past them, putting him face to face with her.

"Cassie! What are you doing here?" His eyes widened when he noticed the swollen bruise on her jaw. He reached for her cheek. "What in the hell?"

She batted his hand away. "It's nothing and don't pull your accidental tourist routine with me. What are you doing here? And don't tell me you were looking for a good book to read."

"Actually, I do need to renew my library card but I'm afraid they'll make me pay all my overdue charges. That stuff adds up after a while."

Cassie folded her arms over her chest. "This is serious, Jake. I'm not kidding." He just stared at her, a mischievous grin spreading from the corners of his mouth. Cassie's lips began to quiver as she choked back a laugh until she couldn't help herself and gave in.

"You really are impossible."

"But in an endearing way."

"That's not the word I had in mind. Am I supposed to believe that this is just a happy coincidence?"

"And if it isn't?"

"Then you should leave."

"Why? Because we can't possibly work together?"

"We're not having this conversation."

"Don't you even want to know how I found you?"

"No." Cassie glanced around and saw Sarah approaching from across the hall. She pinched the bridge of her nose and closed her eyes. "I don't believe this."

"Cassie, there you are," Sarah said. "You ran out so quickly, I wanted to make sure everything was alright."

Jake stuck out his hand. "More than alright. I'm Jake Carter. Global Security. And you are?"

"Oh. Sarah St. James. I'm the curator for the Magna Carta exhibit."

"Then we're all in the right place," Jake said. "I've been assigned to work with Cassie."

Sarah looked at Cassie. "I didn't know there were going to be two of you."

"Neither did I until I got the call this morning," Jake said. "I was in Paris wrapping up another case and they told me to get here as quickly as I could. Don't worry. We'll get the Mag…"

"Not here," Cassie hissed.

Jake smiled, keeping his eyes on Sarah. He didn't want to look at Cassie for fear that her glare would melt him. "Oh, sure. Of course. We should go somewhere private. Your office, maybe."

"Yes, let's do that," Cassie said. She put her hand on Jake's arm, squeezing until he flinched. "But I need to have a word alone with Jake first. We'll meet you upstairs."

Before Sarah could respond, a man appeared at her side. "Excuse me, Dr. St. James?"

"Now what?" muttered Cassie under her breath.

It was the man she'd seen the day before staring at her and Sarah from the bottom of the stairs. He offered his hand.

"It's a pleasure to meet you at last, Dr. St. James. I'm Inspector Gerald Murdoch. Metropolitan Police."

EIGHTEEN

S arah drew in a quick, inadvertent gasp. "Pleased to meet you too… Inspector."

"Allow me to congratulate you on a wonderful exhibit."

"So kind of you to say."

Murdoch leaned in closer, crowding her just a bit. "I'm wondering if I could have a word with you alone. It will only take a moment."

Sarah cast a quick glance at Cassie, who stepped forward, gazing into the detective's face.

"You look so familiar. Where do I know you from? I know! I saw you here yesterday, in the exhibit. Right?"

"Yes. I believe you did. And who may you be?"

"Cassie Ireland. Global Security."

"Global Security? Afraid I'm not familiar with it."

"No reason you would be. Insurers hire us to do security audits of the companies and institutions they insure. Our clients prefer we keep a low profile."

Jake edged between. "Nice to meet you, Inspector. I'm Jake Carter. Cassie and I work together at Global.

The detective raised his eyebrows. "Two security agents? I hope there's no cause for concern."

"Of course not," Jake said. "But we can't be too careful since the Library has one of the world's greatest collections. We're just here on a routine audit."

"And is the Library's collection being well cared for?"

"Top marks."

Murdoch smiled. "A bit odd, isn't it, to conduct an audit during an exhibit like the Magna Carta?"

"That's the best time," Jake said. "Especially since we never tell the insured in advance that we're coming. Look around. The place is packed. Gives us a great chance to see how the Library handles a high-profile event like the Magna Carta exhibit."

"I see, of course. Then I'm sure you noticed the problems with the display cases."

Sarah's eyes fluttered. "Problems? What problems?"

"Yesterday when I was here, I had a chance to take a close look at the Magna Carta display. In fact, I must say I took such a close look that a guard had to remind me to stay behind the rope line."

"Don't worry, Inspector," Sarah said. "We promise not to have you arrested."

Murdoch chuckled. "That's quite decent of you but, as I was saying, I did get a close look and, if I'm not mistaken, the sensors inside the display cases were discolored as if they'd been subjected to high temperatures, which as I'm sure you know, would render them useless. Just the sort of thing that would turn up in a security audit, wouldn't you say, Ms. Ireland?"

"Absolutely. I assure you the display cases were among the first things we examined."

"Ah, then you no doubt also saw that someone had cut or sliced through the acrylic covers protecting the Magna Cartas."

Cassie cocked her head and furrowed her brow. "Um, actually we didn't find any evidence of that or that the sensors were discolored."

Murdoch hesitated, studying Cassie, then turned to Sarah. "Nonetheless, I hope you'll indulge me, Dr. St. James. Let's have a look, shall we? I'd hate for the Library's insurers to spend what I assume is a substantial sum of money on an audit that missed something so important. Don't you agree?"

Sarah folded her arms against her chest. "Indeed...I mean, of course. Let's do that."

Murdoch led the way. When he stepped in front of the rope line, a security guard came toward them until St. James waved him off. Murdoch leaned over the hooded cases and then dropped to one knee, peering intently through the glass.

"It can't be," he muttered as he stood. "It can't be."

"I'm sorry, Inspector," Cassie said. "What is it that can't be?"

Murdoch removed his glasses, wiping them with his handkerchief. "Well, it's just that…"

"There's nothing wrong with the sensors or the acrylic covers?" Cassie asked.

"No, there doesn't appear to be. Tell me, Dr. St. James, has anyone serviced the display since yesterday morning, perhaps replacing the sensors and the covers?"

"Why, no. There was no reason."

He sniffed. "Quite right. No reason." He paused looking again at the Magna Cartas and then at Sarah. "I don't believe I mentioned that I spent a good part of my career assigned to the Arts and Antiquities unit."

"No, you didn't," said Sarah.

"My apologies. Among other things, we investigated thefts and forgeries of…well…of arts and antiquities, priceless objects like these." He swept his hand the length of the display cases.

"That's good to know," Jake said. "We'll be sure and give you a call if anything turns up missing during our audit."

"I'm afraid you'd have to call someone else. Last year, I was transferred to the Serious Crimes Command. Homicide, rape, that sort of thing. Makes me long for the arts, truth be told." He sighed and straightened his coat.

"In that case, I definitely hope we don't need to call you," Jake said. He tilted his head toward the crowd waiting to see the exhibit. "These folks are getting restless. Maybe we should move along and give them a turn."

Murdoch stared at him, his mouth turning down. "Yes, indeed. Can't keep the patrons waiting, can we? One last thing before we go, Dr. St. James."

"Yes?" she said.

"Might I have a look at the Magna Cartas after hours…with the hoods on the display cases open?"

For a fraction of a second, her head tick-tocked back and forth like she was dodging a punch. "Whatever for, Inspector?"

"I'm also a bit of a history buff and I've always had a special place in my heart for the Magna Carta. Can't think of a document more precious to an Englishman. Call it a courtesy from one rare documents lover to another."

Cassie interjected. "I'm sorry, Inspector but I'm afraid that's not possible. The Magna Cartas are very fragile and our client's insurance policy is quite specific on how they are the displayed and handled. Only authorized Library personnel are permitted to examine them and then only under strict environmentally controlled and secure conditions. I'm sure you understand."

"Of course, of course. Don't know what I was thinking. Can't blame a policeman for being curious, now can you." He touched his finger to his brow. "Good day."

NINETEEN

J ake started to say something when Cassie raised her palm. "Not here." Then she turned to Sarah. "We need to go back to your office."

Sarah eyed her watch. "Of course. I'm supposed to interview an applicant for an archivist position in ten minutes. I can get out of it if you need me."

Cassie shook her head. "Go. Do your job like it's any other day. We've got this."

"All right. And, please, my office is your office."

Jake followed Cassie. Each time he caught up to her, she found another speed, ignoring his requests to slow down and talk to him. When he grabbed her elbow, she shook him off. Once in Sarah's office, the door shut tight, Cassie paced, arms crossed, refusing to look at him.

"Why are you so upset?" Jake said. "That went about as well as it possibly could have under the circumstances."

Cassie stopped pacing, dropping her arms to her sides, squinting at him. "You have no idea what the circumstances are."

"I would if you told me."

"You're missing the point. I don't want to tell you."

"I get that. But I know someone stole the Magna Cartas and the ones on display are fakes. And now that Sarah and the cop know we're partners..."

Cassie raised her palm, stopping him. "They think we're partners because you told them we were. Forget that it's both ridiculous and a lie, it could ruin what I'm trying to do here and cost me my job."

Jake was taken aback by the anguish in her voice. "I'm sorry. I just thought after the last time..." He shook his head. "I know it sounds corny, but I never felt more alive."

"I don't do what I do so you can feel more alive, Jake. People tried to kill you and they failed. You had an adventure. It's over. You're a poker player. You're supposed to know when to fold."

He nodded. "Okay, you're right. I'm out. Take care of yourself." He opened the door.

"Wait! What do you think you're doing?"

"Leaving. Isn't that what you want?"

"Ugg! You can't go, not after you told Sarah that you'd been assigned to this case. She'll think we don't know what we're doing and she'll wonder if I can do the job without your help. We lose the client's confidence, we lose the client and the case."

Jake brightened. "Well, we wouldn't want that to happen. And, you have to admit, we make a great team."

"You're a problem, not a teammate. I'm stuck with you until I can figure something else out."

He reached for her. She backed away until she was against the wall. He leaned in and put his hands on her arms. Her biceps tightened and she turned her head to the side. He guided her chin back to center, leaning his forehead against hers, feeling the tension in her body slip away.

"If you're stuck with me, you might as well let me help."

"I don't know…"

"Let's just say until you figure something out."

"Like what?"

"Like we make a good team."

Cassie eased her head back, studying him. "I hope I don't regret this."

"We can agree on that."

She sighed and stepped around him, taking a seat at Sarah's desk and filled him in. Jake listened carefully, impressing Cassie with intelligent questions, reminding her that beneath his glib jokes and casual charm lay a keen, strategic mind.

"Any suspects?"

"There were three guards on duty inside the library that night…"

"The ones that didn't show up for work the next day?"

"How do you know about that? And, for that matter, how in the hell did you find me here?"

"I'll tell you my secrets if you'll tell me yours."

She said, "Not today. The guards are at the top of my suspect list along with a guy named Malcolm Bridges. He designed the exhibit and the security for it. And, he quit his job a couple of days ago."

"Who smacked you in the jaw?"

"He calls himself Aramis. He admitted being involved in the theft but he doesn't match the description of any of the missing guards and we haven't seen him on any of the library's surveillance videos, at least not so far."

"Aramis doesn't sound like a name picked at random."

"No, it doesn't. My guess is that there are two other Musketeers calling themselves Porthos and Athos."

"Don't forget D'Artagnan."

"The fourth Musketeer."

Jake nodded. "Fourth but first among equals. Find him and you may find whoever is calling the shots."

Cassie smiled. "A poker player and a fan of the classics. Who knew?"

"What about Inspector Murdoch?" Jake asked. "Is he going to be a problem?"

"He's a cop and he's suspects something is wrong with the exhibit, so, yes, he's going to be a problem."

"You don't think he was satisfied when he saw that everything was fine with the sensors and the acrylic covers?"

"He knows what he saw. He'll think someone swapped them out. Then he'll wonder why we lied to him and then he'll keep snooping and asking questions we won't want to answer."

"Which means we've got to get the Magna Cartas back before he figures out they've been stolen."

Cassie stood. "Which is why I'm going to see Malcolm Bridges."

"I'll go with you."

"No. You'll stay here."

Jake frowned. "And do what?"

"Figure out how the thieves left the library without being seen on any of the surveillance cameras. Sarah and I were reviewing the footage when I saw you on a live camera feed. There are hours and hours of video for you to review." She handed him the personnel files for the missing guards, pointing out their photographs. "Watch for anyone you see using any of the exits or climbing out a window between midnight and ten a.m. the day the exhibit opened, especially these three." She gestured him to Sarah's chair and explained how the system worked.

Jake looked from her to the computer screen and back to her.

"Really? You want me to sit here and watch videos?"

Cassie kissed him on the cheek. "It will make you feel alive."

TWENTY

Malcolm Bridges and his wife, Gladys, lived in Lewisham, a middle-class borough in southeast London. Their flat was on the fifth floor of a non-descript building on Elmira Street. Cassie rang the bell. A woman answered without opening the door.

"Yes? Who's there?"

"Cassie Ireland. I'm working with the British Library and I'd like to speak with your husband, Malcolm."

The door swung open revealing a short, thin, auburn-haired woman in her forties. She wore slacks and a loose-fitting blouse. Her face was drawn and her eyes were red and puffy.

"Mrs. Bridges?" Cassie asked. The woman nodded. Cassie handed her a business card. She gave the card a quick glance.

"Global Security? What's that got to do with the library?"

"We're working with Sarah St. James to review the library's security system. She told me your husband designed the security for the Magna Carta exhibit and suggested I talk with him but his secretary said he's no longer with Titan. I was hoping to catch him at home."

Her eyes filled and she wiped them with her blouse. "He's not here."

"Do you know when he might be back or where I might find him."

She shook her head. "I don't suppose even he knows that."

Cassie wished she could leave Mrs. Bridges to her misery but that wasn't possible. "May I come in?"

"Suit yourself."

Mrs. Bridges turned and shuffled down the entry hallway, leaving the door open. Cassie followed her into the kitchen. She sat at the table, hunched over a cup of tea. A pile of unopened mail lay on the table. *Final Notice* was printed in bold red on many of the envelopes. The return addresses were for debt collection agencies. She picked up a spoon and stirred her tea.

"I told you I don't know where he is, not that knowing would do much good."

Cassie took a chair opposite Mrs. Bridges. "I'm so sorry you're having to go through such a difficult time."

Mrs. Bridges stopped stirring her tea and shook her head. "What do you know about it?"

"Nothing, but it looks like your husband left you in terrible straits and I know that no woman deserves to be treated like that."

She sat up. "It was the gambling. Lost all our money. I got so I couldn't bear to answer the phone and listen to another bill collector threaten me."

Cassie reached across the table, cupping Mrs. Bridges hands. "How awful for you. Did Mr. Bridges tell you he was leaving you?"

She pulled away, tucking her hands under her arms. "We haven't done a lot of talking lately. Not with all of this," she said pointing to the unopened mail. "We had quite a row last week. He said everything was going to be all right, that he had something big working and that he was going to cash in and quit his job and we'd live the good life. Then yesterday morning, he got a phone call and shot out of the house without a word. Didn't even take his briefcase. I haven't heard from him since."

"Did he keep anything from work at home. If he did, it might be helpful to the library."

"I don't know. Malcolm used the second bedroom as an office. Have a look if you like."

Bridges' office was neat and orderly. Pens and pencils arranged in rows. No papers lying loose on the desk blotter. A laptop computer was plugged in, the lid closed. Cassie opened it, not surprised that it was password protected. She went back to the kitchen.

"Do you happen to know the password for your husband's computer?"

Mrs. Bridges frowned. "I don't know that I should tell you something like that."

"I don't blame you, but I might find something that would help us find him."

She considered that for a moment. "It's Gladys2311. I'm Gladys and my birthday is November 23."

Cassie plugged a flash drive into the laptop and downloaded everything on the hard drive, not wanting to take the time to sort through it now. When she returned to the kitchen, Gladys had folded her arms on the table and lowered her head, crying softly. The doorbell sounded. She looked up at Cassie.

"Would you like me to get that?"

"Please. I haven't the strength."

Cassie made the short walk to the door and opened it. Inspector Gerald Murdoch gave her a bemused smile. Her eyes widened and she sucked in a breath, chiding herself for her involuntary reaction, knowing that it would add to whatever suspicions Murdoch had. The moment passed and she gave him a welcoming smile.

"Hello, Inspector."

"Good day, Ms. Ireland." He paused, taking in the bruising on her face. "Are you quite alright?"

"Yes. Just clumsy. I ran into the bathroom door in my hotel room in the middle of the night."

He raised an eyebrow. "The night can be quite hazardous. You never know what can happen in the dark. Do be more careful."

"Not to worry, Inspector."

"Good, then. I wasn't aware that an audit of the British Library would be so broad as to bring you here."

"We try to be thorough. Malcolm Bridges worked for Titan Security Systems. He designed the security for the Magna Carta exhibit. He's no longer at the company. I hoped to catch him at home but he's not here."

"No, I don't suppose he is. Pity, though. Perhaps he could have explained those mysterious sensors."

Gladys hurried to the door. "Who is it? What's wrong"?

"Mrs. Bridges, I'm Inspector Murdoch, Metropolitan Police, Serious Crimes Command."

"Oh, dear God. What's happened?"

"May I come in?"

"Of course," Gladys said. "It's Malcom, isn't it?"

Murdoch stepped inside. "Let's sit down, shall we?"

Cassie sat next to Gladys on the sofa in the sitting room and held her hand, sensing what was coming.

"I'm afraid it's about your husband," Murdoch said. "I'm sorry to have to tell you that he's dead."

"Dear God," Gladys gasped.

Cassie rose and motioned Murdoch into the kitchen.

"What happened?" she asked.

"Mr. Bridges was found in the front seat of his car in an underground garage, strangled. Should I wonder whether his murder is related to your security audit?"

Cassie pointed to the mail on the kitchen table. "He was a gambler on a losing streak. I'd wonder about that."

TWENTY-ONE

Jake fast-forwarded through the footage from the security cameras covering the front, back and staff entrances to the Library, stopping when he saw any shadow that could possibly be a man. The thieves didn't appear.

Frustrated, he switched from the video to the library's design and construction plans, searching for any pipes, vents or passages big enough to crawl through. Two and a half hours later, he had nothing to show for it but the beginnings of a headache.

The door opened and Sarah came in. "Have you found anything?"

"Not yet," Jake told her. "And, honestly, I don't think I will. These guys planned for everything. They must have come up with a way to get out of the building undetected."

"But how? Every possible exit is monitored."

"There must be one that isn't. One that nobody knows about." Jake stood over the map of the Library still spread across the desk and put his finger on the Manuscript Storage room. "And since this is the last location we have for them, it has to be there, somewhere."

"It isn't," insisted Sarah. "Cassie searched that room thoroughly, and there is no other exit." Jake raised an eyebrow. "All right then." She came around to where he was sitting, edging him out of the way and opened one of her desk drawers. "Here." She handed him a key card attached to a lanyard. "This will get you in. Go see for yourself."

He took it. "Thanks."

Jake rode the elevator down to Basement Level Five and let himself into the Manuscript Storage room. Though the room was massive, he was most interested in the exterior walls. They were concrete, painted white and seamless. No sign of a button that would magically open a secret door. And the room was spotless. If the thieves had burrowed through a floor or wall, they'd have left a mess Cassie wouldn't have missed.

He leaned against the wall, pretending he was the thief, wondering how he would play his hand. The wall began to vibrate, interrupting his thoughts. At first, it was so slight he thought he was imagining the sensation. Then it picked up as if an electric current was buzzing through the concrete accompanied by a distant rumble that soon became a deafening roar. He stepped away from the wall as it began to tremble. He was certain of one thing. The walls were solid. The thieves would have had to blast their way through them.

"Oi, there." Jake jumped and spun around. A slight man in an olive colored maintenance uniform grinned at him. He was gaunt and gray, as if he hadn't seen the sun in a long time. His first name, Timothy, was stitched onto the uniform. "Didn't mean to spook you."

"That's alright. This place is like a giant tomb."

Timothy started to say something but stopped when another train sped past, causing the walls to shudder and growl again.

"Aye, it is a tomb of sorts for all of them dusty, old books and such. I've been here since the Library opened and I can count on one hand the number of visitors I've had."

"Must get lonely."

Timothy stared at Jake. "Suits me just fine. Them that does venture this far down have their credentials but I don't see yours."

"Credentials?"

Timothy pulled a plastic ID card clipped to his belt with a retractable cord. "One of these. Shows you got business being down here."

"Oh, sorry. Haven't had a chance to get one yet. I just got here this morning. I'm working with Sarah St. James." Jake fished his key card from his pocket. "She let me borrow this and told me to have a look around in here. You can call her if you're worried I might walk off with an ancient manuscript."

"Ha! Little as anyone pokes their nose down here, nobody'd notice if you did. Don't stay down here too long or the ghosts might get you," Timothy said with a wink before leaving Jake alone.

Jake waited until Timothy disappeared before exploring more of the Manuscript Room. He opened the door to the equipment room when he heard Cassie's voice behind him.

"Sarah told me I would find you down here."

"How'd you do with Malcom Bridges?"

"He wasn't home. I was having a nice chat with his wife, Gladys, when our friend Inspector Murdoch showed up and told us Bridges had been murdered."

"Holy crap!"

"No kidding. His body was found in his car in an underground parking garage. He'd been strangled, which is a tough way to kill someone. You've got to be very strong and very motivated."

Jake let out a long breath. "Bridges made a bad bet trusting these guys. They're thieves and killers."

"Having second thoughts about going after them?"

He shook his head. "Nope. Makes it easier in a way."

"You prefer killers to thieves?"

"Look, the robbery was planned to perfection, no detail left to chance. Hell, we don't even know how they got out of the building. These guys are smart. But killing Bridges was a mistake because it's going to bring the cops into the case. They just turned a winning hand into a longshot, which means they're probably going to take more risks. And the more chances they take, the better our odds."

"Except those risks could get us killed. Which is why I told Sarah about Bridges. I want to keep her as far in the background as possible. When she told me where you were, I thought I better get down here before you got in trouble."

Jake pointed at his chest. "Me? In trouble? Not likely?"

"No. More like inevitable."

"What are you doing down here? It must not have taken you very long to get through all that video."

Jake shrugged. "The video was making me cross-eyed. Basement Level Five is the last place we know for certain the thieves were. There has to be another way out."

"And you think you're going to find it in this walk-in closet? I already searched it and didn't find anything. Why are you so interested in it?

"I wasn't until you told me you'd already checked it out."

Jake pulled the mops, brooms and buckets out of the equipment room. Then he reached through the shelves to tap on the walls. Cassie watched from the doorway, arms crossed over her middle.

He studied the large piece of equipment in the corner. Sitting on a thick, black rubber mat, it had a half-moon housing over a round, heavy duty brush, wheels at each corner and a pair of handles in the rear. "This thing looks like a cross between a riding mower and a miniature Zamboni. What the hell is it?"

"It's a floor scrubber."

"How do you know that?"

"Because, dummy, it says so on the label next to the bottom of the housing."

"Oh."

He wedged himself behind the handle bars and maneuvered the scrubber out of the closet. Then he rolled back the rubber mat. There was a two square-foot concrete panel cut in the floor beneath where the scrubber and the mat had been.

Jake crouched next to the panel. The cut in the floor was too narrow for his fingers. Cassie nudged him aside. She was holding a pry bar.

"Found this on one of the shelves," she said.

She angled the claw end of the bar into the cut until she felt it catch, then levered it back, lifting the panel. Jake grabbed it and set it aside. They leaned over the opening, peering into a shaft leading to a pitch-black tunnel.

"Son of a bitch," Jake said.

TWENTY-TWO

searched this room. How the hell did I miss a trap door?" Cassie said.

"I checked the plans for this floor after I got cross-eyed watching videos. It's not on there. And, it was hidden under the floor scrubber and the mat. Easy to miss. I just got lucky."

Cassie knew that Jake hadn't gotten lucky. He was smart and she had been careless. And he had the decency not to remind her. That's what a good partner did.

"Lucky or not, it's great work." Cassie knelt next to the opening. "The floor is a foot thick but the panel is only a couple of inches thick. It was cut to fit the opening. There's a lip around the edges of the opening that it sits on. See if you can find a flashlight on one of those shelves."

Jake rummaged around until he found two and handed one to her. Side-by-side, they shined their lights into the shaft. An iron ladder was bolted to the brick surface. Their beams reflected off water running past in the tunnel a good twenty feet below. They gagged and covered their mouths.

"Shit," Jake said.

"Without a doubt. And probably worse stuff than that. Before the library was built, probably long before, this shaft must have been used to get into the sewer. The foundation buried it. These guys found it and figured out they could drill their way into the library without anyone knowing."

"Yeah, but that would have made a hell of a racket. Somebody would have noticed."

Another train flew past, the rattle and roar too loud for them to talk.

"Not with all that noise," Cassie said after the train passed. "All they had to do was time the drilling with the train schedules. Then cover the panel with the rubber mat and the floor scrubber."

"After the robbery, the last one down the shaft would have pulled the panel back in place. Someone on the maintenance crew must have put the mat and the scrubber back without giving it another thought."

"And even if the shaft was discovered, the thieves would have been long gone. All right, let's get down there."

He waved gallantly at the open manhole. "After you, boss."

"Don't call me that."

"How about team leader or captain, my captain?"

"Stick with Cassie and do as I say."

She tested the top rung of the ladder making certain it would hold their weight. Satisfied, she climbed down. Jake followed her. The ladder ended six feet above a tunnel. They dropped from the ladder into a stream of sewage that soaked them halfway up to their knees. The tunnel was rounded and made of brick, tall enough that they could stand. There was a paved ledge on both sides, wide enough for a rat scurrying past them with a half-gnawed chicken bone in its mouth but too narrow for them to walk on.

Cassie raised one shoe above the surface, shaking her black suede pump.

"Crap. That's five hundred dollars down the drain."

"Literally," Jake said.

"If you don't mind the smell, this is the perfect escape route. These tunnels go all over London."

"Which way do you think they went?"

She traced her light in both directions. The thin beam vanished after twenty feet.

"No way to know. They were carrying documents worth a hundred million pounds and a duffel bag full of equipment so they had to go slowly and carefully. If it were me, I'd want to get as far away as I could as quickly as I could but I wouldn't risk getting the Magna Cartas wet any longer than I had to."

"Why don't we go back up and find a map of the sewers. That

way we can identify their most likely route."

She aimed her flashlight at him. "Afraid of getting a little dirty?"

"Too late for that."

"They could have split up and gone in different directions. Our best bet is to stay down here and try to pick up their trail. You're a gambling man. Pick a direction."

Jake shrugged and pointed to their right. "Good as any."

Cassie walked past him in the opposite direction, stopping ten feet from the ladder when the beam of her flashlight revealed a smudge on the wall. "Check this out."

He picked his way through the sludge to join her. "What is it?"

"I think it's a hand print." She held up her hand next to it for comparison. "And it's aimed downward just a bit, like the person was moving. Falling."

She took a step back, then mimed losing her balance in the stream, flailing out a hand to catch herself against another part of the wall, leaving a similar hand print.

"You're right," said Jake. "But for all we know, the person who fell could have been some random sewer maintenance guy."

"Or it could have been someone who doesn't spend all day walking around down here. Like our thieves. I think this is the way they went."

"So, why did you ask me to pick the direction if you were going to go the other way?" He didn't wait for her to answer. "Okay, I get it. This isn't a guessing game."

She smiled. "Let's get going."

They moved slowly at first, avoiding clumps of debris that clung to the brick, as they looked for other signs of the thieves' passage. They reached a Y-shaped junction where two smaller tunnels joined to form the one they were in.

Jake said, "Your call but don't guess."

Cassie peered down both passages, saw nothing helpful, then decided, "Let's stay right."

She picked up a twisted fork lying on the ledge that looked it had been thrown down a garbage disposal. She used one of the tines to scratch a line in the brick beside the right tunnel.

"What are you doing?"

"Marking our route. Works better than bread crumbs. We don't want to end up wandering around in circles down here."

He shook his head. "Where did you learn all this stuff? Asset recovery school?"

"I got an A+ in sewers."

TWENTY-THREE

Half an hour later, they hit a dead end. A steel grate across the tunnel cut them off. Jake examined the lock which had rusted shut.

"Nobody's opened this thing for a long time."

"Okay," said Cassie. "Let's try the other tunnel."

They backtracked to a Y junction. Jake led the way into the passage on the left. This tunnel was smaller, not quite six feet in diameter, and they both had to hunch over as they walked, bobbing and weaving to avoid the foul sludge dripping from cracks in the brick ceiling.

"You still think those three guards pulled this off?" Jake said. "I mean, we're talking about night shift rent-a-cops here, not master criminals. This had to take months to set up and train for."

"They got all the training they needed in the military. And they didn't start working for the library until a month or so ago. By then, the shaft from the tunnel was probably done."

"I still don't see these guys coming up with this caper on their own. My money says somebody hired them and told them how to do it. Plus, the odds are way against their families not having some idea what they were doing."

"People only see what they want to see," Cassie said. "Especially when it's someone they love."

Jake twisted awkwardly to glance back at her. "The voice of experience?"

"No comment," she said, keeping her expression blank.

Jake turned around and let out a shout. "Motherfu...."

He stumbled backward into Cassie who caught him in a bear hug but she couldn't stop his momentum from knocking them off their feet.

"What?" Cassie said.

They scrambled to their feet, dripping with sewage. Jake pointed at a face staring up at them from the water. "That."

Cassie aimed the beam of her flashlight at the face. It was pale. The skin sagged. The eyes were gone. The mouth was toothless. She stepped closer, bent over and picked it up.

"This?"

It was a silicon mask that had gotten snagged on a clump of debris. Jake stood beside her, feeling foolish when he saw what she was holding.

"Are you kidding me," Jake said.

"Nope." She handed it to him. "It's so lifelike. See the hair in the eyebrows and the veins painted on the skin."

"It'd be a killer on Halloween."

"More like a thief." Cassie pulled up a photograph on her phone. "Say hello to Jeremy Bristol-Clarke. The guards didn't steal the Magna Cartas. The thieves wore masks of the guards' faces."

"Like Mission Impossible masks?"

"Exactly. All you need is a 3-D printer. Their families had no idea they were planning a robbery because they weren't."

"So what happened to the real..?" Jake said and stopped without finishing the question.

"I know. Malcolm Bridges is dead. These people don't leave loose ends."

"Not live ones, anyway. You think they left this here to point us in the wrong direction?"

"Not after they went to so much trouble to pin the robbery on the guards. This is their first mistake and our first break. Mr. Fake Galloway probably fell on his ass and didn't realize he'd dropped it."

"We're walking upstream so the mask drifted back here."

"Which means we're headed in the right direction."

They continued walking against the current, reaching another junction, then another, doubling back and searching every tunnel for telltale handprints. A wireless earpiece lying on the narrow shoulder told them the thieves had passed this way. Soon, they came to another shaft with a ladder leading up to a manhole.

Cassie said, "Your turn."

Jake held the end of his flashlight in his mouth and climbed the ladder. A rust coated padlock was looped through one of two clasps bolted to the edge of the manhole cover. The second loop in the door had been severed with a bolt cutter, leaving a gap big enough for the padlock's shackle to pass through. The manhole cover was unlocked. Jake dug his heels into the ladder rungs and shoved. The cover loosened. He pushed it aside and poked his head into darkness.

TWENTY-FOUR

Cassie and Jake climbed out of the sewer and scanned their surroundings with their flashlights. *Fuk the EU* was scrawled in red spray paint on a gray brick wall that curved over their heads and formed a large round passageway twice their height in diameter.

"Great," Cassie said. "Another tunnel."

"But at least it's not a sewer," Jake said. "We're moving up in the world."

They were standing on a platform along one side of the tunnel, overlooking a wide trench. Three thick metal rails ran along the bottom in both directions. A yellow and black sign painted on the middle rail warned, *Danger. High voltage.*

"It's the Tube," Cassie said.

Jake examined a set of double doors leading off the platform, marked *Exit to Street.* The handles were chained together and secured with a grimy padlock.

"This place has been abandoned for a long time," he said.

Cassie said, "They're called ghost stations. A nice spot to pop out of the sewer with a hundred million pounds in stolen treasure."

"They could be using the Tube tunnels as another way to get around the city without being seen." A train approached with a deep rumble. They stepped away from the tracks as the cars sped by in a clattering whoosh of air. "Assuming they could time it well enough to avoid getting flattened."

"Wouldn't put it past them. These guys are good."

Cassie ran her light along the wall, revealing another door at the far end of the platform marked *Emergency Exit.* She tried the door. It was unlocked. They stepped into a spiral stairwell. The steel steps were spotted with patches of rust. Jake craned his head upward.

"Looks like three or four flights."

"I'll lead. You follow," Cassie said.

They started to climb, around and around the central post, the steel joints creaking under their feet.

"If the guards didn't steal the Magna Cartas, who did?" Jake said.

"Professionals hired by someone with serious resources. There are plenty of people with enough money to finance this kind of operation."

"Sure. But how many of them would want to? I mean what's the point? Some rich guy wants to hang them in a secret room where he'd be the only one to ever see them?"

"You'd be surprised how much stolen art is hanging on walls like that" Cassie said. "Or, it could be someone that thinks the cost of the operation is worth it if they can collect the ransom and live long enough to spend it."

"Bad odds. Too many variables. Worse than playing against a stacked deck."

Cassie stopped and turned around toward Jake with a sly grin. "I thought you liked long odds."

Jake smiled in return. "Depends on what's at stake. Are mine getting any better?"

She shrugged. "Maybe."

"And if we find these guys and get the Magna Cartas back before we run out of time on Friday?"

"Could be your lucky day."

"You really know how to make a man feel good about being covered in shit."

"It looks good on you," Cassie said and continued to climb.

They reached a small landing at the top of the stairs and pushed through an exit door into the cold, fresh air. They stood for a moment, winded and dripping sewage, outside a red brick building inlaid with white bricks that spelled *York Road Station*. It was surrounded by a chain link fence. Cassie walked toward the fence and turned around, studying the building.

"What are you looking for?"

"Security cameras. Maybe we can get a look at our guys."

"And we know at least one of them wasn't wearing his mask."

She took a quick tour of the station's exterior. Walking back toward him, she shook her head. "No cameras."

Jake peered through the chain link fence at a used car dealership next door. "Hey, there are three cameras over there."

Cassie joined him. "And it looks like one of them has a direct view of the door we came out of. Gunnar should be able to hack into the footage the night of the robbery. It'll be dark, but we might get lucky."

She called Gunnar and told him what they needed. Then, they climbed over the fence.

"Hey, we're in luck," Jake said. "There's a cab." He stepped into the street and waved. The driver slowed alongside him then sped past. "What in the hell? Why didn't he stop?"

"Maybe because we're covered in shit," Cassie said.

"How about dinner," Jake said when the driver dropped Cassie at her hotel.

"I'd like that. Give me a couple of hours to get the sewer out of my hair."

TWENTY-FIVE

Jake caught his breath when he saw Cassie in the hotel lobby. She was wearing a simple body-skimming, off the shoulder black dress that highlighted the glow in her ebony skin. She'd pulled her hair back, laying bare her long, graceful neck. He wanted to fold her in his arms and kiss her until they both forgot about dinner.

She walked toward him, her eyes twinkling as if she knew exactly what he was thinking. "Hungry?"

"Famished."

"What are you in the mood for?"

He tilted his head. "I'm afraid it's not on the menu."

With an arched eyebrow, she said, "Don't be so sure. You haven't seen what's for dessert. I made a reservation at Hutong. The dim sum is incredible."

The restaurant was on the thirty-third floor of the Shard, a 95-story skyscraper. They were seated in a quiet corner overlooking the Thames, the city spreading out beneath them. A Chinese lantern cast a soft reddish glow across their table.

"We're supposed to get the ransom instructions on Friday which leaves us three days to figure this thing out," Jake said after the server took the order. "So, where do we go from here."

Cassie sighed. "Depends on whether Gunnar finds something on the videos from the car dealership. Right now, that's our best lead. But, you know what?"

"What?"

"Let's just enjoy dinner for now. I have a feeling this will be our last quiet meal for a while."

If this was the new Cassie, Jake was all in. "Works for me."

The food was decadent. The two bottles of Piedmont Barolo were excellent. They fell into easy conversation about food and music and funny stories from their travels, which only got funnier as they drank more wine.

"I realized that I'd picked up the wrong bag, and started looking around for whoever picked up mine," said Jake. "Then I saw this woman... a tiny little white-haired lady... with the identical bag. So, I went up to her and tried to explain what happened. But I don't speak Croatian and she doesn't speak English, so I'm doing my best pantomime..." He mimed holding up a carry-on bag, pointing to it and another imaginary bag beside Cassie with exaggerated gestures, then pretending to swap them. "But she gets the idea that I'm trying to steal her bag. So, she reaches into her purse and pulls out a can of mace. I duck and she sprays and hits the customs agent full in the face."

Cassie laughed. "You totally made up that story, didn't you?"

"Does it matter? It's a great story."

"It would be even better if it were true."

"Ah, well, if you can't trust a professional gambler, who can you trust?"

"That is the question, isn't it?" she said.

They walked back to her hotel and crossed the lobby to the bank of elevators. Cassie pressed the call button, then abruptly turned to face him.

"I didn't ask you to come to London, you know."

"I know."

"And I would have sent you home right away if I could have."

"I know."

She took a breath, then her words came out in a rush. "But you've been a big help and I'm glad you're here."

He gazed at her. "Me, too."

The elevator door slid open. They stood there, wordless, eyes searching each other. When the door began to close, Cassie grabbed him by the shoulders and hauled him into the elevator, planting her lips firmly on his. They kissed furiously as the doors shut and the car started to move, then stumbled out onto the sixth floor, barely pausing for breath. They made their way toward her room. She fumbled with her key card. The door swung open. They crashed against the wall, desperately tugging at each other's clothes.

Her purse tumbled to the floor, the contents spilling at their feet. Cassie pulled away, as if the dropped purse had awakened her from a trance.

Her back stiffened. "This was a bad idea. I'm sorry, I can't."

"I know you think it's risky to get too attached because of what happened to Gabriel..."

"But you don't know what it feels like to lose someone, do you?"

He held her gaze. "No. All I know is how I feel about you and I have a pretty good idea of how you feel about me."

She walked past him into her suite, hugging herself, then turned around. "I wish it was that simple."

Jake stayed where he was. "I can't make it simpler but I'll make it easier. You know how I feel. That's not going to change but from here on out, I'll keep things strictly business. If the day comes when you're ready for something more, you'll know where to find me."

Cassie looked at him, shook her head, then smiled. "You're..." Her phone beeped with a text. She studied the message. "Gunnar just emailed the footage from the camera in the used car lot."

Jake followed her to the desk where she'd set up her laptop. She downloaded the video and pressed the play button. The images were grainy but good enough. The door from the station opened and three figures emerged, one carrying a duffle bag on his shoulder. When they climbed the chain link fence, a street light illuminated their faces. Jake recognized masks of Lloyd Pugh and Tom Galloway. Cassie froze the frame and zeroed in on the man carrying the duffle bag. He wasn't wearing a mask. She enlarged his image until his features were clear.

"Who is that?"

"A dead man," Cassie said. "It's Gabriel."

TWENTY-SIX

T hat's impossible," Jake said.

Cassie closed her eyes for a moment. "Except that it isn't."

She walked to the window. Jake stood next to her, his hand on the small of her back.

"Are you certain it's him?"

She turned around. "You don't forget the face of someone you..." She looked away.

"Loved."

"I was so stupid." He put his hands on her arms. She stepped past him and grabbed a small pillow off the sofa, clutching it to her chest. "I should be happy that he's alive. I should be excited because if we find him, we find the Magna Cartas. But all I can think about is why didn't he tell me. You don't do that to someone you love. Damn him." She flung the pillow across the room. "Damn him."

"Why were you so sure he was dead?"

Cassie sat on the edge of the bed, hands planted on her thighs. Her heart was racing. She took several calming breaths.

"We were in Bosnia. It was so cold Gabriel said it was the next ice age. A Romanian fence named Costin Petrescu was going to put our client's Modigliani painting in a black-market art auction. It was a routine recovery until he and his crew showed up. We got away but they chased us to a clearing in a field where our chopper was waiting. Our car blew a tire. We had to run the last hundred yards. Gabriel was shooting at them to cover me while I climbed in with the painting but...he..." She stopped and cleared her throat. "I was leaning halfway out of the chopper to grab his hand and pull him aboard when Petrescu shot him in the back. I couldn't leave him. I started to jump out but Prometheus stopped me and ordered the pilot to take off. Then, Petrescu kicked Gabriel and shot him again."

"Why was Prometheus there?"

"He'd told us to break off our relationship or he'd get rid of both of us. We said okay but we stayed together figuring we could keep it a secret. He found out while we were on the mission and was so angry he came to fire us in person. But, as it turned out, he didn't have to."

"I'm surprised Prometheus didn't send in a team to rescue Gabriel or at least recover his body."

"He had a backup team standing by. They got there five minutes after we took off but it was too late. I'll never forget the look on his face when he told me Gabriel was dead. It was like he'd lost a son. As soon as we landed, I went back to find Petrescu and waited until he was alone."

"What did you do?"

"I shot him in the heart. He fell on the floor. Then I kicked him and put another round in his head. It was wrong. I knew it then and I know it now. I killed him. And, for what? So, I can see him in my nightmares for the rest of my life?"

"Why did you keep working for Prometheus?"

"It was the only way I could keep my sanity. Keep doing what I'd been doing. One step and one day at a time. He should have told me. He should have told me."

Jake sat next to her. "Maybe he was trying to protect you."

"Protect me? From what?"

"I don't know. We'll have to ask him."

"We?"

"Yes, we. You're not getting rid of me so easily. Like you said. We find him, we find the Magna Cartas."

"He won't be an easy man to find."

Jake walked to the door. "You found me. We'll find him. Fair enough?"

"Fair enough."

TWENTY-SEVEN

Cassie met Jake the next morning in the lobby of his hotel. She handed him a coffee from Starbucks and a muffin.

"This is breakfast?"

"Enjoy it," she said. "Hold still." Jake flinched as she inserted something in his left ear.

"What the hell is that?"

"It's a micro earpiece. We call them comms units. I'm using one too. It allows us to hear and talk to each other."

"For real?"

"For real and don't ask for the secret password. Now, let's go. We've got a lot of ground to cover today." She led him out to the street. "I reviewed the rest of the videos from the York Road station. The thieves split up after they climbed over the fence. Gabriel took the tube and the other two caught cabs. That's the last we have of them on camera."

"Which leaves us where?"

Cassie handed him a list of addresses. "These are the places where Gabriel liked to hang out in London. Talk to anyone that will talk to you. Let them know that you're looking for him and that it's urgent."

"What's the point in that? Anyone who knew him will tell me he's dead."

"If they tell you that much. My guess is that Gabriel reached out to someone he trusted to let them know he was alive and in London."

"Why would he take that chance?"

"Because he knows better than to trust the people he's working for. He'll want a backdoor just in case. The mastermind on this job could easily let them take the fall or decide he'd rather kill them than pay them. Whoever is helping him will get word to him. We won't have to find Gabriel. He'll find you."

"Why would he bother? Why not just get out of the country assuming he hasn't already done that?"

"He's more likely to lay low until things calm down. That's the way he worked. He needs to stay off the street but he can't risk someone running all over London asking about him when he's supposed to be dead. His employer won't appreciate the attention."

"You're saying he'll want to eliminate the risk?"

"First, he'll evaluate the risk. Then," she added with a grin, "he'll decide if he has to eliminate it."

"And where will you be while I'm drawing him out?"

"Close."

"How close?"

"Close enough."

He took another look at Cassie's list. "This is a waste of time. It's like trying to draw to an inside straight ten times in a row."

Cassie raised an eyebrow. "And why is that?"

"Because you're assuming the odds are the same for each place. Plus, it will take all day, maybe longer, for me to cover all of them. And, who knows how long it will take for Gabriel to track me down like a dog. We don't have that kind of time."

"Do you have a better idea."

"Look. You've got pubs, restaurants, coffee shops, a gym and a bookstore on your list. Only one of these is worth a shot."

"Which one?"

Jake pointed to the sixth entry. "Doyle's Rare Books." He looked it up on his cellphone and showed her the website. "It's been owned by the same family for six decades." He scrolled through the page identifying the staff. "They've all been there at least fifteen years."

Cassie nodded. "Okay. I get it. Someone who's been there a long time is more likely to have known Gabriel and remember him."

"That's not all. Any serious collector only buys from someone he trusts. It takes years to build that kind of relationship. The people at Doyle's get to know their top customers better than their own family.

They'll do anything to keep them happy and they know to keep their mouths shut. If Gabriel reached out to anyone from this list, odds are that person works there."

"What makes you so certain?"

"Because I collect rare books about probability. Ben Mitchell is my go to guy. He has a shop on the upper West Side and you couldn't water board my secrets out of him."

"Really? I can't wait to meet him."

"Keep Gabriel from eliminating me and I'll introduce you."

TWENTY-EIGHT

D oyle's Rare Books was in Chelsea. The royal blue exterior stood out from the whitewashed shops on either side. The interior was finished with contemporary polished light brown hardwood floors and walls painted a rich gray. Antique furniture mixed with the sweet smell of rare books for a comforting blend of old and new.

A lanky man with a mop of tousled brown hair dressed in jeans and a sweater sat at a desk in the front of the shop. He had the pale complexion of someone who'd spent his life in the stacks. He rose to greet Jake.

"Welcome to Doyle's. What brings you in?"

"A friend of mine recommended your shop."

"You're a collector?"

Jake laughed. "I tried to quit once but it didn't work out."

"I know what you mean." He looked around the overflowing shelves. "I walked in here when I sixteen and haven't left. Where in the States are you from?"

"It's the accent, isn't it? I live in New York but I grew up in Kansas."

"Dorothy and the Wizard and all of that, eh? We've got a first edition if you'd like to see it. I'm Andrew Finch," he said, shaking Jake's hand.

"Jake Carter. Thanks, but my collection is limited to rare books on probability. I've been looking for a first edition of The Book of Games by Gerolamo Cardona in the original Latin. I think it was published around 1520."

"Afraid that's not in my area. I'll have to check." An older man, bald with a full, closely trimmed beard flecked with silver and black, joined them. "Kevin, this is Jake Carter. A friend of his referred him to us."

"Hello, Mr. Carter. I'm Kevin Doyle."

"You've got a lovely shop," Jake said.

"Mr. Carter is looking for a first edition of…" He looked at Jake.

"The Book of Games by Gerolamo Cardona. In the original Latin."

"I know of it," Doyle said. "Some say the games Cardona describes were the forerunners of poker. Do you play?"

Jake shrugged. "Now and then."

"I've seen a copy up for auction from time to time, but our clients haven't expressed an interest. You say a friend of yours referred you to us. Who might that be?"

"Gabriel Degrande."

Andrew's eyebrows bounced for an instant as he glanced at Doyle whose face remained a calm pool except for a fleeting downward twitch of his mouth. "Isn't he…"

Doyle put his hand on Andrew's arm. "No. You're thinking of someone else. I'm not familiar with Mr. Degrande. Perhaps he meant a different shop."

Jake shook his head. "No. I don't think so. I ran into him last night. He said I'd regret it if I didn't stop in."

"And, we're pleased you did, even if it was in error," Doyle said. "If you tell me where you're staying, I'll make some inquiries about Cardona's book and let you know what I find."

"That would be great. I'm at the Amba Charring Cross. I'm headed there now and I'll be in town until Friday."

"Quite right. We'll be in touch."

"I hope so," Jake said.

***

JAKE'S EARPIECE CRACKLED as soon as he was out the door.

"What do you think?"

"I think hearing your voice in my head is weird."

"No, you dope. What do you think about Finch and Doyle?"

"I think they're liars and not very good ones. The body language was a dead giveaway. And if Doyle wanted to get in touch with me, he'd have asked for my cell number, not my hotel."

"Describe them."

"Finch is tall and skinny, early thirties, and Doyle is sixty, give or take, bald and has a beard."

"Telling them that Gabriel referred you was more plausible than asking for their help to find him. Well done. And, the part about the book you're looking for was smart. Even I believed you."

"Thanks, but I wasn't kidding about the book. It's on the top of my gotta-have-it list. What do I do now?"

"Exactly what you told them you were going to do. Walk back to the hotel. It's about three miles. Take your time."

"You think Gabriel will get there that fast?"

"He's not going anywhere near your hotel. Too risky. If he's close enough, he'll get to you somewhere along the way."

"Got it." Jake consulted his phone. "Google Maps says to take Brompton Road."

"Perfect. That will take you past the Natural History Museum and Harrods. Be a tourist. Site see and shop."

"Why do you think Gabriel will find me in one of those places?"

"Because Andrew Finch is following you and he's on his phone. Care to guess who he's talking to? Keep walking and don't turn around."

TWENTY-NINE

Jake was pleased with the bluff he'd run on Finch and Doyle but he wasn't excited about being a moving target for Gabriel. If they were seated across a poker table, he could read him, get a feel for how he'd play the game. Out on the street, he had no idea what to expect. All he could do was the one thing no poker player ever should do – trust someone else to win the pot for him. Even if Cassie was that someone.

Last night, she'd been a wreck. Today, she was all about the mission, her raw pain squelched, stuffed inside some hidden emotional box. Could she leave it there long enough to get the job done? Or would she peek inside the box and give them away?

But Jake knew his growing anxiety was about more than that. If forced to choose between him and Gabriel, what choice would Cassie make? Competing against a ghost was bad enough. Squaring off against a resurrected lover wasn't a fair fight.

He took his time at the Natural History Museum, wandering through the wildlife photography exhibit and a display of botanical and zoological watercolors. He skipped the virtual reality journey to the great barrier reef, not wanting to linger too long in any one place. The crowd at the dinosaur exhibit insulated him until the tour groups moved on, leaving him feeling small and vulnerable against the skeletons of the massive beasts. He wished he could take the crime scene tour and sift through forensic evidence to catch a killer but his gut told him he'd been there long enough.

Once outside, he glanced around in what he hoped was a natural fashion, hoping to catch a glimpse of Cassie. She was wearing jeans with a t-shirt under an olive khaki jacket and was carrying a messenger bag slung across her body. There was no sign of her. Nor did he see Andrew Finch lurking anywhere. If it was possible to be lonely in a crowd, he was that. Though, knowing that two people were following him was an odd sort of comfort.

He could have lost himself in Harrods but he didn't spend much time there. If Gabriel was going to make a move, it wouldn't be in the wine department. It had been two hours since he'd left Doyle's shop. Time to push the hand he was playing to the final round of betting.

Brompton Road became Knightsbridge. Major renovations were under way on a block-long building. Windows and doors had been re-placed with plywood. Scaffolding overhung the sidewalk. The sounds of traffic mixed with the noise of construction.

"Can you hear me in all this racket?" Jake asked Cassie. When she didn't respond, he had his answer.

Men in work clothes passed him by carrying tools and supplies. One man wearing a scuffed yellow hardhat came alongside him, a length of steel pipe hoisted on his shoulder. He stumbled and pivoted to keep his balance. The pipe struck Jake in the back of his head, stunning him.

"Sorry about that, mate," the man said as he dropped the pipe and grabbed Jake's arm to keep him upright. "You all right?"

Jake blinked and rubbed his scalp. "Yeah. I think so."

"Sorry about that. You look a might glassy-eyed. Let me help you over here where you can get your legs under you."

The man leaned Jake against a sheet of plywood covering a door-way. He gathered the front of Jake's shirt in one hand, holding him up, then gave a swift, sharp kick to the bottom of the plywood. The temporary door swung inside. The man released Jake's shirt and gave him a stiff shove in the chest. Still groggy, Jake tumbled into the open-ing as the man stepped past him and pushed the plywood back in place. From start to finish, the encounter took five seconds.

"On your feet, mate," the man said. He slipped his arm under Jake's and steadied him as Jake widened his eyes and got his bearings. The building had been gutted to the walls. A string of low-wattage bulbs crisscrossed the exposed concrete ceiling, washing the space with

JOEL GOLDMAN & LISA KLINK

dingy light. "Over here now." He used plastic ties to cuff Jake to the arms of a heavy wooden chair, then stepped back, neither asking or explaining.

The room stopped spinning. Jake studied the man. His narrow face and close-cropped dark hair emphasized his retreating hairline. He was a bit shorter than Jake, without an ounce of fat on his lithe frame. He wasn't movie star handsome but there was something compelling about him beginning with the deep brown eyes that bored into Jake.

"Gabriel Degrande?" Jake asked. The man nodded, his eyes brimming with curiosity. "French?" Gabriel nodded again. "Why the phony British accent? If you're trying out for a remake of My Fair Lady, you might want to brush up on your Cockney."

Gabriel switched to English with a slight French accent. "Why did you tell my friends at the bookstore that I sent you there?"

"That's cool. Can you do it with a Russian accent too? You know, you don't look bad for a dead man."

Gabriel ignored Jake's jabs. "Why did you tell my friends at the bookstore that I sent you there." He took a spring-loaded knife from his pocket and popped the blade open. "I won't ask you again."

"Now be careful with that knife. I can't stand the sight of blood. Especially mine. Makes me scream like a little girl and piss my pants. And, let me tell you as one grown man to another, that's something you can't un-see. I'd hate for you to have nightmares on my account."

Gabriel leaned in and pressed the point of the knife against Jake's jugular vein. "You forget that I'm a dead man. No nightmares."

Jake leaned his head back as far as he could. "Okay. You've made your point. Back off and I'll tell you." Gabriel straightened and retreated a step. Jake nodded past him. "She sent me."

"Hello, Gabriel," Cassie said.

Gabriel turned. The knife fell from his hand. "Cassie. You're alive."

THIRTY

Gabriel rushed toward Cassie with open arms. She waited until he was close enough, then smacked her palm against his chest, knocking him back half a step.

"I'm alive?" she said. "I'm alive? What the hell is that supposed to mean?"

"What are you talking about?" Gabriel said. "Prometheus told me Petrescu's crew shot up the chopper as you were taking off. He said you were hit in an artery and bled out."

Cassie said, "And I'm supposed to believe that bullshit?"

"It's the truth. He showed me photos of your body. It was you. I saw the scar next to your breast."

"But you didn't see my body, did you? Just a picture that Prometheus could have photo-shopped with his eyes closed."

"I was hurt pretty badly. The backup team barely got there in time. Another five minutes and I'd have been dead. I was in a coma for a few days. When I was conscious enough to know what was going on, Prometheus told me your body had been cremated and…" He stopped in mid-sentence. "…the bastard told you I was dead, didn't he? He made sure you saw me lying on the ground with a couple of bullets in my back and he broke us up for good."

"Oh, my God, Gabriel." She wrapped her arms around him. Breaking their embrace, she walked toward Jake then turned around. "I can't believe he would do something like that, make us believe that each other was dead. That's the cruelest thing I've ever heard."

"You always thought he was some kind of hero but he wasn't. He was a prick that only cared about the money."

"Then why did you recruit me?"

"Because you were perfect for the job. Smart, beautiful. No family. No ties. No complications. Except for me. After Bosnia, Prometheus said he didn't need me anymore. He paid me for the Bosnia job and gave me a bonus."

"Which was?"

"A warning that if I didn't keep my mouth shut about his operation, he'd finish what Petrescu started."

Cassie didn't say anything for a moment, absorbing what Gabriel had said, then changed gears. "What are you doing in London?"

"You first." He gestured toward Jake. "Who's this clown and why did you send him looking for me when you thought I was dead?"

"Hey, buddy," Jake said. "That's Mr. Clown to you."

Gabriel grimaced. "Where did you get him?"

Cassie sighed. "I know. It's a long story. If you don't untie him, he'll only get more obnoxious."

Gabriel used his knife to slice through Jake's handcuffs. "It's still your turn, Cassie. Why are you looking for me?"

"You have something I want."

"What could I possibly have that you want?"

"Four things, actually," Jake said.

"The Magna Cartas you and your friends stole from the British Library," Cassie added.

Gabriel raised his hands in protest. "How could you possibly…"

"Don't even," Cassie said. She pulled the Bristol-Clarke mask from her messenger bag. "We found your escape hatch in the basement of the library and tracked you through the sewer. You left this behind. A camera at the used car dealer across from the York station got a great shot of you climbing over the fence."

"Well, I was right about one thing. You were perfect for the job but I don't have the Magna Cartas. I don't know where they are and even if I did, I wouldn't try to get them back. They're not worth getting killed over."

"What about Aramis," Jake asked. "Does he know where they are?" Gabriel's eyes flickered for an instant before he caught himself. It was enough for Jake. "So, which one of the Musketeers are you -

Porthos or Athos?"

Gabriel looked at Cassie. "Not bad for a clown," she said.

"Athos," Gabriel said, "not that it matters."

"It doesn't," Jake said. "In the unlikely event you're telling the truth, we'll settle for telling us who's playing D'artagnan. You know, the fourth Musketeer, the guy who didn't want to crawl through the sewer. He'll know where the Magna Cartas are."

Gabriel ignored him and put his hands on Cassie's shoulders. "You've got to trust me. This job's too big for you. I can't tell you how happy I am that you're alive and I want you stay that way."

She turned out of his reach. "What about Pugh, Galloway and Bristol-Clarke? Are they still alive or have you graduated from grand theft to murder?"

"They were fine when I last saw them. I don't know where they are now but I was told they would be released soon."

"They better be. And, you know I'm not going to back off. The question is why did you sign on for a caper like this? You're a better man than that."

"Was a better man, though I'm not even sure about that. My skill set is not exactly transferable to the corporate world. And, the money spends the same. Something you should consider. Don't throw your life away chasing after the Magna Cartas. Whoever hired us to steal them is probably going to tuck them away somewhere only he can see them."

"Then why the ransom note demanding a hundred million pounds by Friday?" Jake said.

"I don't know anything about a ransom note. That was never part of the plan. It had to have been Aramis. He hung back for a minute after we grabbed the Magna Cartas. He's probably free-lancing and taking a helluva chance at that. Shaw will have his head."

"Who's Shaw?" Cassie said.

"It's his operation but the name is just another name. I have no idea who he is. I'm telling you…no, I'm begging you, Cassie, to leave this alone."

"Don't worry about her," Jake said. "She blew Petrescu away because she thought he killed you. I think she can handle Shaw."

Gabriel stared at Cassie whose eyes filled with tears. He hung his head and ambled toward a pillar in the center of the room. He braced himself against it and stared at her again.

"Pity," he said and the room went black.

"Hey," Jake called out. "Cassie? What happened? Are you alright?"

Using her cellphone's light, Cassie navigated to the pillar where she'd last seen Gabriel. Jake did the same. They shined their lights up and down its length.

"Here," Cassie said. She flipped a switch mounted in a recessed cavity on the pillar and the overhead lights came on.

"He's gone," Jake said.

"Of course. Vanishing is what he does best."

"What now?" Jake said.

Cassie opened an app on her phone. "We give him a head start."

Jake looked at her screen. The app showed a GPS display of the surrounding streets and a blinking red triangle as it advanced along Knightsbridge before turning off onto a side street where it soon turned again before coming to a stop.

"You're tracking him? How is that possible?"

She reached into her jeans pocket and showed him a tiny, wafer thin disc with an adhesive on the back. "I put one of these on his jacket when I hugged him."

"But how did you know we'd find him and you'd want to tag him like that?"

"I didn't. These are so I don't lose track of you. There's one under your collar. I put it there when I fitted you with the earpiece. You were too excited to notice."

Jack ran his fingers across the fabric, feeling the tag under his thumb. "Huh, so I'm what, like a fish you catch and release so you can follow me through the wild?"

"Yeah. I like watching you swim upstream." She looked at her screen again. "Gabriel stopped a couple of blocks from here. We'll keep our distance until he starts moving again."

They left the building and followed Gabriel's path, stopping where he turned off Knightsbridge.

Jake said, "He hasn't moved an inch."

"You're right." Cassie frowned and studied her phone, then jammed it into her pocket. "That bastard!"

She broke into a run with Jake chasing after her until they reached a Dumpster in an alley off a side street near Knightsbridge. Gabriel's jacket lay rumpled on a pile of garbage.

"You're right," Jake said. "Vanishing is what he does."

THIRTY-ONE

W here is that woman?" Sir Robert muttered as he checked his Rolex.

It was eight minutes after the scheduled time for the Trustees' meeting and the second time they'd gathered since the robbery. They were all there, except for Lady Liliane Tresch who had summoned them.

"You know our Lady Lili," said Alexander Crossley. "She called the meeting for ten a.m. and you know she loves a dramatic entrance."

Lady Liliane swept into the conference room three minutes later. "Do forgive me. The roads are beastly today." Then she looked back at someone standing just outside the door. "Come in, my dear."

Sarah St. James stepped into the room, her eyes wary. Lady Tresch enjoyed Sir Robert's jaw dropping reaction, then turned to the others.

"You all know Dr. St. James from her marvelous work on the exhibit. She has also been working with the agent Sir Robert so graciously engaged without consulting us to recover the Magna Cartas."

"How did you…?" Sir Robert began, as a surprised murmur passed through the room.

Liliane favored him with a smile. "Secrets are such hard things to keep, Robert. It was quite simple. Your agent had to work with someone who knew everything about the exhibit and the Magna Cartas. After you told us that dim bulb, Ian Thorpe, couldn't be trusted, Dr. St. James was the only logical choice. As this concerns all of us, I thought we'd appreciate hearing a progress report on the recovery effort."

She fixed her dark eyes on Sarah, who returned them with her own steady gaze before breaking off to look at the others.

"All right," Sarah began. "It appears that three security guards were involved in the theft and now they've gone missing. Most likely, they we're working from information obtained from Malcolm Bridges at Titan Security Systems."

"What? Bridges?" Sir Robert said, his face reddening.

"Yes. He quit his job rather abruptly and now I'm afraid he's dead," Sarah said. "The police said he was strangled."

Lady Tresch said, "So now we know the kind of people we're dealing with. Sir Robert, if this agent of yours fails to recover the Magna Cartas before the ransom deadline…"

"She won't," Sarah interjected. "I have every confidence in her ability to get the Magna Cartas back safely and…"

"My dear. I most fervently hope that you're correct. Like the Magna Cartas, your future depends upon it. I suggest we reconvene at five-thirty this afternoon for another update from our curator."

Sir Robert straightened and cleared his throat. "Very well. However, we must be prepared for the worst. To that end, I have opened a secure account at my bank in which I've deposited my share of the ransom." He passed out slips of paper to each of them. "This is the information you'll need to wire your funds into the account in the unlikely event…" He glanced at Sarah. "… that we're obliged to pay the ransom. I suggest you do so immediately so there are no last-minute delays. If it comes to it, I'll transfer the funds as we're instructed and we'll await the return the Magna Cartas."

"If they're in a generous mood," Lord Sommerton muttered.

Sir Robert said. "It's all we can do."

THIRTY-TWO

A fire escape ended six feet above the Dumpster where Cassie and Jake found Gabriel's jacket. She slammed the Dumpster's lid down and vaulted onto the steel surface, then jumped and grabbed the bottom rung of the ladder.

"Where the hell are you going?" Jake asked.

"To the roof. Maybe I'll be able to see him from there." She pulled herself up one rung at a time. "Get back on Knightsbridge," she said over her shoulder. "If I find him, I'll tell you where to go. Once you've got him, keep your distance until I'll catch up with you."

The building was four stories tall. Cassie swung her legs onto the flat, asphalt covered roof. A waist-high brick wall wrapped around the perimeter. She pulled a small pair of binoculars from her bag. Racing from one side to the next, she scanned the streets below. There was no sign of Gabriel until she saw a hatless man, hands in his pockets, strolling down the street like he had no better place to be. He stopped in front of a shop window with a mirrored display giving her a clear view of his face. It was Gabriel.

"Jake, I've got him."

"Where?"

Cassie studied the GPS display on her phone. "He's heading east on a side street between Kinnerton and Wilton Place."

"I'm almost to Wilton."

"Great. Go south on Wilton. He's wearing a brown sweater and tan pants. Let me know when you've got a visual."

Thirty seconds passed. "Okay," Jake said. "I see him. He's on Wilton a block ahead of me."

"Hang back. I'm on my way."

***

WILTON PLACE WAS a two-lane street lined on both sides with apartment buildings three to five stories high. Trees and shrubs dotted the front of the buildings, none tall or wide enough to provide cover for Jake.

To keep Gabriel in sight, Jake hustled between parked cars, popping up when Gabriel wasn't looking until he saw him turn into the courtyard for St. Paul's church further down on Wilton. A double-decker bus churned past heading toward the church with tourists hanging over the sides and snapping pictures. Jake trotted behind the bus, using it for cover.

A white panel van bearing a logo for Spark Electrical Service was parked at the corner across the street from the church. Jake waited there, peeking around the back end. The bus stopped in front of the church and the passengers climbed down and streamed inside. There was no sign of Gabriel.

Until Jake turned around and Gabriel grabbed him by the throat and slammed him against the side of the van. Pinning him with one hand, Gabriel snagged Jake's earpiece, threw it on the ground and crushed it under his heel.

"You're terrible at this," Gabriel said.

Bug-eyed and gasping, Jake launched his knee at Gabriel's crotch but Gabriel clamped his free hand on Jake's thigh, blocking him and squeezing his throat and his leg until Jake threw up his hands in surrender.

Gabriel released him. "I mean really terrible."

Jake caught his breath. "What can I tell you. Rookie mistake." He straightened his collar and threw himself at Gabriel, wrapping him in a bear hug. Gabriel head-butted him. Seeing stars, Jake let go and slid to the pavement.

Gabriel crouched in front of him, cupping Jake's chin and gently patting his face until Jake's eyes focused.

"I'm only going to tell you this once so pay close attention." Jake nodded. "If I see you again, I'll kill you. Understood?" Jake nodded again. "Say it."

"Understood."

"Good lad. Now lie down on your stomach and crawl under the van and stay there until Cassie finds you."

"Go to hell."

"I'm afraid that was decided long ago."

Gabriel smacked Jake in the jaw with a furious backhand, knocking him over. Jake rose to his knees and drove his head and shoulders at Gabriel's legs. Gabriel sidestepped him, letting Jake flop onto the concrete. He helped Jake to his feet and propped him against the van. Jake was woozy and slack, his arms hanging at his sides.

"You give up yet?" Jake asked.

Gabriel shook his head, slid the van's door open and shoved Jake inside. Tools and coils of electrical wire were stacked on a rack welded to the opposite side of the van. Gabriel cut two lengths of wire and tied Jake's wrists to the rack.

"Goodbye, Jake. And remember what I told you," Gabriel said, then slammed the van's door shut.

Jake tugged at his wrists, quitting when he realized he was only tightening the knots. He could reach the van door with his legs and began kicking, hoping the racket would attract attention. Moments later, the door slid open. It was Cassie.

"Get me out of here," he said.

Hands on her hips, Cassie said. "I should probably leave you. What part of keeping your distance didn't you understand?"

"The part about him sneaking up on me. How did you find me?"

Cassie picked up a pair of wire shears and cut him loose. "I heard a racket in my earpiece like you'd hit your head. When you didn't answer, I ran to where the tracker said you were when I heard the noise. What happened?"

"He's tougher than he looks."

"Well, you've got a knot on your forehead big as a quarter and a welt on your cheek to remind you."

Jake climbed out of the van. "If he thinks he can scare me off by threatening to kill me…"

"Save it, Jake. He probably will kill you the next time except there isn't going to be a next time since we have no way to find him."

"Open the app you were using to track me."

Cassie tapped her phone. Her eyes widened as she watched the blinking red triangle advance across the screen. She looked at Jake. "How did you…"

"I pulled the tracker off my collar and tagged him when I did the bear hug thing. He won't notice it until he takes his sweater off. Maybe not even then."

A smile spread across Cassie's face. "Let's go nail the bastard."

THIRTY-THREE

Gabriel stopped at Hyde Park Corner. "That's three-tenths of a mile from here," Cassie said, consulting the GPS map on her phone. "Wherever he's going, he won't take a direct route. He'll switch between walking, taking a cab or the bus or the tube or all of them to make sure he's not being followed. This would be a lot easier if we had our own car."

"There's a cab parked across the street," Jake said.

"Where to, mate?", the driver said when they climbed into the back seat.

The registration clipped to the dashboard said his name was Derek McNulty. He had a ruddy complexion, lively eyes and a bushy mustache that stretched jowl to jowl. He wore his tweed cap pulled down to his eyebrows.

Jake said, "We don't know but we can give you directions. This might take a while. Hope you don't mind."

"I've got all the time you need so long as my meter's running."

Cassie sighed and leaned back against the seat. She handed Jake her phone and closed her eyes for a moment.

Jake told McNulty, "Let's start with Hyde Park Corner but don't get too close."

Cassie opened her eyes. Jake offered her the phone but she shook her head. "You're the navigator."

"And your head must be about to explode. I mean it's not every day that a dead lover comes back to life especially on the wrong side of a caper like this."

"No, this is definitely not an everyday thing."

Jake knew he was on tricky terrain but pressed on. "He thought you were dead. That's a pretty good reason for not telling you he was alive."

"Why are you sticking up for him?"

"I'm not. It's just that you were so upset because you didn't think he loved you and…"

"And you're just trying to make me feel better so I'll fall into your arms?"

"Maybe I just want you to feel better."

"That's Hyde Park Corner up ahead. What now?" McNulty said.

They squared around, facing the front seat.

"Hand me the phone," Cassie said. She studied the GPS screen and gave McNulty his instructions.

Gabriel took the kind of circuitous route Cassie anticipated. Together with the congested traffic, an hour passed with no clear idea of his destination.

"Where are we?" Jake asked McNulty.

"East end. Limehouse District they call it."

"What's around here?"

"A bunch of derelict warehouses and a few shops that are just hanging on. Some of the gentry are tryin' to bring it back, tearing down the old and putting up flats the likes of me will never see from the inside. But, it's still mostly abandoned buildings nobody but bums and stray dogs have a taste for. This here is Commercial Road, what you Yanks would call the main drag. Back behind them warehouses," he said, pointing out the window, "is the Limehouse Cut. That's a canal leads to the Thames. Used to be for the barges. Not so much anymore."

"Pull over," Cassie said. "We'll walk from here."

McNulty stopped in front of a business that sold tires and serviced cars. The adjacent lot had gone back to nature and was covered with a thick overgrowth of trees. It separated the service station from an abandoned warehouse that filled the rest of the block

Cassie waited on the broad sidewalk while Jake leaned in the driver's window. He handed McNulty a wad of bills. "This cover it?"

"More than covers it, mate. She's a fine woman, that one is, eh?

I'd wager you're glad you found her? Well, as my old pop used to say, don't screw it up, lad."

"I'll try not to."

"You want me to stick around?"

"Might be a good idea. Do you mind?"

McNulty patted his meter. "I'll pull in here. I'm in the market for new tires as it is."

Jake joined Cassie. He said, "Why did we give up the cab?"

"Because Gabriel likes derelicts, bums and stray dogs when he's on the run. Keeps him off the grid. Look," she said, holding up her phone. "He's been in that warehouse for the last ten minutes."

Jake checked the address, then searched it on his phone. "It's old alright. Goes back to the 1800's. The owners made supplies for sailing ships. They shut down in the early 1970's and it's been left to go to hell ever since then. Check out these pictures of the interior. Looks like a bomb went off."

"I like this one," Cassie said, pointing to a photo of an exterior stairway leading up half a flight to a narrow doorway. "It has to be in the back or on the side. Better than trying the front door."

The main building was a brown brick, three-story structure with a pitched roof. The boarded up and broken cast iron windows testified to its neglect. The warehouse behind it was a ramshackle mess missing portions of ceilings, walls and windows. The Limehouse Cut, a foul ribbon of brackish water, snaked behind them. The dense overgrowth of trees and shrubs bordering the warehouse made it impossible to locate the exterior stairs from the street.

"Let's each take a side," Cassie said. "Whoever finds the entrance, text the other. But," she added, poking his chest with her finger, "don't even think about going in on your own. Got it?"

"Got it." He turned toward the far side of the building.

"Hey." Cassie grabbed his shoulder from behind, spun him around and kissed him, crushing her mouth against his. "Now you can go."

"If that's what I get for leaving, I can't wait to see what I get for coming back."

"Depends on what you bring me. Now move it."

Cassie wove her way toward the rear, careful not to make any noise that might carry inside the open-air warehouse. She was nearing the back when she emerged from a thick stand of trees to find the wooden stairs tucked into a recessed section of the exterior wall.

After texting Jake, she crept up the dozen steps leading to a slightly ajar door that gave her a narrow view inside. Rain water was puddled in scattered pools across the uneven, cement floor. Steel girders supported a second level wrap-around balcony where rusted heavy equipment had been abandoned. A gigantic iron hook, taller than a man, hung suspended from a heavy wire coil centered at the far end of the balcony opposite Cassie's position, the cable stretching across the length of the room. Birds flew in and out, perching on the hook and basking in the sun that washed through vacant ceiling panels.

Gabriel, Aramis and another man whom she guessed was the third thief, Porthos, stood in the center of the barren warehouse fifty feet from her door. Aramis and Porthos were side-by-side. Gabriel was ten feet away from them, his back to her.

Aramis said, "You called this fuckin' meeting. Now what's it about?"

Gabriel said, "Where are the Magna Cartas?"

"Shaw's got 'em far as I know. What's it to you? Your piece of this is done."

"I signed on for a heist, not a ransom play."

"Ransom? What are you talkin' about? There's no fuckin' ransom," Aramis said.

"The note you left demanding a hundred million pounds for the safe return of the Magna Cartas was what? A joke? Because I'm not laughing."

"You know about that, do you. How's that?"

"Doesn't matter. Point is, I know. The job was to grab the Magna Cartas, not to ransom them. If I'm going to be looking over my shoulder for the rest of my life, I want my cut of the hundred million."

"See now, it does matter because I didn't tell you. It had to be someone from the library. Like maybe this little bird." Aramis held up his phone, showing Gabriel a photograph. Cassie didn't need to see it to know it was her. "Now, strictly speaking, she doesn't work at the library, does she?"

"I wouldn't know. I've never seen her before."

Aramis pulled a gun from behind his back and pointed it at Gabriel. "I think you have. Her name is Cassie Ireland and she works for an outfit called Global Security. They're in the business of getting back what gets stolen. And I'm thinkin' the two of you are intendin' to steal the Magna Cartas from Shaw and collect the ransom yourselves."

Gabriel raised his hands in protest. "That's crazy. I don't know anything about the woman or Global Security and I'm not fool enough to double-cross Shaw."

"Then why'd you bring Cassie to our little parlay?" Gabriel dropped his arms to his sides, casting furtive glances around the warehouse as Cassie ducked her head out of the open doorway. "That's right, mate. We've been following her and that bloke tagging along with her all day. And no need to be lookin' around for them. They'll be along soon enough."

Cassie heard footsteps behind her and turned, holding a finger to her mouth to quiet Jake only to see a broad-shouldered man dressed in black aiming a gun at her. He had the mashed face of a man who'd lost more fights than he'd won despite his sledgehammer arms. He motioned with his gun for her to raise her hands.

"Inside, Missy," the gunman said.

THIRTY-FOUR

Going inside as an unarmed prisoner was a bad option. That would give Aramis more leverage and shorten the odds for both her and Gabriel. Cassie didn't have time to sort out her concern for him, especially after hearing Gabriel demand a cut of the ransom. It was hard enough to admit to caring what happened to him.

She began walking down the stairs toward the gunman, never taking her eyes from him. He gestured at her again.

"I said, inside."

There was nothing between Cassie and the gunman she could use as a weapon. Her one chance was to get close enough to disarm him. That hadn't worked with Aramis and she welcomed the second chance.

"Don't make me shoot you," the gunman said.

Cassie kept going, almost to the bottom of the stairs. "You won't shoot me. Aramis wants me alive."

The gunman stayed out of her reach. "He didn't say nuthin' about not putting a bullet in your knee, so get yourself inside."

Before she could make another move, Jake slipped out of the trees carrying a length of iron pipe cocked over his shoulder like a baseball bat. The gunman spun around as Jake swung, raising his arm to block the blow. The center of the pipe caught him on the wrist, shattering it and causing his gun to fly out of his hand. Jake's follow through caught the gunman's chin, dropping him to his knees.

Cassie picked up the weapon, then twisted the gunman's injured arm behind his back and forced him to his feet. He groaned as she wrenched his arm up toward his neck and pressed the barrel of the gun against the base of his skull.

"You have a name?"

Chin hanging on his chest, he muttered, "Rugger."

"Well, Rugger. If you don't want your day to get any worse, you'll do exactly what I tell you. Got it?" He nodded. "Are there any more of you roaming around outside?" He shook his head. She forced his damaged arm higher. "Because if I find out you're lying to me, I'll put a bullet in your knee. So, one more time. Is there anyone else?"

He answered through gritted teeth. "One other."

Jake motioned to Cassie with the pipe. "I've got him." He slipped back into the trees before Cassie could stop him.

Rugger asked, "Now what?"

"Like you said, time to go inside."

Cassie shoved Rugger ahead of her into the warehouse, keeping a firm grip on his damaged arm. Gabriel was on his knees facing her. Aramis was behind him, his gun aimed at the back of Gabriel's head. Porthos stood nearby, gun in hand, arms slack at his sides.

Porthos saw them first. "Oi!"

Cassie pressed her gun against Rugger's temple. "Aramis, your nose is a mess and those black eyes make you look like a raccoon. Did you walk into a door or did you let a girl beat you up?"

"Keep talkin', missy. When I get done with your boyfriend here, you're next and I'll be glad to take my time with you."

"Let him go and I'll let Rugger go."

Aramis sneered. "Or, what? You going to shoot poor Rugger?"

"First you, then Rugger."

"Huh? Can't have that."

He swung his gun toward them and shot Rugger in the head. Cassie shoved his body aside and rolled across the floor, coming up in a shooting position as Porthos fired wildly at her. She returned fire, hitting him center mass and toppling him over.

Gabriel pivoted, sweeping his legs against the back of Aramis' knees and knocking him off balance, forcing his second shot to miss Cassie. Gabriel leapt on Aramis, wrestling for control of his gun, knocking it free and sending it skidding across the floor. Aramis flipped Gabriel onto his back and began hammering him with massive blows.

Cassie looked up as Jake appeared on the balcony and jumped

onto the giant hook. He released a lever and the hook flew down the cable. As he sailed past, Jake struck Aramis in the back of the head with his iron pipe, dropping him like a dead weight onto Gabriel. The hook slowed and Jake jumped to the floor.

Gabriel crawled out from under Aramis and stared at Jake. "What was that?"

Jake shrugged. "Zip line. Lot of fun. You should try it."

He turned to Cassie. "Who is he? And why are you pointing that gun at me?"

Cassie said. "Forget about him. I want the Magna Cartas."

"Shooting me won't get them back. Besides, we both know you won't do it."

"Not this time." She found a rag and wiped Rugger's gun clean, then put it in his hand, finger around the trigger and squeezed off a round.

"What was that for?" Jake asked.

"Rugger needs powder burns on his hand if we want the police to think he shot Porthos. What about the other guy outside?"

"Rugger was bluffing."

Cassie pressed two fingers against Aramis' neck. "He'll wake up with a bad headache." She went through his pockets until she found his wallet, then did the same with Porthos. Well, now we know their real names. This one," she said, pointing at Aramis, "is Max Dekker. The other one is Lionel Kent."

Gabriel said, "We never knew each other's real names. That's the way Shaw wanted it."

"Was it just the three of you in the Library?"

"Yes."

"Did you ever meet or talk to Shaw?"

"No. Aramis - I guess I can call him Dekker now – he dealt with Shaw."

"Then how'd you get the job?"

"Dekker. He said Shaw told him how to reach me. How did you find me?"

"She didn't find you," Jake said. "I did. I tagged you with a tracker while you were beating the crap out of me."

Gabriel shook his head. "Unbelievable."

"I know," Cassie said. "You have to help us get the Magna Cartas back."

"No, I don't. After this, Shaw is going to come after me with everything he's got. I'm not going to put you in his crosshairs too. I can't let Dekker tell Shaw what happened."

He took Dekker's gun and aimed it at his head. Cassie clamped her hand around the barrel. "I can handle Shaw and you owe me. I just saved your life."

Gabriel stuck the gun in his belt and took her by the arms. "And I don't want you to regret it because I may not be able to save yours if you don't let this go." He peeled off his sweater and stuffed it under her arm. "Goodbye, Cassie. This is the last time. It's for the best."

"What are you going to do?"

"What I've always done. Survive. You should try it."

THIRTY-FIVE

Sirens sounded in the distance, rapidly closing in on the warehouse. "That didn't take long. Someone on the other side of the water must have heard the gunfire and called the police," Cassie said. "We can't go back the way we came."

Jake said, "There's a footpath that runs along the Limehouse Cut that I used to get around the back of the warehouse. We can stay in the trees and follow it until we get back to the service station. McNulty is waiting for us."

She stared at him. "You told McNulty to wait for us?"

"Gotta plan ahead. Sometimes the next card matters more than the ones on the table."

They made it into the cab as a trio of police cars skidded to a stop in front of the warehouse. McNulty eased into traffic going the opposite direction and studied Jake in the rearview mirror, his raised eyebrows asking a silent question. Jake shrugged in reply.

"Where to?" McNulty asked.

Cassie's phone pinged with a text message. She studied it, then answered. "Someplace far from here and private."

Jake watched as her fingers swarmed over her phone, pulling up one webpage after another. He liked watching her work, how the corners of her mouth twitched and her eyes flashed as she moved from screen to screen. She was on the hunt and enjoying it. He started to ask her what she was doing but stopped when she shook her head, as if anticipating his interruption.

Half an hour later, McNulty pulled to the curb alongside Cavendish Square Gardens, a public square with a perimeter hedge around a lush lawn, shrubs and flower beds beneath broad-leafed oak trees. He cut the engine and opened his door.

"Hey, where are you going?" Jake asked.

McNulty said. "The lady requested far away so I took you from the East End to the West End. And you can't get more private than my cab. Take your time. The meter's running."

He got out, closed his door and walked into the Gardens.

Cassie turned to Jake. "That text I got was from Gunnar. It was a link to a message on a secure server we use. Fifty thousand pounds was deposited into each of the missing guards' bank accounts a week ago."

"But we know the guards didn't do it. That's a lot of money to throw away on a setup."

"It's a rounding error compared to a hundred million. Gunnar traced the guards' money and the Malcolm Bridges' million pounds back through a rat's nest of offshore accounts and shell companies. Each payment had one thing in common. The money passed through a charitable foundation in London called the Dawn of Hope."

She handed Jake her phone. The screen was open to the foundation's home page.

He read out loud. "Creating a brighter future for children across the globe."

"A charitable foundation is perfect for laundering money. Lots of small donations come in from lots of different sources and they can distribute it to whoever they want." She took her phone back, scrolled to another page and showed Jake a photograph. "That's Lord William Tresch, founder and chairman of the board."

Tresch looked to be in his late fifties. He was tall with silver hair brushed back tight against his scalp. Crow's feet crept from the corners of his eyes, his gaze flinty. His lips were pressed in a bloodless, hard smile.

"He looks like he'd rather foreclose your mortgage than kiss your baby. You think he's Shaw?"

"Could be. From what I just read, he comes from a lot of old, old money. Enough to set up a job like this. When he was young, he made regular appearances in the tabloids. Drinking, gambling, fighting, unsuitable girlfriends… the usual 'blue blooded bad boy' stuff. Until ten years ago when he met Lilly Moore and she supposedly made him behave." She pulled up a press photo of Tresch and his bride coming out of Royal Albert Hall on their wedding day.

Jake took in the sharp contrast between the scowling Lord and the vivacious beauty. "That's a mismatched pair."

"Except they both had money," said Cassie. "She was a commoner and he had a title. The press treated it like a Cinderella story when she became Lady Liliane Tresch."

Jake's mouth fell open. "As in the Lady Liliane Tresch who's one of the Magna Carta trustees? You think they're in it together. She would have known how the security was set up."

"Doubtful. Lord Tresch had Malcolm Bridges for that. And, they've been going through an ugly divorce for the last year. She put up with him gambling away his family fortune. But when she caught him cheating on her, she gave him the boot."

"Stealing the Magna Cartas would embarrass the hell out of her."

"And he'd collect her share of the ransom."

"Where do we find this royal asshole?"

Cassie clicked back to the foundation's home page. "Scotland. The foundation is having its annual fundraising gala tomorrow night at Culzean Castle, which is about four hundred miles from here."

"Hate to break this to you, but I didn't bring my tux."

She patted his cheek. "Don't worry. It's a costume ball. Let's go ask McNulty if his meter runs all the way to Scotland."

They found him on a bench beneath one of the many wide-spreading oak trees canopied over the neatly manicured grounds, earbuds plugged into his phone. Sitting stock-still, he watched them approach, waiting until they were standing in front of him before removing them.

"Amazin' thing," he said, holding up his phone. "I've got a police scanner app. Gets all their chatter if you've a mind to listen. You two kicked up quite a ruckus back at that warehouse."

Cassie said, "I don't know what you're…"

Jake held up his hand, keeping his eyes fixed on McNulty. "Forget it Cassie. He knows we were there."

The cabbie's face was implacable and he wouldn't be fooled. "Aye. Saw you disappear into that thicket up by the warehouse and saw you come out from behind the tire shop. Easy enough to figure. Chatter says there's two dead bodies. Both shot."

"What else are they saying?" Jake asked.

"Might be they shot each other. Might be they didn't."

"Does it matter to you?"

"What matters to me is collectin' my fare. Besides, you don't look like the killin' kind. Too soft. Now the lady," he said with a nod to Cassie, "I'd hate to tangle with her."

"You'd be right about that. Why didn't you call the police?"

"How do you know I didn't?"

"Because, if you did, we'd have been arrested before we got out of your cab."

McNulty allowed himself a small smile. "True, that."

"So, why didn't you?"

"Not my nature." He sniffed. "I'm not in the habit of making other people's troubles my own." He stood, his hand out. "I'll be takin' my fare now."

Jake handed him a hundred-pound note. "Good enough?"

McNulty pocketed the bill without a glance. "More than enough. Good luck with your troubles."

"Ever been to Scotland?" Jake asked.

"Course I been to Scotland."

"Want to go back? Now."

McNulty crossed his arms. "Now why would I want to do that?"

"For a thousand pounds. Round trip."

McNulty pushed the bill of his cap up. "What sort of trouble am I buyin' with your money?"

Jake looked at Cassie. She clenched her jaw and shook her head. He took a breath and looked at McNulty.

"Those men at the warehouse were part of a gang that stole the last four original Magna Cartas from the British Library two days ago. We're going to get them back. The man that hired them is in Scotland."

"Bollocks," McNulty said. "A thing like that'd be all over the news.

I've taken a dozen fares to the library since that exhibit opened."

"The library substituted fakes. The guy in Scotland wants a hundred million pounds by Friday or he'll turn the Magna Cartas into confetti. He's throwing a big party tomorrow night at a castle in Scotland and we need a ride. It could be dangerous. You heard what happened at the warehouse."

McNulty bristled and handed Jake the hundred-pound note. "I've been in more scrapes than you've had birthdays. And, nobody fucks with England."

THIRTY-SIX

W e can't take your cab," Cassie said. "The police will check video from the neighborhood. There's a good chance they'll see us with you and at the warehouse. They'll come looking for you and when they can't find you, they'll start looking for the cab."

"Over there," McNulty said, looking at his watch and cocking his head toward a glass-enclosed structure on the edge of the grounds. It looked like a bus stop shelter. "There's an elevator that takes you to the car park under the Gardens. It's six-fifteen. I'll meet you on the bottom level in the northwest corner in fifteen minutes and we'll be on our way."

Cassie waited until McNulty was out of earshot before lacing into Jake. "Are you out of your mind? I can't believe you told him. He's probably on his way to call the police and the newspapers while he posts it all on Facebook."

"He's not going to do any of that. He'll be back with a car."

She threw her arms up. "You don't know that."

"I do. When he said nobody fucks with England, he meant it. Besides, we had no choice. You're right about the video. We can't rent a car or buy a train, bus or plane ticket because the cops are going to be looking for us if they aren't already."

Cassie didn't back down. "It wasn't your call."

"But I made it. I played the card. If it blows up, it's on me."

She folded her arms over her chest. "I can't tell you what a comfort that is." Her cellphone rang. She looked at the caller ID and sighed. "Prometheus. Perfect."

She opened her phone and listened, then answered. "Yes, I know we're running out of time but we've got a good lead." She explained about Lord Tresch and listened again. "That makes no sense…let me talk to…understood." She ended the call, jammed the phone in her pocket.

"That good, huh?"

"The trustees have caved. After Bridges' murder, they don't want to take any chances. We're supposed to sit tight until we get instructions on where and when to pay the ransom and make sure everything goes okay with the exchange. They've all deposited their shares in an account controlled by Sir Robert." She shook her head. "It makes no sense, especially after Prometheus told me that Tresch has been a regular buyer on the black market – art, antiquities, rare documents – whatever he can get at a good price regardless of where it came from, so he doesn't mind doing business with fences."

"Which means he's got the contacts to recruit a team of thieves. Why did the trustees fold?"

"All Prometheus said was that they decided it was too risky but I don't buy that. Sarah might know something." She called her and left a message when Sarah didn't answer.

"Do you still trust Prometheus after what he did to you and Gabriel?"

"I trust him to do whatever he thinks he needs to do regardless of the consequences for someone else."

"But you didn't tell him about Gabriel or me."

"And I'm not going to until this is over. I don't need to give him a reason to pull me off the case."

"Do you trust him when he says the Trustees wants us to back off?"

Cassie sucked in a deep breath and let it out slowly. "Why would he make up something like that."

"The guy has his own agenda and keeps it to himself. That's why he told you Gabriel was dead. I don't trust him."

"You don't have to," Cassie said.

"Neither do you. If you did, you would have told him about me."

"What's your point?"

"My point is that if you don't trust him enough to tell him about

Gabriel and me, why should you trust him when he says the trustees have folded?"

She looked away, then back at Jake. "Maybe I don't…Maybe I… I don't know."

"You're in a tough spot but I'm sure you'll do the right thing. See you around." He turned and walked toward the elevator.

"Wait a minute. What are you doing?"

Jake kept walking, answering over his shoulder. "Prometheus doesn't know about me and I don't take orders from him so I'm going to catch a ride to Scotland. Care to come along?"

"Wait for me," she said and ran after him.

THIRTY-SEVEN

M urdoch found Inspector Amit Patel in a low-ceilinged, beige-on-beige conference room at the Metropolitan Police Lime-house station. Patel had circulated a request asking for help identifying two persons of interest in a double-homicide. The request included an enlarged frame from a surveillance video. The grainy image showed a man and woman standing on a sidewalk beside a black London cab. The man's face was shadowed but Murdoch recognized the woman, which meant that the man was Jake Carter.

Patel was studying the murder board, a large, dry erase surface on wheels. Photographs of the crime scene and head shots of the victims were pinned along the perimeter. There was also another enlarged surveillance frame, this one clear enough to confirm that Jake Carter was the man accompanying Cassie Ireland. A diagram of the interior of the warehouse, complete with outlines showing the locations of the dead bodies, filled the center of the board. Two more detectives sat at a long, rectangular table drafting reports and sorting through witness statements.

Murdoch knocked on the open door. Patel turned around. He had a younger man's smooth, boyish face and an abundance of wavy black hair that made Murdoch run a hand over his own balding pate. Patel's flat expression told Murdoch he didn't appreciate the interruption. Murdoch wasn't surprised. Every detective jealously guarded their turf, especially young, ambitious ones, and that's how Patel struck him.

Patel said, "Can I help you…?"

"I'm Inspector Murdoch. Serious Crimes." He pointed to the photographs on the murder board. "Have you ID'd that pair?"

"We're working on it. Why the interest?"

Murdoch ignored the question and walked to the murder board. He tapped his finger on the woman's face. "Her name is Cassie Ireland. She's an American security consultant. That much is for certain. And the bloke she's with is Jake Carter, also American. He's a card sharp, a professional poker player. Though I'd wager they're both much more than what they claim."

Murdoch knew that as much as Patel wanted to crack the case, like every cop, he didn't want to do it riding someone else's coattails.

"And what else might they be?" Patel said.

"Worst case - murderers and thieves, if I'm any judge."

"And you came here to do what? Round them up and save the day?"

Murdoch pursed his lips as he studied the youthful detective. "That's what I'd have wanted when I was your age." He shrugged. "Now I'm content to let you save the day if that means we can round them up. I'll tell you what I've got and then you can do the same."

The other detectives stopped what they were doing and gathered around Murdoch. He told them about Bridges' murder, described meeting Ireland and Carter at the British Library and his subsequent meeting with Ireland at Bridges' apartment, then concluded, "I suspect that the three of them were working together."

Patel furrowed his brow. "Working together on... what, exactly?"

Murdoch would have paid a month's wages to have a definitive answer to that question. "Not certain, yet. But it cost Bridges his life."

"And you think Ireland and Carter killed him?"

"They're persons of interest at this point, but, yes. Your turn."

Patel walked him through the crime scene. "At 1:18 p.m., we received reports of shots fired in an abandoned warehouse on Commercial Road. Units arrived on the scene six minutes later to find two white males, both DOA."

"And the surveillance images, when were they taken?" Murdoch asked.

"The one attached to my request for assistance was at 12:53 this afternoon. The subjects were in front of a repair shop on Commercial

Road fifty meters from the warehouse. The second was taken at 1:24 at the same location. We were lucky that the shop owner didn't make us run to a magistrate for an order to have a look at his video."

Murdoch examined the murder board, putting the photographs into context with the warehouse. "You've got them coming and going. Beating your boys by a few minutes."

"That's the way it looks to us."

"I don't suppose either of the victims had a connection to the British Library?"

"None that I know of. But we've only identified one of our victims so far." He took down the crime scene photo of Rugger, lying on the grimy concrete, a bullet hole in his forehead. "This is Roger Higgins, otherwise known as Rugger. He's quite well known to us. A regular leg-breaker. Hired himself out as muscle." He considered the picture. "Not an intellectual, was our Rugger. I'd be rather surprised if he'd ever seen the inside of a library. What's the British Library got to do with your case or mine, for that matter?"

Murdoch balked. Suggesting without proof that the four remaining original Magna Cartas had been stolen could ruin his career. Failing to come forward with his suspicions would also ruin him if he turned out to be right. Going public would ignite a scandal especially if no one saved the day. Confiding in a climber like Patel would add foolishness to his recklessness.

"All I know for certain is that Bridges' employer handled the security for an exhibit at the British Library and now he's been murdered. Our mutual persons of interest are connected to him and your two victims. That's three dead in two days." Murdoch pulled down the photo of the other dead man. He was pale and blond with wide open blue eyes. "No identification on this one?"

"No. His wallet was missing."

He followed the implication. "Do you suppose our friends took it?"

"Possibly, but we know there was at least one other person in the warehouse. The red line on the diagram is the blood trail he left going out the back exit. And, we found shell casings from three different guns that were fired from several different locations. But we only found one gun. Someone made off with the other two. We also found a length of iron pipe. It was bloody and several hairs were caught in the blood. Forensics is studying it."

"There must be other cameras pointed at the warehouse. What did they show?"

"Not much, I'm afraid. The warehouse has been abandoned for years and it's badly overgrown. Which, I imagine, is was why they used it."

A young man joined them. "Excuse me, Inspector. We managed to enhance the registration number on the cab on the video. I'll call the Public Carriage Office and find out who drives it."

Patel added, "And when he last reported in." Then he turned back to Murdoch. "The image quality on the video isn't great but neither of the Americans appear to be injured and we can't make out any evidence of blood splatter on their clothing."

"Let me know when you collect the driver and the Americans. I'd like to be there for the questioning."

"As an interested observer, of course."

Murdoch nodded. "Of course. How else could you save the day."

THIRTY-EIGHT

Cassie stared out the front passenger window of McNulty's Audi Q3 as dusk fell on the English countryside, the descending darkness matching her mood. Crashing Lord Tresch's masked ball seemed like a good idea a couple of hours ago because it was the only idea they had. But the further they got from London, the more terrible it sounded.

Shaw had recruited Max Dekker, Lionel Kent and Gabriel to steal the Magna Cartas. Gabriel was on the run. Kent was dead. Dekker, whom they'd left unconscious on the warehouse floor, was no doubt in custody by now. That didn't mean Shaw was vulnerable. He wouldn't rely only on the three thieves to protect him any more than he had relied on Malcolm Bridges to keep his mouth shut. If Lord Tresch was Shaw, he'd be ready for them. The trail of dead bodies was proof of what lay ahead.

It was bad enough that she was responsible for Jake, but now she had to worry about McNulty. They'd taken advantage of his patriotic fervor and if he lost his livelihood – or his life – that would be a burden she'd never put down. Judging from the tune he was whistling, McNulty shared none of her concerns. The melody was haunting and beautiful.

"What song is that?" she asked him. "It's familiar but I can't place it."

"Greensleeves," he said. "An old English folk song. Goes back centuries."

"Do you know the words?"

He shook his head. "No, but I'd recognize 'em if I heard 'em."

"Alas my love, you do me wrong." Jake said from the backseat.

Cassie turned to look at him. "Excuse me?"

"Alas my love, you do me wrong. That's the first line of the song."

McNulty nodded. "Aye, that it is, lad. I remember it now." He began to whistle and Jake began to sing, breathy and off-key, while looking at Cassie with puppy eyes and covering his heart with his hand.

"Alas my love, you do me wrong.
To cast me off discourteously.
And I have loved you oh so long
Delighting in your company."

Cassie rolled her eyes and covered her ears with her hands. "Stop before I kill myself!"

Jake and McNulty ignored her protests and started over, Jake making up in volume what he lacked in talent. Cassie giggled, then broke into full-throated laughter. McNulty was next. He gave up whistling and joined her, pounding the steering wheel as his eyes watered.

"Hey, I'm serious about my music," Jake said and continued acapella until Cassie pulled off her shoe and threw it at him. "Okay, okay. I can't help it if you have no appreciation for the arts."

"How is it possible," Cassie said, "that you know the lyrics to Greensleeves?"

"Blame my high school choir teacher. But, hey, I also know the words to the Gilligan's Island theme song if you'd like to hear that. This is the tale of our castaways…".

Jake stopped when Cassie threatened him with her other shoe. He handed her the first one, brushing her fingers. Cassie let his touch linger, wondering if he was trying pick up her spirits or just being a goof. Or whether he was using the lyrics to *Greensleeves* to tell her how he felt. One more thing for her to worry about.

They were on the M40, approaching Oxford, when McNulty's phone rang. It was resting in the center console. He glanced at the caller ID and didn't answer. A few minutes later, his phone rang again and he still didn't answer, not bothering to see who was calling. He kept his expression neutral, but Cassie saw the muscles in his neck grow tense.

After a third rejected call, Cassie asked, "Is that your boss or your wife?"

"No such creatures. Long as I keep up my license, I report to no man. Or woman." Then he told her, "It's the Public Carriage Office. Likely calling to ask about my whereabouts this afternoon. They can bloody well wait until I'm back from my vacation in Scotland."

Cassie picked up his phone and turned it off. "Take the first exit for Oxford. We need to make a stop."

Cassie bought half a dozen burner cellphones at a discount electronics store. Back in the car, she explained that the store clerk had recommended a coffee shop with free Wifi and told McNulty how to get there. They settled in a booth with steaming cups. Cassie opened one of the new burner phones and downloaded an app.

Jake peered over her shoulder and said, "That doesn't look like the iPhone app store."

"That's because it's the Global Security app store." She opened the app and said to McNulty, "Give me your phone."

She turned it on and laid it alongside the burner. McNulty's screen blinked and a message appeared confirming that the two phones were connected. Cassie tapped her keyboard and a ball began to swirl on McNulty's phone. Beneath the ball, the screen read *syncing*.

"What the devil?" McNulty asked.

"I'm downloading everything on your phone to this new one."

"What in the world for?"

"So you don't lose your data when we get rid of it. You're probably right that the Public Carriage Office is trying to reach you because of what happened at the warehouse. That means the police got your license number either from a witness or a surveillance camera. If your phone is on, they can track it and find us."

"Then why not just turn it off and destroy the sim card?" Jake asked.

"Because we want them to follow McNulty's phone. We just don't want them to follow us."

McNulty scratched his chin. "And you can copy my phone just by letting it sit there?"

"The app does the copying. Law enforcement does it all the time with what they call an extraction device. My company developed this

JOEL GOLDMAN & LISA KLINK

app which can connect to any device with a Wi-Fi connection and does the same thing. When this is over, I'll buy you whatever phone you want and we'll put everything back on it, your contacts, your email, your funny cat pictures, all of it. And, you'll be able to use your old number. For now, don't make any calls with this one unless it's an emergency."

McNulty asked, "What about your phones?"

"I doubt that they've identified either Jake or me but we're keeping our phones turned off."

"Can I use the apps on my new phone?"

"Sure," Cassie said.

McNulty opened his police scanner app and set the phone on the table with the volume turned down so only they could hear it. Five minutes later, they listened as Cassie and Jake were identified by name as persons of interest in the double homicide at a warehouse in the Limehouse District.

"I think that's our cue," Jake said.

Cassie removed the sim cards from her phone and Jake's and crushed them under her heel. "I don't care if they find McNulty's phone but I don't want them having what's on ours."

On their way to the car, Cassie dropped McNulty's phone through an opening on the side of an eighteen-wheel truck carrying sheep. Moments later, they were back on the M-40.

THIRTY-NINE

M urdoch drove away from Inspector Patel's crime scene in the warehouse mulling his investigation of Malcolm Bridges' murder. The wife, now widow, had identified the body. The crime scene techs had finished their work and would deliver their preliminary reports tomorrow. Officers were canvassing the area around the car park where Bridges was found, looking for witnesses and video cameras that might have captured useful footage.

The next step was to reconstruct Bridges' final days and hours to find the moment that had set his murder in motion. That meant talking with the people who knew him and had last seen him. The wife had given him a handful of names of friends and relatives and he'd arranged with Titan's HR director to interview Bridges' co-workers.

All that was routine, right out of the Catch-the-Killer manual, and would keep him occupied for the next several days. But nothing about this case felt routine to Murdoch since he'd run into Cassie Ireland at Bridges' house. He wanted to talk with her next, though he didn't expect her to be strolling thru Piccadilly waiting to be nabbed on Patel's person-of-interest alert, not after what had happened at the warehouse. And, if Patel got lucky and found Cassie before he did, Patel would have first crack at her and Murdoch hated waiting his turn.

Instead of starting on the list Gladys Bridges had given him, Murdoch drove to the British Library hoping that Sarah St. James would know where he might find Cassie. He was certain Sarah had lied to him about the damage to the motion sensors and acrylic covers in the Magna Carta display cases. She might have been covering for herself or Cassie and Jake or all three of them and may be tempted to lie to him again until he tells her that she could be covering for a pair of murderers.

Before bracing Sarah, Murdoch decided to have a word with Ian Thorpe. He'd dealt with the Library's Director of Security back in his Arts & Antiquities days. The man was disagreeable, defensive and only borderline competent but may be useful. Thorpe's secretary, Edna, showed Murdoch into his office.

"Inspector Murdoch," Thorpe said. "I haven't seen you since that business about the forged Martellus World Map. What brings you around?"

Murdoch took a chair opposite Thorpe's desk. "Afraid I'm not in Arts & Antiquities anymore. They moved me to the Serious Crimes Command."

Thorpe leaned back in his chair, making a steeple with his fingers. "Homicide and all that?"

Murdoch nodded. "Yes, and all that."

"Don't see how I can be any use to you then. Haven't run across a single corpse in all my time here."

"Don't be so certain. What can you tell me about Cassie Ireland?"

Thorpe's steepled hands collapsed into a stranglehold. "Ha! Not except that she barged in here Monday morning with her knickers in a twist, telling me I better cooperate with her or else."

"Cooperate with her about what?"

He curled his fingers into air quotes. "A security audit of the library. Like I don't know my job, which is rubbish. You know me better than that, Inspector."

"I take it you didn't retain her services?"

"You take it right. Sir Robert Howell went behind my back and he had no cause to do that. No cause at all."

Murdoch frowned. He'd seen Sir Robert's name listed in the program for the Magna Carta exhibit. "Does Sir Robert speak for the Library?"

"He speaks for the Magna Carta Trustees and that's all but he's one of those high and mighty that expects the common folk to stand at attention when he speaks. Threatened me with my job if I didn't cooperate, he did."

"What sort of cooperation did Ms. Ireland want from you?"

"Stay out of her way, was how I took it. That, and she wanted to know which guards had been on duty…"

Thorpe turned away and didn't finish the sentence. Murdoch let Thorpe dangle in the awkward silence, then took a chance and finished it for him.

"The night before the Magna Carta exhibit opened."

Thorpe looked at him, mouth open. "How could you know that?"

Murdoch hadn't known until Thorpe told him. He felt the electrical charge he always got when a case began to come together and he wasn't going to let Thorpe ask the questions.

"Who were the guards and why was she so interested in them?"

"Lloyd Pugh, Tom Galloway and Jeremy Bristol-Clarke. And she didn't say why she was interested in them. Just that she wanted to review all the guards' personnel files beginning with the ones that had been on duty inside the library that night."

"Then why did you hesitate to tell me about them?"

Thorpe reddened. "Because they didn't clock out after their shift. Made me look bad even though it wasn't my fault. But I can't blame them for quitting. The pay barely buys a pint."

"They quit?"

"And never came back. Didn't answer when I called them and their families said they never came home."

Murdoch said, "Did you report them as missing?"

"Why should I? They quit and left me hanging. That's all I cared about."

"How well did you know Malcolm Bridges?"

"Sat in meetings with him when they were putting the Magna Carta exhibit together. Talked to him about security. He did a good job."

"If the motion sensors inside the display cases were damaged, would you know about it?"

"Of course. I'd have had them switched out and made sure I knew what happened."

"Of course, you would have. I won't take any more of your time. I would like to take a close look at the display cases without arousing the guards if you don't mind."

"I'll let them know," Thorpe said. "What's any of this to do with homicide?"

"Malcolm Bridges was murdered. Strangled, poor fellow."

Thorpe sank back in his chair. "I suppose none of us are safe anymore."

"When did you last see Bridges?" Murdoch asked.

"A week ago. We did a final walk-thru on the exhibit."

"How did he seem to you?"

"Same as ever. Pleasant fellow except when he was badmouthing Titan. Said he loved the work but hated the company."

"Did Cassie Ireland talk to you about Bridges?"

"Not a peep. Are you thinking she had something to do with his murder, because I'd like to see the look on Sir Robert's face when he got that news."

Murdoch rose and waved off his comment even though he'd been asking himself the same question. "I'm suggesting nothing of the kind. Just being thorough. You know how this business goes."

Thorpe came around his desk and shook Murdoch's hand. "Indeed, I do. We're in the same game, aren't we now."

Murdoch held his tongue. "Of course, we are."

FORTY

The jam-packed crowds that had swarmed the Magna Carta exhibit when it opened had thinned to an irregular flow of visitors, making it easier for Murdoch to closely examine the display cases. He nodded to the security guard on duty who touched his brow in reply, acknowledging Murdoch's permission to cross in front of the rope barrier.

He quickly re-confirmed that the motion detectors and acrylic covers were undamaged. There was no visible means of opening the glass hoods, no key locks or keypads and no buttons to push. He stepped back to study the wide pedestal bases. The exteriors looked to be oak, though he assumed it was a veneer covering a steel structure because that would be the most secure design.

Since the glass hoods couldn't be opened from the outside, he realized that the pedestals would have to be disassembled to gain access to the Magna Cartas, probably by releasing an internal lock. The veneer was no doubt cemented to the steel and couldn't be removed without destroying it. He decided that there must be hidden screws holding an access plate in place, screws that could be located with a nail finder. Removing the screws would damage the veneer but less so than ripping it off entirely.

It was a smart design that was intended for a one-time use. He'd encountered similar models while investigating several museum thefts. When the exhibit was over, the pedestals would be torn down and the Magna Cartas removed. But, if it was necessary to open the glass hoods during the exhibit, it could be done with minimal damage to the pedestals.

Murdoch knelt next to the pedestal on the far left of the display and ran his hands across the highly-polished surface, searching for any irregularities. He felt a slight depression with his fingertip mid-way down the length of the base, then opened the flashlight app on his smartphone and shined the beam on the oak veneer. And there it was. A small circular defect the size of a screw head patched and touched up, probably with a colored marker. From the other side of the rope, it blended in with the wood grain, attracting no attention. He found three more defects, each another corner in a square. There were similar defects on the other pedestals.

Someone had opened the display cases. The questions were who and why. The motion sensors may have failed, requiring them to be replaced. If that happened too close to the opening of the exhibit to replace the damaged veneer, there would be an innocent explanation for the defects. Not so if thieves had broken into the cases.

Murdoch scanned the exhibit gallery. There were cameras and motion detectors, reliable but not impregnable measures. He looked at the ceiling, glad there were no skylights. In the movies, black-suited burglars descended from skylights on nylon ropes, hanging suspended inches above the floor while dodging laser beams but not in his world.

He'd seen the steel curtain recessed into the ceiling at the entrance to the gallery. Not many people would be authorized to open the gate. From past experiences, he expected that Ian Thorpe, Sarah St. James and Malcolm Bridges would on that list. Bridges was dead and now, more than ever, he was certain that Sarah St. James was a liar.

Murdoch caught up to Sarah in the hallway outside her office. She stopped when she saw him walking toward her, her suddenly slack jaw confirming that his visit was neither expected or welcome.

"Mrs. St. James," he said with a slight nod.

Sarah was carrying a file tucked under her arm. With her free hand, she brushed the front of her knee-length, navy blue dress and straightened her already straight collar.

"Inspector Murdoch. What a surprise."

Murdoch pointed to her file. "I hope you're not in such a hurry that you don't have a moment for me."

Sarah glanced at her watch. "Actually, I'm afraid this isn't a good time. I'm late to meeting."

Murdoch cocked his head to one side, giving her a half smile. "I won't keep you long. Just a few questions."

Sarah sucked in a breath. "Well then, I suppose you can walk with me. The meeting is just down the hall in our executive conference room."

He fell in step alongside her. "You seem a bit worked up. Who are you meeting with that has you in such a state."

She glanced at him. "I'd rather not say. Confidential library business and all that."

"Of course. How's the Magna Carta exhibit going?"

"Quite well, actually. The turnout has been more than we expected."

They reached the solid wood, double-doors to the conference room. Sarah reached for one of the handles but Murdoch laid a palm on the door, holding it closed.

"I must say," he said, staring hard at her, "you did an excellent job patching up the holes in the pedestals after you opened them up."

The color drained from Sarah's face. "I...I...I don't know what you're referring to, Inspector."

"Mrs. St. James," he began, but was cut off by Lady Tresch.

"Sarah," she said with a steely smile, "who is this gentleman that is keeping us from our meeting?"

"I'm Inspector Gerald Murdoch, Metropolitan Police, Serious Crimes. And who might you be, madam?"

She raised an eyebrow, tilting her head back. "Lady Lillian Tresch."

Murdoch dipped his chin in small acknowledgement of her status. "Lady Tresch."

"What brings the Metropolitan Police to a meeting of the Magna Carta trustees?" she asked.

"I came to see Mrs. St. James, though I'm pleased to know that her meeting is with the trustees."

Lady Tresch gazed at him. "And why is that, Inspector? Does your business with our curator concern us?"

"It may, my Lady."

She pulled the door open. "Then, by all means, please join us."

Murdoch followed Lady Tresch and Sarah into the conference room. Eight men and women were seated around the table, chattering. He recognized Sir Robert Howell sitting at the far end. Some of the other faces were familiar but he couldn't summon their names. All conversation stopped when they saw him.

Lady Tresch said, "This is Inspector Gerald Murdoch of the Metropolitan Police. I found him outside our door questioning Sarah about some matter he says may concern us. I invited him to our meeting so that we might learn more. And, since he tells me he's in the Serious Crimes Unit, I trust that whatever it is, we should take it seriously." She took a seat at the end of the table opposite Sir Robert and looked up at him. "How might we assist you, Inspector?"

Murdoch recognized that he was on shaky ground. He'd hoped to get Sarah to admit that she'd lied about the motion sensors and leverage that confession into information about Cassie Ireland and Jake Carter. He couldn't question her in front of the trustees. Nor could he raise doubts about the integrity of the Magna Carta exhibit without one or more trustees complaining to the Commissioner about what they would characterize as his unfounded speculation that, if made public, would damage their reputations and the fortunes of the library. But, he could still use this opportunity to his advantage.

"Thank you, Lady Tresch. Pardon me for distracting you from your business. I'm investigating the murder of Malcolm Bridges." He watched their reactions. Most looked down or away and fidgeted in their seats.

"Yes," Sir Robert said. "Terrible business. You have our complete cooperation, though I'm not certain how we can be of any help."

"I'm aware that you engaged the services of Global Security."

"That's right," Sir Robert said. "We asked them to conduct a security audit of the library. Strictly routine, of course."

"Of course. I met their operatives, Ms. Ireland and Mr. Carter, here on the first day of the exhibit. I ran into Ms. Ireland again at the Bridges' residence when I went there to inform Mrs. Bridges that her husband had been murdered." He paused, letting that sink in without further explanation. The fidgeting increased, some of the trustees shuffling papers, others sneaking a peek at him. "I didn't think much of it at the time," Murdoch continued. "Mr. Bridges had designed and supervised the construction of the Magna Carta display cases and the installation of the security systems for the exhibit. It was natural that she would want to speak with him."

"It's unfortunate she didn't have the opportunity," Lady Tresch said.

"Yes, it is, isn't it," Murdoch said. "However, earlier today, things took a bit of a nasty turn. Two men were found shot to death in a warehouse in the Limehouse district. Ms. Ireland and Mr. Carter were seen walking toward the warehouse immediately before the shooting and away from the warehouse immediately after. My colleague, Inspector Patel, has declared them persons of interest in these murders and has issued an alert so that they might be found and questioned. At the moment, they seem to have disappeared. I was hoping Mrs. St. James might know their whereabouts."

Lady Tresch shot Sarah a sharp look. "And, do you, Sarah?"

Sarah swallowed, her face still pale. "No, my Lady. But I will tell the Inspector the moment I hear from them, if I do."

"As shall we all," Sir Robert said. "And, speaking for the trustees, I must say this is quite shocking news and we will immediately terminate their services. Now, may we be of any further assistance, Inspector?"

"No," Murdoch said. "I believe I have all I need for the moment."

FORTY-ONE

Cassie, Jake and McNulty stopped in front of the office of a motel on the outskirts of Liverpool at ten o'clock. It was a non-descript, one-story, gray brick building. There was no sign promising free wifi or a free breakfast. Just the word *Motel* written in neon, the letters flickering as if they wouldn't make it through the night. A light was on in the office illuminating a sign in the window offering rates by the week, night or hour.

"I think we can do better," Jake said.

"I don't," Cassie said. "Less chance we'll be remembered at a place like this." She handed McNulty a hundred-pound note. "Get us rooms." McNulty left. She turned to Jake. "I'll find costumes tomorrow in Liverpool, but we won't need them if you can't get us tickets to the ball."

Jake's phone pinged. He read the text, grinned and tapped a reply. "Got 'em. A Duke I bailed out of a bad hand a couple of years ago let me have them for twenty-five thousand pounds."

"Twenty-five thousand pounds," Cassie said. "Are you out of your mind?"

"Plus, tickets to the final round of the World Series of Poker. Don't sweat it. Global Security is good for the money. What's the plan once we're inside the castle?"

"We look for proof that Lord Tresch is – or isn't – Shaw," Cassie said.

"It's a castle. Probably a big one. We can't exactly go on a treasure hunt without attracting attention."

"Really? Well, I guess we'll just have to ask him. If he admits to being Shaw, we can tell him we'd really like him to return the Magna

Cartas and stop trying to kill us. That could work."

Jake said, "I know you too well. You've probably got it figured out. Tell me."

"We start by finding out who he's been talking to. The best way to do that is to copy the data on his phone. Just like I did with Mc-Nulty."

Jake perked up. "If he's like most people, he can't stand not having his phone even if he's wearing a damn costume. All you've got to do is bump into him, lift the phone without him realizing it. That sort of thing. I can't do it but I'm sure you can."

She looked down her nose at him. "You think I'm a common pick-pocket?"

"Are you saying you got an A in sewers and an F in pickpocketing at asset recovery school?"

"Trust me. I could lift your socks and your shoes would never know it. Your idea might work. I'll find some out of the way place to copy the data and slip the phone back in his pocket."

"Wrong," Jake said. "Better to pass the phone to me and let me do the copying so you can keep an eye on Tresch."

"Makes sense. I'm glad I brought you along."

"You didn't. I brought you along. Show me how to use the app."

"Nothing to it, really. Just lay them side-by-side and follow the prompts."

McNulty returned, holding a key in each hand. "Two rooms is all they had left." He cast a knowing glance at Jake. "How do you want to divvy them up?"

Cassie snatched one of the keys. "I'll see you boys in the morning. Sleep tight."

FORTY-TWO

Jake followed McNulty into their room. The walls, once white, had dulled to gray. Flakes of paint were scattered along the baseboard. The ceiling was a kaleidoscope of water stains. The lone window, a narrow rectangle of opaque glass, was clouded with steel mesh bolted to the frame. The only light came from a dim lamp on the nightstand wedged into a corner between the wall and the double bed. When McNulty turned on the light, a pair of cockroaches zigzagged across the floor.

Jake wrinkled his nose. "What's that smell?"

"Equal parts bleach and cat piss, I'd say." McNulty pulled back the thin blanket and frayed sheet covering the bed and lifted a corner of the mattress, bending over for a closer look. "Nothing movin' that I can see but I'd wager a pint that the bedbugs will be glad for our company."

"We'll live. It's only one night."

McNulty winked. "And you'd pass it a might more comfortable if you was to share it with Cassie instead of the likes of me."

"She'd rather I dance with the bedbugs."

"Why? It's plain as day the two of you fancy each other."

Jake shrugged. "You'd have to ask her." He raised his palm. "But don't. Let's just say we're bouncing back and forth between lip lock and deadlock."

"Is there someone else?"

Jake let out a sigh. "Yeah. She thought he was dead until we found out he was part of the gang that stole the Magna Cartas."

"Blimey. I don't envy you cutting through that thicket though she's a woman worth the scratches and scars. I can tell you that." He clapped Jake's shoulders. "But either way, I'm sleeping in my car. There's just some things I won't do and spending the night with you in that bed in this room is one of them."

After McNulty left, Jake sat on the bed, nearly falling backward as his butt sank until the mattress was nothing more than a wafer between him and the bedsprings. He hoisted himself up and onto the cold floor, legs stretched out, back against the wall.

Tired but unable to sleep, he used his phone to research Culzean Castle, including watching an episode of *Ghost Hunters* that had been filmed there. He downloaded and studied the castle's floorplan, memorizing the location of rooms close to the ballroom where he could copy Lord Tresch's phone.

Jake wanted to show Cassie the floorplan. He got to his feet and was halfway out the door when he retreated to his room. If he knocked at this hour, she'd think he had more in mind since he could do that in the morning. She wouldn't be wrong and if she was suddenly okay with that, she knew where to find him.

***

CASSIE STRIPPED HER BED, shook the linens off outside and remade it. She climbed on and stretched out, cushioning her head and shoulders with two lumpy pillows stacked against the wall. Eyes closed, she focused on her breathing, letting the steady in and out rhythm soothe her. Twenty minutes later, she opened her eyes, stood and worked through a series of yoga poses to loosen the interconnected kinks woven through her muscles like braided iron.

Finished and refreshed, she used her phone to find a costume rental shop online and reserve outfits for Jake and her, grinning at his. She also made reservations at a Hotel in Maidens, a village a few miles from the castle, where they could change.

That done, she laid on the bed and closed her eyes again knowing she needed the sleep but she couldn't stop replaying the day's events and imagining what might happen tomorrow. Resigned to insomnia, she called Sarah St. James.

"I hope I didn't wake you."

"Oh, no," Sarah said. "Not at all. To be truthful, I can't remember the last time I slept. I'm afraid I have some bad news."

"I know. The trustees got cold feet after they found out about Malcolm Bridges. We're supposed to sit tight until the ransom exchange."

"It's worse than that. You've been sacked."

Prometheus hadn't said anything about that. "Fired? When did that happen?"

"Late this afternoon at a meeting of the trustees."

"Hang on a sec." Cassie pulled up the call log on her phone. Prometheus had called her at three-seventeen. "What time was the meeting?"

"Five-thirty."

Cassie checked her phone again. She hadn't missed any calls or texts from Prometheus. She sent him a text. *Understand we've been fired, not just told to back off. Can you confirm?"*

She asked Sarah, "What happened?"

Sarah told her how Inspector Murdoch had caught her by surprise and complimented her on patching up the screw holes on the pedestals. "The next thing I knew, Lady Tresch was at the conference room door and invited him to the meeting and he told the trustees that you and Jake had disappeared and that you were persons of interest in a double murder in some warehouse. Are you persons…I mean did you…"

"Yes, the police want to talk to us but we're in the clear. How did the trustees take that news?"

"It was an epidemic of heart attacks and strokes. If you ask me, they were mostly afraid of seeing their pictures on the front page of the tabloids. Sir Robert said that they would sack you and then Inspector Murdoch left."

"Anything else I should know?"

"It was awful. They're cowards if you ask me. All, that is, except for Lady Tresch. She was furious with them for agreeing to pay the ransom and for sacking you. She blasted Sir Robert for making a mess of the whole thing and said it was a tragedy that the only trustee with the balls to stand up to the thieves was a woman. She said the rest of them were so weak they'd blow away in a stiff breeze if they didn't have rocks in their pockets. And, that if you had killed anyone, she bloody well hoped it was the thieves. Difficult as she is, I must say I admire her for her spine. The woman is made of steel. She reminds me of you in that regard."

"Thanks for the compliment."

"So, what now? Are you and Jake just going to walk away?"

Cassie was reluctant to draw Sarah into their plans. The risks were too great. But, they might need her help. "Are you sure you want to know?"

"Sure? Are you crazy? What assurance is there that the thieves will keep their word? They are thieves, after all. I've staked my career on getting the Magna Cartas back. Lord knows how many laws I've already broken. I'd rather cast my lot with you and Jake than a bunch of dithering old men."

She told Sarah about Lord Tresch, the foundation and the gala at Culzean Castle. "It's the only lead we have. I'll let you know what we find out."

"Dear God. If Lady Tresch had a hint of this, she'd draw and quarter her husband. Shall I tell her?"

"Don't say anything to her. They're in the middle of a nasty divorce. I don't want to make things worse if it turns out we're wrong."

"Very well. But if you change your mind, you can tell her yourself. She mentioned the gala and said she would be there because the children that benefit from the foundation shouldn't suffer just because her husband is a jackass."

Cassie ended the call thinking she should tell Jake what she'd learned. All she had to do was send him a text asking him to come to her room. She stared at the door picturing what would happen after she let him in. They'd sit on the bed because there was nowhere else to sit. They'd banter and flirt. Then one of them would brush against the other, pretending it was unintentional, knowing it wasn't. His hand, her knee, his shoulder, her arm. It wouldn't matter. There would be no turning back. Her pulse quickened as a surge of warmth and longing washed over her. Perhaps it was time.

Cassie opened her phone and typed the message. Her finger hovered over the send icon. The anger and hurt Gabriel had caused her and her fear of loving and losing Jake welled up and paralyzed her. She erased the message and rolled over, frustrated that she kept succumbing to these negative emotions. If she did that with her work, she'd fail and she was tired of failing at love. No more, she told herself. No more.

FORTY-THREE

McNulty pounded on Cassie and Jake's doors as the morning sky began to lighten. They stepped outside, faces drawn from a restless night.

"Time's a-wasting. We've a long drive ahead."

Jake said, "In case you forgot, we missed dinner last night. I need food."

"Fair enough. They serve a tasty fry-up at a tidy little café down the street. Had my full while you two were still sleeping."

"What's a fry-up?" Cassie asked.

"Just the best breakfast in the world. Couple of bangers, some Irish bacon, beans, tomatoes and some runny eggs plus a bit of fried bread if you can find the room for it." He patted his belly and smiled. "I know I did."

"Perfect," Jake said. "Point me in the right direction."

They took a booth against a wall with a window facing the street. McNulty sat on one side by himself. Jake slid in on the other side ahead of Cassie. The short bench seat left them hip-to-hip. She matched his gusto for the food. Finished, she eased away from the table, holding a mug of steaming coffee with both hands.

"I talked to Sarah St. James last night," she said. Jake and McNulty listened as she summarized her conversation.

"Does this change our plans?" Jake asked.

Cassie said, "Just means we're working for free. Are you okay with that?"

"Sure," Jake said, "but we may not be out of the money if we pull this off. At least Lady Tresch fought for us. Maybe she can help us smoke out her future former husband."

"Too risky. If we're wrong about him, we'd just make things worse for her and that wouldn't be right after the way she tried to help us."

"But, if Lord Tresch is Shaw, we should let her know so that she isn't blindsided."

"If we can without compromising the investigation, we will." Cassie looked at her watch. "McNulty's right. Let's go. We've got a long drive and a couple of stops to make."

"Where? For what?"

She patted Jake's rough-whiskered cheek. "Neither of us is gala-ready. I don't know about you, but I need clean underwear and you need a shave. And, we can't go to the ball dressed like this. We need costumes."

"Oh, boy. I can't decide whether I want to be a pirate or a Knight in shining armor."

"Wait for Halloween. I've already taken care of it." She gave directions to McNulty for the costume store. "I'll just run in and pick them up. There's a store on the same block where we can get everything else. There's a village close to the castle called Maidens. I got us rooms at a hotel where we can clean up and change."

"Hold on. You picked my costume without asking me? When did you do that?"

"Last night before I went to bed. I found this shop online. There was no time to ask your opinion."

"What do you mean there was no time? I could have come to your room and we could have picked them out together."

Cassie raised an eyebrow. "You and me. In the same room. Late at night. Is that what you're saying we should have done."

Jake stared at her, his voice soft. "Yeah, that's what I'm saying. Would that have been so terrible?"

She flushed and gazed into her coffee mug. McNulty cleared his throat. "You children carry on. I'll go bring the car around."

Jake waited until McNulty was gone. "Well?"

Cassie had made a promise to herself before falling asleep and now was the time to keep it. She squared around and leaned toward Jake, their faces and bodies inches apart. His eyes widened. With a sly smile, she draped her right arm around his neck and reached her left arm past him, bringing them even closer. Jake tried to kiss her but she turned her head and pulled away holding a sausage from his plate in her left hand.

Her eyes dancing, she said, "You going to eat this?"

Jake shook his head. "I'd rather you do it."

"I'm sure you would." She dropped the sausage on her plate and scooted out of the booth. "But, we're in a hurry and I'd hate to rush a thing like that."

**

Cassie came out of the costume shop with boxes under each arm, having insisted that Jake wait in the car. She tucked them into the Audi's trunk with their newly purchased underwear and toiletries and got in the front seat. McNulty headed back to the highway.

"Really," Jake said. "You're not going to let me see my costume?"

"I want it to be a surprise."

"What if it doesn't fit. You don't know my size?"

She turned around. "Remember our stroll on the nude beach in Portugal? I know all about your size."

McNulty laughed and gave the horn two sharp blasts. "Here's hoping it was a balmy day."

Jake said, "Well, in that case, I hope you got an extra…"

"Easy, cowboy. Don't lie in front of McNulty."

"At least give me a clue."

"Fine. It's a two-person horse costume. Guess which half you get?"

"At least I'll enjoy the view."

FORTY-FOUR

Murdoch called Inspector Patel while he was on his way to Titan Security Solutions to interview Malcolm Bridges' co-workers.

"Anything new, Inspector?" Murdoch asked.

"A bit."

Murdoch sighed. "Are you in a sharing mood this morning?"

"We're very busy here."

"Not too busy, I hope, for a fellow copper who could help you make your case while standing behind you."

"It's not that, Murdoch."

"Glad to hear it," he said, knowing that was exactly it. "Tell me what you've learned. Maybe I can put it together with whatever I dig up."

"Fine," Patel said, his irritated tone telling Murdoch that he just wanted to be done with the call. "Video traces McNulty's cab to an underground car park beneath Cavendish Square Gardens. He went straight there from the warehouse. The cab never left but we picked McNulty out leaving in an Audi Q3 with two passengers. We couldn't make out their faces but we assume they are your friends, Ireland and Carter."

"Where'd they go from there?"

"North. Out of London. I've put out an alert to local police along all the northern routes and to bus and train stations and hotels. We covered the airports as well. And, we included their photographs."

"If the images were so poor, where did you get their photographs?"

"McNulty's is on file with the taxi authorities. We pulled Ireland's from the video outside the warehouse and we got Carter's from the

Internet. What's a professional poker player doing mixed up in this?"

"Going all in on a bad bet."

FORTY-FIVE

The hotel in Maidens offered beautiful views of the Irish Sea, a charming restaurant and a dozen comfortable rooms, only one of which was available when Cassie gave her name to the desk clerk.

"But I reserved two rooms on your website last night."

"I'm sorry, m'lady. Our website was overly generous. But the room has a king-sized bed, a large flat-screen…"

"We'll take it," Jake said.

Cassie declined Jake's offer to wash her back and took the first shower. When Jake stepped out of the bathroom with a towel cinched around his waist, she was wearing her costume - a bold red, strapless gown with a sweetheart neckline, fitted bodice and full princess skirt.

"Holy, smokes, Your Majesty. You look gorgeous. The women will hate you and the men will promise you their fortunes."

"You don't think it's too much? I feel like my boobs are going to pop out."

"They deserve to be set free."

She pointed to a box on the bed. "Your turn."

"Ah, at last. My costume." He returned to the bathroom to change.

He came back dressed in a red and purple jester costume. The long-sleeved tunic and puffy pants were divided into different patches of color and gathered into ruffles at the ankle and wrist. The shoes, one purple and one red, were oversized with upturned toes. There was also a hat with four crescent moons stretching from the crown, gold bells dangling at each end. Grinning, he danced a jig, spun his hat around and bowed deeply.

"How else might I amuse you, m'lady?"

Cassie laughed. "You're not mad at me?"

"Mad? It's brilliant. No one will take me seriously. One glance, and I'll be forgotten. And, while we're not on the subject, what's going on with us? That thing you did this morning with the sausage - which, by the way, was the perfect blend of sexy, crass and hilarious - and your crack in the car about knowing all about my size weren't exactly platonic gestures."

"No, I suppose they weren't. I guess I laid it on a bit thick. Let's just say that…"

McNulty banged on the door. "Open up, you two. His Lordship awaits."

"He has the timing of an in-law," Jake said. With a sigh, he opened the door.

McNulty took one step into their room and stopped, eyes bulging, mouth agape. "Bloody, bloody…bloody hell. Cassie, darlin', you're a vision of beauty no man has a right to expect. As for you playing the fool, Jake, I'd say Cassie got it right."

"Thanks, McNulty," Jake said. "Good to have you in my corner. Let's go."

Cassie held up her hand. "Not yet. We've got to practice the phone handoff so we don't end up like the relay team that drops the baton. We'll keep an eye on Lord Tresch. If he's like every other phone crack-head, he won't go ten minutes without checking it for something. Once I know which pocket he uses, I'll make sure he asks me to dance. When you see me rub my hand across his back, you'll know I have it."

"Then what?"

"We do a brush pass. You slide past me and I hand you the phone without anyone noticing. Don't make eye contact and don't stop moving. Pretend that the hand-off isn't even happening. Now let's practice."

They walked past each other, barely touching as they passed the phone. Jake smiled. "Easy enough."

McNulty said, "Not by half. You looked down at your hand. Right quickly, but I saw it. Like this." He darted a downward glance.

Cassie said, "Okay, let's try it again."

After four more practice passes, they were satisfied. McNulty headed out the door followed by Jake until Cassie called to him.

"Hey, fool."

Jake turned around. "Who you calling a fool, lady?"

"You, mister." She put her hand behind his neck and drew him toward her, then kissed him. "That answer your question?"

"Yeah, and look," he said, pointing to his shoes. "You made my toes curl."

In the parking lot, McNulty led them to a gleaming black limousine and opened the back door.

"Where did you get this," Cassie said. "And, where's the Audi?"

"We couldn't very well pull up to the castle in that pile of junk. There's bound to be security and one look at my Audi and they'd tell us to turn right around. While you two were doing, well, whatever you were doing, not that it's any of my business," he said with a wave of his hand, "I was chatting up the gent that owns a service station down the way. He keeps the limo for the occasional rental. He's holding the Audi as collateral and you owe him a hundred pounds."

Cassie kissed him on the cheek. "McNulty, you are a treasure."

He drove them through the Culzean Country Park until they reached a line of cars waiting to cross a narrow stone bridge leading to the castle. A security guard stood at the entrance to the bridge, checking the names of arriving guests.

Jake told him, "Tell him I'm the Duke of Lincolnshire accompanied by his lovely lady."

The guard motioned them through without giving them a second glance. They cleared a patch of trees and crossed the bridge where they got their first view of Culzean Castle. Perched at the top of a cliff overlooking the Firth of Clyde and brightly illuminated for the night's festivities, it was an imposing stone fortress straight out of a fairy tale, with round towers topped by crenellated parapets where medieval archers once fired on the enemy below.

McNulty pulled up to the massive granite arch at the entrance to the castle, got out and opened the door for Cassie with an exaggerated bow. She flashed a quick smile at Jake.

"Here we go."

FORTY-SIX

The wrought iron chandelier hung from a thick chain in the castle's large entry hall casting a warm glow on the rough stone walls and high, vaulted ceiling. A large shield bearing the clan Kilpatrick coat of arms - a green cross on a white field, surrounded by bows and arrows and a large, leaping stag - was mounted at eye level opposite the main door.

Beside the coat of arms was an open doorway, draped in gold and purple fabric. A man in an 18th century butler's uniform of black pants and coat over a crisp white shirt nodded politely, and waved them toward the door.

"Welcome, my Lord, my Lady."

Cassie noted his earpiece and the telltale bump of a gun under his long coat.

They followed a runner of royal purple carpet down a short passage to a large double door where another security guard masquerading as a butler opened the heavy door, releasing a flood of music and light.

The grand ballroom was at the base of a round tower that stood on the edge of the cliff. Seventy-five feet in diameter with floor to ceiling windows along one curved section of the wall, it overlooked the moonlit water of the Firth of Clive. Large framed mirrors bordered with gold and purple fabric and strings of twinkling light hung on the pale, yellow walls making the ballroom appear even larger. Ten tuxedoed musicians sat on a raised platform, playing a lively waltz. Dozens of couples crowded the dance floor in a swirl of brightly colored costumes. Servers dressed in white tie formal wear circulated among the guests offering crystal flutes of champagne to go with Beluga Caviar, foie gras and oysters.

As they took in the glittering scene, Jake shook his head, laughing softly.

"What is it?" Cassie asked.

"I grew up in a small town surrounded by wheat fields. My escape was books. *The Once and Future King* was my favorite. I used to pretend I was one of the Knights of the Roundtable. But I never imagined that one day I'd be dancing with a beautiful woman at a fancy masquerade ball in a Scottish castle."

"Want me to pinch you?"

"Maybe later." He gave her a courtly bow. "Would you care to dance, my Lady?"

"Indeed, I would."

He took her right hand in his left and placed the other on the small of her back, sweeping her into a waltz. They moved in unison, as naturally as if they'd spent years dancing in each other's arms. Cassie saw her reflection in one of the mirrors. Even with a mask covering her eyes, she looked the way she felt - happy – and drew Jake closer.

She surveyed the guests. There were kings and queens, lords and ladies, soldiers and sailors, a sprinkling of pirates and wenches and a few jesters, all hiding their eyes behind masks.

"What's the plan, Mata Hari? How do we find Lord Tresch?"

"We don't. We make him find me."

Jake looked her up and down, his gaze lingering on her chest. "Well, that dress is a good start."

Smiling, she tipped his chin up. "Eyes right here. Tresch's mind is on money. We'll give him a prospective donor to cultivate."

"And you're the whale."

She twirled gracefully, her full skirt flaring out. "Tonight, I'm Katherine York. I'm rich, thanks to my late, successful father and grandfather. I adore children, especially disadvantaged ones, and I'd love to support the foundation's very important work."

Jake nodded. "Tresch has a lot of friends in this room. They'll make sure he knows about the woman in the killer red dress. But what if he checks you out?"

"I hope he does. Prometheus created Katherine York's complete, fake family history when I started working for him, along with several others I've used."

Jake leaned his head back. "But, you really are Cassie Ireland, aren't you?"

She pressed her hand against his cheek. "Trust me. I'm the real deal. Head for the sidelines and let me work the room."

Over the next hour, the Red Baron told her war stories and gave her tax advice. A very tipsy Cleopatra extolled the virtues of coffee colonics. Julius Caesar invited her to join him for a weekend in the Bahamas and Mary Queen of Scots did the same.

Alone for a moment away from the dance floor, she sipped champagne. A tall man approached, dressed in full Louis XVI regalia, including a pale blue brocade coat with matching knee breeches and a powered wig. She recognized his long, angular face and thin-lipped smile.

"I do hope you're having a nice evening," he said.

"Yes, I am."

"I'm so glad to hear it." He offered her a white gloved hand and she took it. "Lord William Tresch."

"Katherine York. This is a lovely event and for such a deserving cause."

"So kind of you to say. The foundation's work is quite gratifying but none of it would be possible without our generous donors. Tonight's affair is our way of thanking them."

"And warming them up for your next solicitation."

Tresch smiled. "Ah, yes. Our guests know that their tickets to the ball are the least expensive part of the evening. After dinner, I'll give a rousing speech complete with testimonials from starving children whose lives we've saved after which our benefactors will fight to see who can make the largest pledge." He paused, shook his head and reached inside his long coat to retrieve his cellphone from his right hip. "Please accept my apologies. I hate these damn things but they've become an irritating and unavoidable necessity."

"Of course."

Tresch turned away. Cassie looked around the room for Jake but another guest caught her attention. A woman wearing a pale blue brocade dress and a towering, powdered white wig, decorated with ribbons, gems and a single peacock feather on top. She was Marie Antoinette to Tresch's Louis XVI and she was glaring at him with guillotine eyes.

"Is everything alright?" Cassie asked when Tresch ended the call.

"It seems there's a shortage of foie gras. The chef wishes to substitute Beluga caviar but hesitates to make so monumental a decision without my approval."

Cassie chuckled. "Heavy lies Your Majesty's crown. That woman across the way dressed as your queen has not taken her eyes off you and, if you don't mind my saying so, her gaze is not a warm one."

Lord Tresch's back stiffened when he saw who she was looking at. "Are you married, Ms. York."

"No."

"Then you must avoid it at all costs. That woman is my wife until her lawyers finish pecking the flesh from my bones. Now, about the foundation. Perhaps I can encourage you to join our cause."

Cassie cocked her head to one side, then emptied her glass. "Perhaps you might ask me to dance first. I'm much more pliable after champagne and a waltz."

"I'd be delighted."

He led her to the center of the dance floor. She made eye contact with Jake, letting him know to get ready. He approached a young woman whose ample breasts were blossoming from her hand maiden's dress and escorted her onto the dance floor. Cassie gave him a raised eyebrow review of his choice. He responded with a shrug and a grin, then spun and twirled his partner to within a few feet of her.

Cassie leaned her head back, closed her eyes for an instant, then opened them and let out a breath. "Oh, my. I'm afraid I may have had a bit too much champagne." She stumbled and braced herself with her right hand on Tresch's shoulder while slipping her left inside his long coat and lifting his phone from his hip. Tresch propped her up until she straightened and shook her head.

"Are you alright, Ms. York?"

Cassie smiled wanly. "Embarrassed but otherwise fine, William."

Tresch's eyes lit up. "I'm so glad, Katherine."

Cassie swept her hand across his back, signaling Jake.

FORTY-SEVEN

Don't look at your hand, Jake repeated to himself. *Look at...* For a moment, he blanked on his partner's name. *Anya.*

He focused on Anya's deep brown eyes as they waltzed toward Cassie. When she reached down to adjust her voluminous skirt, he lifted his hand from Anya's back and let it drop to hip level as they whirled past Cassie and Tresch, feeling his fingers brush hers as he took the phone. He palmed it, tucked it into the waistband of his puffy jester pants and returned his hand to his partner's back in one smooth motion. The maneuver had been flawless and he was grateful for a lifetime of keeping a poker face.

Jake escorted Anya to the edge of the dance floor where he bowed and kissed her hand. "If you'll excuse me."

He went to a room designated on the floor plans as the china closet. Inside, he pushed a stack of dishes out of the way and laid Tresch's phone alongside his, then turned on the app. A little spinning ball appeared as the two phones synced.

When the download was complete, he hid the burner inside his waistband and palmed Tresch's phone. Back in the ballroom, Jake found Cassie in her red dress. She was laughing at something Lord Tresch must have said. Their eyes met and he nodded, telling her he was ready.

He couldn't find Anya. Then he saw Marie Antoinette wearing an elaborate wig and blue dress that matched Lord Tresch's Louis XVI outfit. Giving himself five-to-one odds that she was Lady Tresch, he approached her and bowed deeply, the bells on his hat jingling as they brushed the floor.

"Your Majesty."

When he looked up, she was smiling. "My loyal subject."

"Loyal and true. May I request the honor of a dance?"

He held out a hand and she took it.

"You may."

They danced to a slow sonata. "I must say, Mr. Carter, I'm surprised to see you here."

Jake had several first rules of poker. One was to never act surprised when the unexpected card turned up. "And, why is that, Lady Tresch?"

"Well done, Mr. Carter. Aren't you going to ask how I knew it was you?"

"I don't need to. You knew my name because you're a trustee of the Magna Carta Trust and you knew what I looked like because you found photographs of me on Google."

"But none with a mask," she said.

"Batman wore a mask and everyone except the Joker knew he was Bruce Wayne. You're a good fiduciary. You did your homework."

She nodded. "And my fiduciary duty requires that I ask what you are doing at my husband's gala."

"I just got fired. Can't go to Disney World so I chose the next best thing."

"Ah, Mr. Carter. I do hope you're a better poker player than you are a detective, or whatever you and Ms. Ireland call yourselves. You were fired and yet you're still on the job. I'll ascribe that to strength of character. I'm more interested in knowing why you're here, dancing with me while your partner is dancing with my husband. One might think you suspect he is somehow connected to the theft of the Magna Cartas."

Cassie maneuvered Lord Tresch toward them. Jake passed Tresch's phone to her as she swept by while the Lord and Lady pretended not to notice one another. He kept his eyes on Lady Tresch as they made the switch.

"Should we suspect him?"

"I'm hardly an unbiased source."

"Doesn't mean you'd be wrong."

"William is an unfaithful spendthrift. I suspect that from time to time he's acquired…valuables…whose provenance is suspect or, at best, obscure. I don't know whether that makes him a criminal or just clever. I'm afraid I wouldn't begin to know how one would carry out such a crime so I can't say whether he would have the necessary resources but I daresay he lacks the courage."

"Could he have taken advantage of your position to learn about the security for the exhibit?"

"How do you mean?"

"If you had any information about it on your personal computer, he could have had someone hack into it."

She stopped dancing and guided him by the hand to a quiet corner. "Some months ago, he was at my flat during one of the few moments we haven't been at each other's throats during this nasty business. He insisted on coming over in the hopes that we could reach an agreement without the lawyers. He arrived before me. I'd forgotten that he had a key. I found him in my office at my computer. He had one of those things you stick in the side of the computer…."

"A flash drive?"

"Yes. That's it. He yanked it out as soon as he saw me. I thought he was after my financial records or email. The trustees were provided with confidential information about the exhibit including the security. It was on my computer. It never occurred to me that he could have been after that. In any case, I got so angry that I threw him out. My lawyers demanded that he disclose what information he'd stolen."

"And did he?"

"Yes. But there was nothing about the Library or the Magna Carta exhibit." She paused and took a deep breath. "What he did wasn't honorable. What he found wasn't either. Emails and text messages between me and a certain gentleman. My husband and I both abused our vows."

"We've all done things we regret."

"Indeed. I regret letting him keep that key."

Jake looked past her, watching Lord Tresch and Cassie leave the dance floor for the other side of the ballroom. Tresch reached for his phone and pressed it against his ear, glancing toward the hall leading to the china closet. Jake followed his gaze, locking onto the hulking figure of Max Dekker standing in the shadows wearing all black. Jake recognized his costume. He'd come to the party as an executioner.

FORTY-EIGHT

F orgive me, Katherine," Lord Tresch said when he ended the call. "There's something I must attend to."

"William, don't tell me the chef has run out of foie gras and Beluga?"

"Nothing that serious. Promise you won't move from this spot."

Cassie pressed her palm against his chest. "I promise you won't have to look for me."

She watched Tresch circle the dance floor, then step into the same corridor Jake had used. Scanning the ballroom, she saw Jake on the other side chatting with Lady Tresch. They'd come to the gala to copy Lord Tresch's phone and that job was done. Sticking around hoping to find something more was risky. She'd seen half a dozen security guards and assumed there were others. They were unarmed and outnumbered. It was time to signal Jake and slip away.

The exit was behind her. She turned around and ran into a man decked out in forest green, his face hidden by a black mask covering his eyes and a hooded cloak. He stood there, blocking her.

Cassie smoothed her dress and said, "Out of my way, Robin Hood."

"Cassie," he said and she froze. She knew that voice as well as her own.

"Gabriel. How did you…"

"It takes more than a mask for you to hide from me."

She straightened, regaining her composure. "You weren't invited. How did you get in?"

"I borrowed my costume from one of the guests. Like that job we did in Melbourne, remember?"

She did. She also remembered the long, sleepless night they spent together after the job.

Gabriel pressed her. "What the hell are you doing here?"

"My job."

He took her by the arms. "Dammit, Cassie, I told you to let this go."

She grabbed his wrists and broke his hold. "You, of all people, don't get to tell me what to do."

"If Dekker sees you, you're dead."

"Dekker? Last time I saw him, he was out cold at the warehouse. The police should have carried him out of there."

"He's a hard man to put down." Gabriel tipped his head toward the far side of the ballroom. Cassie glanced over her shoulder and saw Dekker dressed as an executioner and standing at the entrance to the corridor where she'd last seen Lord Tresch.

"The costume certainly fits. Why are you here? Dekker won't be glad to see you."

"I'm not going to spend the rest of my life on the run from Shaw."

"Meaning what?"

"Meaning I'm going to persuade Shaw not to kill me."

"What if he won't listen to reason?"

"Then I'll make sure he can't kill me."

If all Gabriel cared about was saving his own skin, he was of no use to her. But if he wanted to make things right between them, they might yet be able to work together.

"And the Magna Cartas?"

"One problem at a time. I can't do anything about that if I'm dead."

His answer was encouraging but she needed more if she was going to trust him. "But you don't know who Shaw is or how to find him."

"That's why I've been following Dekker. I knew that he'd eventually lead me to Shaw."

"And has he?"

Gabriel looked at her. "You don't really expect me to give you the first crack at him."

"That's exactly what I expect. You owe me."

He nodded. "You're right. I do owe you. And I can never pay my debt. But, you can't win this one. I can get to Shaw but you can't. Whatever you're planning, he's already thought of it."

"Then help me think of something he hasn't."

He was quiet for a moment, his dark eyes fixed on hers. Cassie felt a stirring of hope. Then he said, "You know I can't."

She was disappointed but not surprised. He hadn't changed and never would. "You mean, you won't."

Before he could say anything else, Jake joined them and asked Cassie, "Who's your friend?"

Gabriel said, "Walk away, Jake. This doesn't concern you."

"Well, look at you," Jake said. "The Walking Dead returns. Listen, Gabe, Cassie and I are a team so whatever…"

Cassie stopped him. She'd give Gabriel one last chance. "It's okay. He was about to tell us who Shaw is."

"We don't need his help. Lord Tresch is Shaw. I just saw him talking to Dekker and…oh, shit." Jake aimed his thumb behind Cassie. "Not good. We're busted. The Executioner is on his way over here and he's bringing his buddies."

Dekker and two other black-clad enforcers were crossing the dance floor. Dekker reached inside his vest, drew a gun and palmed it against his side.

"This way," Gabriel said.

They hustled toward the double-swinging doors leading to the kitchen. Two butlers the size of refrigerators lingering near the doors intercepted them. Dekker caught up to them.

He pushed Gabriel's hood back and pulled his mask off, then grinned. "I can't fuckin' believe it. You've got some kind of stones showing up here. Not much in the way of brains, though." He turned to Cassie and yanked off her mask. "I see you've brought along your bit of quim." Finally, he looked at Jake, laughing as he took in the jester outfit. "And the tragic clown. Brilliant." He snatched Jake's jester hat and handed it to one of the butlers. "Hang on to his hat. We'll fill it with what's left of him when we're done." Then he motioned to the three of them. "You'll be coming with us now."

Cassie said, "I promised Lord Tresch that I wouldn't move from this spot. He won't be happy if I'm not here when he gets back."

"Funny you say that because I promised his Lordship I wouldn't let any uninvited guests ruin his party. He was none too happy when I told him that Katherine York wasn't your real name."

Jake stood his ground, looking around at the crowd of guests. "Wow. Look at all these witnesses. I'll bet none of them have ever seen a triple murder."

The big man stepped closer, pulling out a six-inch knife and pressed the blade against his ribs. "Then I'll have to be real quiet-like, won't I?"

Jake didn't move. "Not me. I'm a real screamer."

Cassie pulled him away from Dekker. "Not here. Bad odds."

Dekker laughed. "And I'll wager they won't be getting any better."

FORTY-NINE

Dekker led them single-file down a long, chilly hallway. Cassie was behind Jake and Gabriel followed her. They were flanked by two guards on either side pointing handguns at them. Dekker was right. The odds of getting out of the castle alive were dropping with every step they took.

Their costumes made matters worse. Her dress was made for show, not fighting and Jake's upturned jester shoes were a slip and fall waiting to happen.

Cassie eyed the suits of armor once worn by long dead knights that lined the corridor, each with its own weapons. There were swords, pikes, battle hammers, maces and daggers close enough to touch but there were too many guards with too many guns for her to reach for one.

Jake tapped Dekker on the shoulder and stopped walking. Everyone else did the same. She and Gabriel were standing between two suits of armor, one on each side of the hall. Cassie bit her lip. Jake was making a play. She wished she knew what it was.

Dekker turned around and scowled. "What is it, Jester?"

"Hang on a second. These goofy shoes are killing me." He pulled them off and tossed them to the side. "That's better. Now, first of all, I'm sorry about smacking you in the head back at the warehouse. I snuck up on you and that wasn't really fair."

Dekker rubbed his head and waved his gun at Jake. "What the fuck…"

Jake raised his hands. "Apology accepted. Fantastic. Let's get down to business. Shaw ordered you to kill us but where's the profit in that? We can do more for you alive than dead so what's it going to take?

Name your price and you'll be a wealthy man before you know it."

"That's rich, is what that is, Jester. You thinking you can buy me off."

"Hey, a hundred million pounds goes a long way. If we don't give it to Shaw, we can give it to you. And, your crew can have a taste if you want to cut them in." Jake turned to the guards. "Don't worry. If Dekker stiffs you, you'll still have your jobs."

The four guards wrinkled their collective brows and stepped closer to Jake, guns leveled at him. One of them said, "A hundred million? For what?"

Jake said, "For returning the Magna Cartas Dekker stole from the British Library. Tomorrow is the big payday. But, if he's holding out on you, we'll guarantee you fifty grand each for letting us go. That's got to be more than you take home in a year. Easiest money you'll ever make."

"This is bullshit," another guard said. "Nobody said nothing about no big fuckin' payday. What about it, Dekker?"

"Uh, oh, Dekker," Jake said. "Your boys don't sound happy."

"Shut your yap," Dekker told Jake, "before I shut it for you." He gestured to the guards. "And that goes for the lot of you. Just do your fucking jobs and don't pay this asshole any mind. He doesn't know what he's talking about."

"He's right about one thing," the first guard said. "A hundred million pounds goes a long way. And, we'll be having our cut."

The four guards formed a semi-circle behind Jake, their backs to Cassie and Gabriel. Well played, Cassie wanted to tell Jake. She and Gabriel exchanged quick glances and nods.

Cassie grabbed a two-foot long battle hammer, with a spike on one side and blunt hammer on the other. Gabriel yanked a five-foot long pike with a still sharp blade from the suit of armor next to him. They each took out a guard with swift blows to the backs of their heads before the other guards were on them.

One of the two remaining guards tackled Cassie. She let go of the battle hammer and grabbed the guard's gun hand as he tried to aim the barrel at her face, forcing his shot to go high and wide, the sound

JOEL GOLDMAN & LISA KLINK

ricocheting down the hall. Cassie slammed her elbow into the guard's nose, then jammed her thumbs in his eyes. He rolled onto his side and she put him out with a double-fisted blow to his temple.

Jake drove his foot into the side of Dekker's knee as he tried to shove Jake out of the way. Dekker howled as his leg gave way and Jake knocked the gun from his hand. Dekker clamped his other hand around the back of Jake's neck, forcing him to the floor and pinning him with his good knee planted in the center of Jake's back. Dekker yanked Jake's hair, arching his neck, then wrapped his arm around Jake's throat and squeezed until Jake's eyes widened and rolled skyward.

Cassie found her battle hammer, took a roundhouse swing and connected with Dekker, breaking his hold on Jake. Gabriel finished the other guard then drove the back end of his pike into Dekker's midsection and whipped it against his head until Dekker collapsed in a heap.

Jake struggled to his feet, rubbing his neck. "Thanks, but next time don't wait so long before saving my life."

Cassie smiled. "I'll put you at the top of my list." She retrieved a dagger from another suit of armor and cut her dress off above the knee.

"Radical, but practical," Gabriel said. "My kind of woman."

Cassie looked at him. "I am not your woman." She handed Jake the battle hammer and retrieved a short sword from a knight, hefting it and tossing it from hand to hand. "Nice weight. Good balance. I'll take it."

"It suits you," said Gabriel. "But you might want one of these."

He started to pick up one of the guard's guns when two more guards came running down the hall toward them, semi-automatics blazing.

"Follow me," Jake said.

Relying on his memory of the castle's floorplan, they lost the pursuing guards in the maze of hallways and stairs. Each time they got close to an exit, they saw more guards waiting for them

"They've blocked all the exits," Cassie said.

"I know," Jake said.

"So where do we go?"

Jake pointed at the ceiling. "Up."

FIFTY

Jake led them to a hexagonal rotunda with a domed skylight ceiling fifty feet above a marble tiled floor. A sweeping double staircase curved along the walls to a second story landing bordered by a wrought iron railing with intricate scrollwork between the posts. As they raced up the right side of the staircase, two heavily muscled black-clad guards burst through a door on the ground floor. One had a pony-tail and the other had a ring of barbwire tattooed around his neck.

"Give me a break," Jake said. "Where do they get these guys? Hulks R Us?"

The guards spotted them and opened fire with semi-automatic pistols. They fell to their knees, crawling as fast as they could. The iron scrollwork gave them cover even as it showered them with shrapnel.

The guard with the ponytail started up the stairs while the other took the left side to intercept them on the landing. Gabriel rolled onto his back and hurled his pikestaff at the first guard as he rounded the curve of the stairs. The blade sunk deep into the man's belly and he fell backward screaming, his arms pin-wheeling.

Jake and the other guard reached the landing at the same moment. The guard took aim at Jake as Cassie threw her dagger, hitting the guard in the arm. Grinning, he pulled the blade from his bicep like it was a splinter. Jake charged him, driving the battle hammer's spike into the guard's thigh. His momentum took them to the floor. The guard raised his gun and Cassie slapped it out of his hand with the flat side of her sword. Jake got to his knees and slammed the blunt side of the hammer against the guard's skull, leaving him limp.

Cassie plucked a comms unit from the guard's ear and tucked it into hers. "Now we can listen in."

"Gotta go," said Gabriel, as he joined them, carrying his bloody pikestaff in one hand and the dead guard's gun in the other.

He nodded toward three more guards that were heading toward the stairs, shooting at them. Cassie picked up the other guard's gun and they returned fire before her gun ran out of ammunition.

"This way," Jake said and led them down the second-floor hallway, consulting his mental map. "There's another set of stairs at the end of the hall."

Cassie caught up with him. "Careful. They might be using those, too."

She was bleeding from a shallow cut at the top of her right shoulder. The track of a bullet that had barely missed her skull.

"You've been shot."

She glanced at the wound. "A little."

"A little? How can you…?" He stopped short as they heard guards coming from both directions.

"We're trapped," Gabriel said.

"In here," Cassie said, and opened a door in the center of the hallway.

Jake locked the door and studied the room. There was a window overlooking the sculpture garden that didn't open. There were no other doors. The walls were painted a soothing pale blue and padded settees were arranged across the floor in rows as if for an audience. A grand piano occupied one corner and a variety of antique instruments were on display. The wall opposite the door was lined with shelves stuffed with antiquarian books. The large, comfortable space looked familiar.

Jake said, "This is the music room."

"Good guess, Sherlock," Gabriel said. "We're still trapped. Tresch's army will be pounding on the door any second." He examined the slide bolt. "And, this lock won't hold very long."

Jake went to the bookshelves, running his hand along the spines of each book.

"Jake, I know you're a collector," Cassie said. "But I don't think this is a good time."

He ignored her and began pulling out books only to push them back onto the shelf. The footsteps in the hallway stopped outside the music room. The side bolt jiggled. The door opened a fraction but the bolt held. Then the pounding started. Cassie and Gabriel took up positions on either side of the door, sword and pikestaff ready.

Cassie said, "Jake, what are you doing? We could use a little help over here."

Jake eyed a book with dark brown leather binding. The Latin title, *Ibi Reconditum*, was spelled out in gilded letters on the spine. He repeated the title out loud, trying to remember enough of his high school Latin to translate it.

"Ibi Reconditum, Ibi Reconditum, Ibi Reconditum."

The lock began to give. Cassie and Gabriel braced their backs against the door.

"Jake, what are you saying?" Cassie asked.

"I'm trying to remember my high school Latin so I can translate this title. *Ibi* means *there*, but I don't know what *reconditum means…*"

"Oh, for Christ's sake," Gabriel said. "The translation is *There Is Stored*. Now get over here and lend a hand before we're overrun."

"There is stored, huh," Jake said. "Makes sense." He tilted the book toward him until he heard the click of a latch within the bookcase. He turned to Cassie and Gabriel.

"That was it."

"What was it?" Cassie asked.

"*There is stored* means hidden passage." He pulled the section of bookcase toward him. It swung open, revealing a dark narrow passageway in the space between two walls. "Saw it on Ghost Chasers when they did a special on the castle but I couldn't remember which book it was."

Gabriel said. "Go, both of you. I'll hold them off as long as I can."

Using Jake's battle hammer, Cassie shattered the window and broke off the jagged edges of glass. "They'll think we jumped." She motioned to Gabriel. "C'mon. You can be the hero another day."

Cassie followed Jake into the dark tunnel, turning sideways to fit through the slender opening. Gabriel ran and joined them. Jake grabbed the handle on the back of the bookcase, and pulled it shut as the door to the music room cracked and splintered. Pounding feet and shouted curses filled the room. They stood silent in the blackness, not daring to move. Or even breathe.

FIFTY-ONE

The shuffling of feet in the music room stopped. Cassie eavesdropped with her stolen comms unit.

"It's Dekker," she whispered. "They think we're outside. He's on his way to the sculpture garden."

"Would somebody please kill that guy," Jake said.

Gabriel answered, "Next chance I get." He opened the flashlight app on his phone, casting a gloomy glow. "Where does this lead?"

"It'll take us to a closet in the master suite," Jake said. "When Lord Edwin Kilpatrick lived here, he used the hidden passage to sneak out of the bedroom while his wife slept so he could visit his favorite housemaid. At least, according to the Ghost Chasers. From there, we can take another staircase to the third floor, maybe all the way up to the roof. If they think we're outside, the staircase might be clear."

"And I suppose you have a helicopter waiting," said Gabriel.

"Not exactly. But we do have a limo and driver."

"On the ground," Cassie pointed out, brushing an ancient cobweb off her face. "Why go up to the roof?"

"Because Dekker won't expect that. There's a big trellis covered in ivy on the south side we can use to climb down. It's above a duck pond. Worst case, we pretend we're cliff diving in Acapulco. I'll text McNulty to meet us there."

The passageway ended at a door that opened into an empty closet. They emerged into a large bedroom furnished with a four-poster, canopy bed draped in richly embroidered red silk. Two naked party guests lay on the bed, entwined, eyes closed and moaning. Discarded pieces of their pirate and Southern belle costumes were scattered along a path from the door to the bed.

The woman opened her eyes, shoved her lover to one side and started to scream. Gabriel clamped his hand over her mouth. The man scrambled off the bed, armed only with his erection. He was older, with dark, thinning hair and a flabby midsection. "Who are you? Get out of here."

"It's all right," said Cassie. "We're on a scavenger hunt."

"Where is everybody?" Jake asked Cassie.

She listened to her comms unit. "Outside. They've cleared the sculpture garden and are spreading out on the grounds."

"So far, so good. You folks be sure to get some rest," Jake said to the couple.

He led them down the hall, toward the tower that anchored one corner of the castle. They reached the tower and climbed up a spiral staircase with narrow stone treads wound around a central iron post, passing the third floor until they reached the roof.

They stood for a moment in the cold, clear night air, looking out over the acres of parkland that surrounded the castle. The nearest artificial lights were distant pinpricks in the dark. Jake oriented himself and pointed south. "This way."

Jake trailed Cassie and Gabriel as they ran side-by-side across the battlements encircling the castle. The duck pond was somewhere between them and the next tower.

"I guess you aren't going to work things out with Tresch," Cassie said to Gabriel.

Gabriel shook his head. "He'll just keep coming after me... after us, unless we stop him."

"We?"

Jake caught up to them and interrupted. "McNulty will meet us at the duck pond. I told him to expect an extra passenger but you'll have to pay half the fare."

Cassie smiled, pleased by Jake's peace offering. Then she saw a muzzle flash from the tower, the sound of the rifle coming an instant later as Gabriel fell.

They flattened themselves on the stone floor, hidden in the darkness from the sniper as a flurry of bullets ricocheted off the battlement wall. When the firing stopped, Cassie glanced over her shoulder at

Jake who gave her a thumbs up. She knew the sniper would open fire again as soon as they raised their heads.

For an awful moment, she was back in Bosnia, watching from the helicopter as the man she loved was shot in the back, collapsing in the snow as a pool of blood spread around him. She couldn't watch Gabriel die again. She inched toward him.

"It's my right leg," he said.

Blood was soaking from a wound in the middle of his thigh. She pulled his belt off and cinched it tight around his thigh above the wound, staunching the flow of blood.

"Can you move?"

"I'm not staying here."

He handed her the gun he'd taken from one of the guards. "I've got a few rounds left."

Cassie said to Jake, "How close are we to the duck pond?"

"Best guess, fifty feet, give or take."

"Help Gabriel up and stay behind me, low as you can."

Jake slung Gabriel's right arm around his shoulders and looked at Cassie. "Ready."

"Go!"

The sniper got off two quick rounds before Cassie fired back, driving him to cover. They reached the south wall directly above the duck pond. She was out of bullets. An instant later, the sniper opened fire again, bullets cascading around them.

They climbed over the wall and out of the sniper's field of view, the last of his shots landing harmlessly above them. Clutching the trellis Cassie studied the duck pond. The near edge appeared to be a few feet from the castle wall, though she knew her height three stories above ground skewed her perspective. It was impossible to gauge the depth of the murky green water. They began their descent when another guard opened fire from a third-floor balcony.

Cassie yelled, "Jump!"

They plunged into the icy water. The bottom was deep enough to cushion the impact without breaking their legs. Pushing off, they stayed underwater for as long as they could and made their way to the far side of the pond. Gasping, they pulled themselves out of the water.

"You guys okay," Cassie asked.

"Any landing you can walk away from," Gabriel said.

"Next time, I'll take the elevator," Jake said.

McNulty's limousine broke through the trees beyond the pond, fishtailing and skidding to a stop, headlights blinding them for a moment. They stumbled and ran toward the car as gunfire erupted from the other side of the pond. Cassie and Gabriel fell into a sodden heap in the back seat. Jake took the front passenger seat and slammed the door as a hail of bullets rattled the limo.

He told McNulty, "Kill the lights and get us out of here!"

McNulty gunned the engine, heading back the way they'd first driven onto the castle grounds, letting the moonlight guide him.

"Not that way," said Jake. "They'll trap us on the bridge. There's got to be another way to get back on the main road."

McNulty said, "There may be. I drove past a service road but it dead ends in a pasture."

"Go for it."

Moments after reaching the service road, a black SUV appeared behind them. McNulty stepped on the gas but the SUV drew closer. Someone was leaning out the window and shooting at them. Jake couldn't see who it was through the glare of the headlights but had no doubt it was Dekker.

Bullets pinged off the limo, shattering the rear window as McNulty weaved back and forth. The SUV pulled up along McNulty's side. Dekker raised a short-barreled shot gun. McNulty jerked the steering wheel hard left, crashing into the SUV and forcing Dekker's blast high, the impact knocking the SUV off the road and into a ditch, it's wheels spinning in mud.

A gravel road appeared ahead, forking off into the woods.

"That way," Jake said, then "Shit!"

Dekker's SUV had caught up to them again, bumping the limo from behind. Cassie found an ice bucket tucked under the seat, leaned out the window and threw it at the SUV, cracking the windshield without slowing its pursuit. Dekker opened fire again. Bullets crisscrossed the interior of the limo as McNulty continued weaving side-to-side.

Cassie told Gabriel, "Give me your cloak."

She flung it through the back window. Soaked from the pond, it landed on the SUV's windshield with a heavy splat, blinding the driver. He hit the brakes and careened off the road, flipping the SUV. It landed upside down, smoke belching from beneath the crumpled hood. McNulty hooted and hammered the horn as they left Dekker behind.

FIFTY-TWO

They stayed on the gravel road until it petered out on the edge of a plowed field. There was a farmhouse a quarter of a mile away set on a small hill and surrounded by trees. There were no lights on but the tendrils of smoke wafting from the chimney suggested someone was home.

"Stop the car," Jake said. "I have an idea."

"More of them will be coming," McNulty said.

"I know. I'll be quick."

The cabbie stopped the limo. Jake jumped out, went around to the driver's side and opened the door.

"Come on out. Just for a sec."

Frowning and shaking his head, McNulty got out. "I don't think we have time for..." he began, as Jake slipped into the drivers' seat, closed and locked the door. He rolled the window down a few inches.

"Sorry about this. But you've done more than enough for us. If they catch us, they'll kill you, too."

"You dodgy wanker!" He pulled at the locked door handle.

"Go to that farmhouse and ask for a lift to Maidens. Pick up your car and get back to London. We'll get you your money and more and we'll take care of the limo."

Jake turned the car around and went back the way they'd come.

Gabriel spoke up from the back seat. "That was good of you but you realize you're driving us right back at them."

"And away from McNulty. Got to play one card at a time."

They reached the service road. Jake turned away from the direction of the castle. The woods fell away, wide pastures flanking both sides of the road, the tall grass silvery beneath the moon and stars.

He glanced in the rearview mirror. Cassie had torn off a piece of

Gabriel's shirt and was pressing it against his wound. Gabriel stared at her. She met his gaze. It was a tender and forgiving lover's look. The last thing he wanted to see. He turned his attention to the road and cleared his throat.

"How are you guys doing back there?"

"I'll live," Gabriel said.

"It's a through and through wound," Cassie said. "Missed his femur and femoral artery. All the blood makes it look worse than it is."

"That's good to hear," Jake said.

Cassie looked at his reflection in the rearview mirror, her brow furrowed with concerns he couldn't decipher. Afraid that he was losing her, he kept his poker face and drove on.

A short time later, Jake saw pinpricks of light coming toward him. It was another car, headlights bouncing in the darkness. Checking his side mirror, he saw lights from two more cars closing from behind. He didn't need to see the drivers' licenses and registration to know who they were.

"Trouble," he said.

The distance between the limo and the advancing cars was closing swiftly.

"They're boxing us in," Cassie said.

Jake pressed the accelerator to the floor and turned on the headlight high beams.

"What are you doing?" Gabriel asked.

"Bluffing."

He kept the limo in the center of the road so that no one could pass him and so that the trailing drivers couldn't see how close the approaching vehicle was. The cars behind them sped up, keeping pace. The driver in front of them didn't slow down at first but as Jake closed to within a hundred feet, he slammed on the breaks, spinning clockwise, wheels locked as the car slid sideways toward the limo.

Cassie gripped the back of the front seat. "Jake, what the hell..."

At the last instant before colliding, Jake killed his headlights and angled the limo to the right, clipping the front fender of the oncoming car before going airborne off the road and landing in the pasture. The limo shook and rattled but kept going as Jake eased off the brakes.

Behind them, the first following car slammed into the advancing car, catapulting over it, both vehicles exploding in flames. The second following car, a large Land Rover, swerved and followed the limo.

Jake fought the wheel as the limo rumbled over the uneven terrain until the front end fell into a narrow creek hidden by the tall grass. The rear of the limo jackknifed, then crashed to the ground. The engine died and steam rose from the limo's hood. Stunned, Jake shook his head. Gabriel moaned. Cassie was silent.

A bright light swept over the interior of the limo. Jake blinked, shielding his eyes. The light fell away.

"End of the line, boyo," Dekker said. "Out of the car."

Jake pushed the door open, got to his feet and leaned against the side of the car. One of Dekker's thugs had opened the rear door and was shining a flashlight on Cassie and Gabriel, neither of whom moved or made a sound. Another aimed a semi-automatic rifle at them. When Jake turned to look at the backseat, Dekker whipped him around by his shoulder, shoved him against the car, then grabbed his wrists and bound them with plastic cuffs. Then, Dekker swept Jake's legs from under him, leaving him laid out, face down.

Dekker yanked Gabriel from the car, tossed him belly-first on the grass and handcuffed him after which he stepped on Gabriel's wounded leg, smiling when he grunted in pain.

The first thug reached into the back seat for Cassie. "I think this one's dead."

"Get her out of there," Dekker said, "and cuff her all the same. Dead or alive, I don't trust that bitch."

Cassie lay near Jake, her head facing his. Her eyes were closed, her face was slack and her lips were slightly parted. His heart thumped and rage welled up within him as he promised himself that he would kill Dekker.

He whispered to her. "Cassie. C'mon, Cassie. You can't die...I love you."

She winked at him. "I know."

One of the thugs was nearby. "Oi, the slag ain't dead. I heard them talking."

"About what?" Dekker asked.

"Don't know. Just heard 'em is all."

Dekker grabbed Cassie by the hair and pulled her to her feet. "Playing dead, now are you? Well, you'll be doing it for real soon enough."

Cassie looked him in the eye, lips peeled back. "I'll dance on your grave first."

Dekker stared hard at her, his mouth turned down and grim but she didn't back off. He looked away and shoved her toward his men.

"Get her and the others in the Rover. Now!"

FIFTY-THREE

Gabriel was in the middle row of the Land Rover. His chin hung on his chest and his breathing was labored. Jake and Cassie sat next to each other in the third row of seats in the rear of the car. One of Dekker's men also sat in the middle row, gun in hand, watching them. Jake turned to Cassie, keeping his voice low.

"Were you knocked out or faking it?"

"I saw stars, that's for sure. My head cleared pretty quickly but I decided to play dead until I had a better sense of what was going to happen."

Jake took a deep breath. "About what I said…"

Cassie stared out the window. "Don't worry. You thought I was dead. Doesn't count."

The drive back to the castle took half an hour. They passed a steady stream of cars going the opposite direction filled with costumed guests from the gala. It was an orderly procession, not the panicked escape from a running gun battle Jake would have expected. Nor were there any flashing lights and sirens from police rushing to the scene. Either the gala was so loud and the castle so large and soundproof that the guests didn't hear any gunfire or Tresch convinced them it was a fireworks display gone awry.

Once they were out of the Land Rover, Jake and Cassie, still hand-cuffed, pressed their bodies against Gabriel to keep him upright.

"You're going to be alright," Cassie said, and brushed her lips across his cheek.

He smiled wanly. "Wouldn't have it any other way."

The castle door opened and Lady Tresch was led out by two rugged men gripping her arms. Still in her Marie Antoinette costume, there was a red welt on her cheek. She grimaced as she struggled to break free but the men held firm as they hurried past and shoved her into the backseat of a silver Mercedes parked nearby. Palm pressed against the window, she stared at them mouthing *I'm sorry* as the Mercedes drove away.

Dekker herded them into the castle's entry hall. Lord Tresch was waiting for them. He was wearing dark slacks with a deep blue shirt under a waist cut leather jacket, holding a thin briefcase.

"Cut them loose," Tresch said. "If they misbehave, shoot them."

Dekker clipped their handcuffs. They rubbed their wrists and when Gabriel began to totter, they wrapped their arms around his waist, keeping him upright.

Cassie said. "This man has been shot. We have to take him to the hospital."

"You're in no position to make demands, Ms. Ireland," Tresch said. "Whether he lives or dies is no concern of mine."

"His name is Gabriel Degrande. You hired him to help steal the Magna Cartas from the British Library. You owe him."

"Yes, he was part of the crew, though I've never met him until now. Mr. Degrande, would you be so good as to take a step or two forward. Without the help of your friends. Let's see how badly you're injured."

Gabriel hobbled forward until Tresch raised his palm, telling him to stop. Tresch pulled a handgun from his jacket pocket. Using the barrel to raise Gabriel's chin, Tresch studied his face and frowned.

"As the lower class often does, Mr. Degrande forgot his place when he demanded a share of the ransom." He whipped Gabriel across the face with his gun, opening a cut beneath his eye. Gabriel shuddered, somehow kept his feet and didn't make a sound.

Cassie screamed, "Stop it!"

She started to lunge at Tresch but Dekker threw his arm around her neck from behind and pressed the barrel of his gun under her chin. It was enough to keep both her and Jake where they were.

Tresch ignored Cassie. "That I can forgive because he's a criminal and that's what criminals do. But," he said, his voice rising, his face turning crimson, "I cannot forgive that he brought you and your misfit associate to my doorstep. That is treachery," he said, hitting Gabriel again, now shouting. "And, I cannot abide traitors." Tresch hammered Gabriel's head and neck with the butt of his gun until Gabriel collapsed on the floor.

Tresch nodded at Dekker who released his hold on Cassie. She knelt beside Gabriel, glaring at Tresch.

"If he dies, I'll kill you."

"Perhaps, but if you don't do exactly as I say, you won't get the chance. Though I am pleased to know how much Mr. Degrande means to you."

"At least let me take care of him. There must be a first aid kit around here somewhere."

Tresch sighed. "Ms. Ireland, do not try my patience. I told Dekker to kill the three of you but, thus far, he hasn't been up to the task. Which, is all well and good because I've decided you may be of more use to me alive, at least for now. So, I'll allow you to tend to Mr. Degrande. There's a first aid kit on the plane."

"What plane?"

"The plane that's taking us back to London, of course. We have a busy day tomorrow but you can't go dressed in what's left of your gown." He pointed to jeans, a sweater and ankle-high shoes laying on a side table together with a black leather jacket. "Those belonged to Lady Tresch but she won't be needing them any longer."

"Why? What have you done with her?"

Tresch smiled. "Let's just say that we've reached an unamicable settlement of our divorce. You are about her size. Put those clothes on."

FIFTY-FOUR

They boarded a Gulfstream G650. It was waiting at a nearby airfield. There was a row of three seats against one wall of the cabin that folded into a bed. Jake retrieved the first aid kit while Cassie helped Gabriel lay down. She cut away his pants around the gunshot wound, cleaned and stitched it up, then cleaned and dressed the cuts on his head and face.

"That'll have to do for now," she said to Tresch, "Where's the whiskey?"

Tresch nodded at Dekker who brought Cassie a bottle of single malt Scotch. She raised Gabriel's head and tipped the bottle to his mouth. He took a healthy swallow and then another before smiling and closing his eyes.

Jake and Cassie took seats opposite Tresch and Dekker.

"You have a literary flair," Cassie said. "Naming your crew after the Three Musketeers. You should have come to the gala dressed as d'Artagnan. I'm guessing Shaw is for George Bernard Shaw."

Tresch smiled. "A brilliant dramatist, second only to Shakespeare. I own first editions of all his plays."

"He is prodigiously fluent of speech, restless, excitable, possibly a little mad," Cassie said.

"From *Man and Superman*. You're well read, Ms. Ireland."

"At least you fit the bill," Jake said, "the nuts part I mean, not the Superman stuff."

"Enjoy your little joke while you can, Mr. Carter."

"Got to take what I can get." He pointed at Tresch's briefcase. "Are they in there?"

Tresch opened the briefcase and showed them the Magna Cartas, each sealed in a protective sheath, then closed the case.

"Why?" Cassie asked.

Tresch raised an eyebrow. "For the money, of course."

"And to embarrass Lady Tresch."

"Humiliate, not embarrass. Which is worth almost as much as the money."

"Was that worth killing Malcolm Bridges?"

Tresch waved his hand. "He was greedy and tried to blackmail me. Entirely his fault."

Cassie looked at Dekker. "His handiwork?"

"Let's just say that like any good leader, I wouldn't ask my people to do anything I wasn't also willing to do."

"And the guards that should have been on duty that night at the Library? Did you demonstrate your leadership to them or did Dekker follow your example?"

"Dekker is a model employee. Loyal to a fault and usually quite good at what he does. The three of you being a notable exception."

"Two more men died at that warehouse. Plus your goons at the castle and the ones in the cars that blew up. How many more people have to die to line your pockets and make a fool of your wife?"

"I understand that you get the credit for one of those men. But, I take your point. If you do as I say, no one else need die. So, you see, it's all in your hands."

"What's that supposed to mean," Jake said.

"It means that Ms. Ireland is going to accompany whomever the Library and the Trustees designate to receive the Magna Cartas after they pay the ransom. The exchange will happen in a public place. Dekker will be my representative."

Cassie sat back in her chair and folded her arms across her chest. "And why would I do that?"

"Because if you refuse or if anything goes wrong, if anyone tries to follow Dekker, if the money isn't immediately transferred to the account Dekker tells you, I will cut your friends' throats after what I promise will be very unpleasant preliminaries. There will be no second chances, no excuses. If you do not do exactly as I tell you, they will die. Do you understand?"

Cassie nodded. That was all she could do for now. "I understand."

Tresch pointed a finger at her. "I hope you do for your friends' sake." He paused. "There is one other…small detail that you'll have to take care of for me if you want your friends to live."

"What's that?"

"Are you familiar with the Codex Leicester?"

Jake interrupted. "It's a compilation of Leonardo da Vinci's scientific writings from the late 1600's. Bill Gates bought it a few years ago for thirty million dollars."

Tresch nodded. "Mr. Gates has sent it on an international tour of select museums. It arrived at the British Library yesterday. I should like to add it to my collection." He handed her a cellphone. "When you have the Codex, open the phone and press 1. I'll answer and give you delivery instructions. Your deadline is noon tomorrow."

"Forget it, Tresch," Jake said. "You'll have to check that book out yourself. Cassie doesn't have a library card."

"Ignore him," Cassie said. "I'll do it."

Jake said, "Don't be stupid, Cassie. He's going to kill us anyway."

"Do you think I'm going to kill you and your friends, Ms. Ireland?"

"We both know you'll try, but I'll take my chances."

"You're the poker player, Mr. Carter," Tresch said. "Wouldn't you agree I'm holding all the cards?"

"I'd say you're holding a full house, aces over eights."

"Is that a winning hand?" Tresch asked.

"No. It's a dead man's hand," Jake said.

FIFTY-FIVE

Sarah St. James stared at the clock on her nightstand. 3:46 a.m. Another sleepless night. She'd been anxious enough in the days before the exhibit opened. But her worry paled in comparison to the terror she'd lived with since the Magna Cartas were stolen five days ago.

The thieves' ransom note said they would provide instructions for the exchange sometime today. And that made any thoughts of sleep impossible.

She'd hoped that Cassie and Jake could recover the Magna Cartas before the deadline, but that had proved to be a fantasy. Now they were on the run, suspected of murder, and chasing after Lord Tresch, as if there was any chance he was behind all of this. It was hard to tell what was real and what wasn't.

And even if, by some amazing stroke of good fortune, the thieves did return the Magna Cartas, what damage will have been done to them. Did they know how to properly care for eight-hundred-year-old documents? But that was a secondary concern. The important thing was getting them back. *Please, God*, she prayed silently. *Let us get them back safely.*

"You all right, luv?" Michael's voice in the darkness startled her. She had told him everything when she'd come home on the night of the grand opening. He'd urged her to go to the police, despite the warning in the ransom note, but had ultimately respected her decision and given her unwavering comfort and support ever since.

"I'm petrified."

Michael pulled her close. He didn't offer any platitudes or empty reassurance. He was just there for her, warm and solid. And she loved him for it. She kissed him, gripping the back of his neck, wanting to lose herself in the feeling. Michael responded with equal passion. They made love in the quiet, pre-dawn hours, letting her push aside for the moment thoughts of what the day might bring.

The alarm clock blared an hour and a half later, jolting her back to reality. She had to go to work. She showered and dressed, then checked her phone to make sure she hadn't missed any calls. Maybe she'd have a message from Sir Robert, letting her know that they'd already made the ransom exchange and he had the Magna Cartas in hand. No such luck. She tried to check in with Cassie, but got no answer. As she headed for the door, Michael stopped her.

"Call as soon as you hear anything, yeah?"

"I will."

She kissed him and left the apartment. She parked in the underground car park at the St. Pancras Railway station, then stopped at her favorite tea shop at the station and ordered their special herbal blend.

As she stirred in some honey, a stranger bumped into her as he passed, the man muttering, "Sorry."

Sarah reached into the pocket of her coat for her phone and felt a slip of paper that hadn't been there before. She pulled it out. It read, *Regent's Park rose garden, 11:00. Be prepared to wire $.* These were the instructions for the ransom drop. It was really happening, just over two and a half hours from now. Heart pounding, she looked around the crowded shop for the man, but she hadn't even glimpsed his face.

***

INSPECTOR GERALD MURDOCH was on his way to the British Library, intending to brace Sarah St. James again when his phone rang. It was Inspector Patel.

"Good morning, Inspector," Murdoch said.

"I wish it were."

"No luck finding your suspects?"

"I thought they were our suspects."

"My apologies," Murdoch said. "Our suspects."

"We had a lead but it didn't pan out. A hotel desk clerk in Maidens…"

Murdoch interrupted, "Maidens? In Scotland?"

"Aye. The clerk recognized them and alerted the manager who got busy and forgot to call us until the clerk saw them leaving. Ireland and Carter were dressed in costumes. McNulty drove them off in a borrowed limousine."

"And you thought that was a good lead?"

"Not until we sent the local police to the hotel to check the surveillance video showing them checking in and confirmed it was them."

"But why the costumes?"

"We're told there was a costumed charity gala benefitting the Dawn of Hope Foundation at Culzean Castle. Maidens is the closest village. The Maidens police force had been detailed to provide security at a golf tournament and didn't send anyone to the castle until this morning. They arrived at the same time as the caretaker who was the only one there. He confirmed there had been a gala the night before but knew nothing else."

"Why would they go to the gala? What do we know about the Dawn of Hope Foundation?" Murdoch asked.

"It's a children's charity founded by Sir William Tresch and his wife, Lady Lillian Tresch."

Murdoch thought for a moment. "Lady Tresch is one of the Magna Carta trustees."

"Which is why I called. You asked whether any of my murder victims were connected to the British Library but you didn't say why you were interested. Is the Tresch connection relevant to your case?"

"Perhaps."

"Well, then, do remember where you got this information if it proves useful," Patel said.

"Indeed, I will, Inspector."

Murdoch got out of his car in the St. Pancras Railway Station underground car park when he saw Sarah St. James walking toward an elevator that led to the main hall of the station. Happy at the chance of talking with her away from the Library, he followed her.

He slipped into the tea shop while Sarah was stirring her tea. The shop was too crowded for private conversation. He decided to wait until she left and then invite her to go somewhere quiet to talk.

A burly man pushed his way toward the front of the line, brushing against Sarah, then kept going until he was out the door. Murdoch kept his eyes on Sarah. A moment later, she reached into her coat pocket and drew out a slip of paper. Reading it, her chin fell and the color drained from her face. She stuffed the note back in her pocket and hurried out, leaving her tea behind without noticing Murdoch. He caught up with her outside the shop in the Station's main hall.

"Mrs. St. James," he said.

She whirled around, hand to her throat. "Inspector Murdoch? What are you doing here?" She arched an eyebrow before he could answer. "Are you following me?"

"Why would you think that?"

"Because...because,..." She drew herself up. "Because you've been nosing around all week, popping up every time I turn around."

He shrugged. "I can't help it. It's what a policeman does. May I have a word?"

"Have I done something wrong? Are you here to arrest me?"

"Of course, not. Though I must say you look quite vexed. Is everything alright?"

Sarah swallowed. "Everything is fine. It's just that I have a very busy day and no time for idle conversation. If you'll excuse me."

"What was in the note that man passed you? Is that what's upset you so?"

Sarah stared at him goggle-eyed, then marched off without a word.

FIFTY-SIX

O h, thank God you're here," Sarah said when Cassie walked into her office. "I've been trying to reach you. I've been out of my mind with worry. Is everything alright?"

The words tumbled out of Sarah's mouth in a torrent. She was sitting behind her desk, tapping a pen with one hand and drumming her nails with another. She jumped out of her chair and threw her arms around Cassie in a bear hug.

Cassie peeled her away and held her hands. "Sorry about that. Everything's fine."

Sarah took a step back. "Well, you don't look fine. You're always so put together but you look like you were thrown together. When was the last time you slept?"

"There will be plenty of time to sleep when this is over. Bring me up to date."

"I was at the tea shop in Pancras Station this morning when a man bumped into me and stuck this note in my coat pocket saying to be at Regents Park at 11:00."

She handed the note to Cassie.

"How far is Regents Park?"

Sarah said, "About a mile. I'd barely gotten out of the shop before Inspector Murdoch popped up. He'd seen what happened with the man and the note and wanted to know what it said. Of course, I didn't tell him but between the man, the note and Murdoch, I've been coming undone."

"I doubt Murdoch just happened to be there. Either he was on his way to the Library or he's been following you."

"I don't care which it is. I just want this to all be over. Sir Robert will wire the money once I call him and verify that the Magna Cartas are authentic." She gave a short, unhappy laugh. "That would be ironic, wouldn't it? If the thieves tried to sell us their own set of forgeries? We could put them on display right next to mine."

"It's going to be alright. I promise. I'll come with you."

"Would you? I'd feel so much better. We'll walk. Finding a parking place on the street is impossible."

While Sarah gathered her things, Cassie scooped up the keycard Sarah had left lying on her desk. She'd need it to navigate the Library after hours, even though every swipe of the card would leave an electronic trail leading back to Sarah. At best, Sarah would be accused of negligence. At worst, she'd be charged with conspiracy. One more mess Cassie would have to clean up if she survived the next twenty-four hours.

"Give me your phone," Cassie said when they reached the street.

Sarah handed it to her. "Who are you calling?"

"A friend. Keep walking. I'll catch up in a minute."

Cassie waited until Sarah was half a block in front of her before calling Gunnar.

"It's Cassie."

"You've really stepped into this time. Wanted for double-homicide. I've got strict orders from Prometheus to bring you in if you call. He knows you and Jake are wanted by the police and it's the Jake part that he's really angry about."

"He'll get over it and if he doesn't, that's fine by me but I'm not coming in until this is over. I need you to do something for me."

"Ha. You never were much for following orders. What is it?" Gunnar listened as Cassie explained. "I can do my piece but how are you going to do yours?" he asked her.

"I'll figure it out. Just be ready. It's going to be close," she said and ended the call.

It was a cold, gloomy day and there weren't many visitors in the park. As they walked across the York Bridge, Cassie swept the landscape for anyone following them while evaluating the threat potential of each person she saw. Though no one stood out, she knew better than to let her guard down.

They reached Queen Mary's Rose Garden at 10:55. The February weather had reduced it to a sad-looking collection of bloomless shrubs arranged in a circle with pathways radiating out like the spokes of a wheel.

Cassie chose a wrought iron bench in the middle of the circle. From there, she had a clear view over the tops of the rosebushes for thirty feet in every direction. Within that perimeter, there was nowhere for someone larger than a toddler to hide.

There was more cover in the trees outside the perimeter where she caught a glimpse of someone in the shadows. She could make out a man in a long coat wearing a hat but that was all. He retreated deeper into the trees until Cassie lost sight of him. One of Tresch's men, she thought, backup for Dekker if anything went wrong. There was nothing to do but sit and wait.

"What do we do if they won't give the Magna Cartas back?" asked Sarah. "I mean, even after we pay the ransom?"

Cassie said, "I don't think that will happen. This is a business deal. Keeping them puts the thieves at greater risk. The Trustees and the Library would have to go to the police. There'd be nowhere for the them to hide and no one willing to buy the Magna Cartas. This way, they get their money, the Magna Cartas go back in the display cases and no one, except for us, are the wiser. It's as close as they can get to a perfect crime."

"Let's hope they are as rational as you are."

At 11:00 a.m., Max Dekker sauntered down the garden path as if on a leisurely morning stroll. He was carrying Tresch's slender briefcase.

"Oh, God, this is it." Sarah clutched Cassie's arm.

"Just do what he says and you'll be fine."

The women stood as Dekker approached. He stopped a couple of feet away and looked around, then nodded and raised the briefcase.

"Go ahead and wire the money."

Cassie said to Sarah, "Stay here." Then motioned Dekker to follow her. She stopped when they were out of Sarah's hearing. "Call Tresch. I want to make sure Jake and Gabriel are okay."

Dekker shook his head. "Not part of the deal, Missy and, in case you forgot, you're not calling the shots."

Cassie crossed her arms over her chest. "Fine. Deal's off. Go home."

Dekker's jaw dropped. "Oi, you can't do that."

"I just did. Go home and tell Tresch you screwed up the exchange and cost him a hundred million pounds. You'll be the first one he kills."

"You're bluffing. You wouldn't let him kill your lover boys."

"We both know they're already dead. The only question now is whether you live or die."

Dekker hesitated, grinding his teeth, then called Tresch. "She wants to make sure the blokes are still breathing." He listened for a moment, wincing, then handed the phone to Cassie.

"Who's this?" Cassie said.

"It's Jake."

"Are you okay?"

"Never better. You can't beat these all-inclusive vacation packages."

"And Gabriel?"

"Still with us."

"Take care of each other and I'll see you tomorrow," Cassie said.

Cassie gave Dekker the phone and they walked back to Sarah. She faced Dekker, the top of her head inches beneath his chin.

Sarah said, "Let me see the Magna Cartas. Please."

"You have the money?" he asked.

"It's ready to transfer to your account." She pulled her cellphone from her coat pocket and held it up. "As soon as I give the word."

"Right." Dekker opened the briefcase and spread the Magna Cartas, each in a plastic sheath, across the iron bench.

Sarah gasped. "You haven't been keeping them in this flimsy plastic, have you? Do you have any idea of the irreparable damage you might have caused?"

She took a jeweler's loupe from her bag and knelt beside the bench, carefully examining each document. After several minutes, she stood, brushing damp earth from her knees. "I would need to run tests in the Conservation Centre to be absolutely certain…"

"Yes or no?" Dekker said.

"Yes," she told him. "They're authentic. Give me the wire instructions and I'll call Sir Robert."

Dekker recited the instructions with the stilted cadence of a schoolboy who'd memorized his lesson. Sarah made the call. Dekker watched the screen on his phone, a satisfied smirk creasing his face as one hundred million pounds appeared in the designated account.

"That was easy enough," Dekker said.

"We'll take the briefcase too," Cassie said. Dekker didn't answer. "We don't want anyone to see us walking through the park carrying the Magna Cartas under our arms like the morning paper. Something could go wrong.

Dekker's eyes shifted from the bench to the briefcase in his hand, then he handed the case to her. "All yours," he said and walked away.

FIFTY-SEVEN

Sarah let out a deep breath. "I'm so glad he's gone. That man blocks out the sun even on a cloudy day."

She returned the Magna Cartas to the briefcase.

"Mind if I carry it," Cassie said. "Just to be on the safe side."

"Thank you. That would be lovely. My hands are shaking enough as it is." She gave Cassie the case, then locked arms with her. "By God, we did it, didn't we? It's over. It's finally over. I'll put them back on display tonight after we close and then you and I are going out for a drink. My treat."

"I'd like that," Cassie said.

She looked around the garden a last time, searching for the man in the trees but there was no sign of him. She kept a close watch around them as they started back.

They were on Eversholt St. when she glanced over her shoulder and saw the man that had been hiding in the trees following them. He was on the other side of the road, a block behind. Same long coat. Same hat, now pulled down over his brow so she couldn't see his face. A trio of trucks and buses passed them, cutting off the man's view. She tugged on Sarah's arm and hustled her onto a side street, using the distraction to lift Sarah's phone from her coat pocket.

"What are you doing? That's not the right way," Sarah said.

"It is now. We're being followed."

Sarah swiveled her head around. "By whom? Where is he?"

"Doesn't matter. Don't look back. Pick up the pace."

They zig-zagged from one side-street to another, cutting across parking lots until they were standing at the mouth of an alley that opened onto Ossulston Street across from the Library. Cassie scanned the plaza in front of the entrance but didn't see the man.

"Okay, let's go. Be quick but don't hurry."

When they were through the entrance, Cassie looked back across the plaza. The man was coming toward them at a brisk clip, head up, hat pushed back. She wasn't surprised. He must have known where they were going and didn't care what route they took. She lingered a moment longer to see his face.

"It's Murdoch. I don't have time for him," Cassie said, handing Sarah the briefcase. "Go to your office."

"Where are you going?"

"Better you don't know so you don't have to lie when Murdoch knocks on your door."

"What shall I tell him?"

"Anything you want as long as it isn't about me or the Magna Cartas."

Cassie caught an elevator going down and Sarah caught one going up, doors closing as Murdoch marched into the Library.

***

SARAH WAS STUDYING her computer screen, her back to her open door when Murdoch arrived.

"Where is she?" Murdoch said, without knocking.

Sarah swiveled her chair around. "Good day to you, too, Inspector. Are you going to keep popping up out of nowhere the entire day? I shall have my assistant put you on my schedule."

"You can save your innocent act for another time. Where is Cassie Ireland?"

"I don't know."

"How can you not know? The two of you walked to the Rose Garden in Regents Park and met with a man who gave you that briefcase," Murdoch said, pointing to the one standing next to Sarah's desk, "and then you came back here not five minutes ago."

Sarah stood, hands on her hips. "You've no right to harass me. Who I take a walk with is none of your concern."

Murdoch paused, then said, "Have you ever seen a dead body?"

Sarah did a double-take. "What a terrible thing to say."

Murdoch opened his phone. "It's even worse to see," he said and showed her a photograph of a dead man lying in a pool of blood. Sarah gasped and covered her mouth with her hand. "His name is Roger Higgins. He was shot to death a couple of days ago in a warehouse in the Limehouse District." Murdoch scrolled to another bloody photograph. "And, this is Lionel Kent. He was also murdered at the warehouse."

Sarah turned away. "Why are you showing me those awful photos?"

"Because we suspect Cassie Ireland and Jake Carter murdered these men."

Sarah stiffened her jaw. "They did not."

"How can you be so certain? Did Cassie tell you that?"

Sarah hesitated, stammering, struggling with how much to tell Murdoch. "Yes. I spoke to her by phone the other night, after you barged into the Trustees meeting."

"And you believed her?"

"Of course, what reason would I have not to?"

"We have video putting her and Jake Carter inside the warehouse at the time of the murders. Did you tell her that the police were looking for her?"

Sarah sucked in a breath and twisted her fingers into a knot. "Yes. I…thought she should know."

"And if she was innocent, wouldn't you have expected her to go to the police to clear her name?"

"I…I suppose…I don't know about such things."

"Did she tell you that Jake Carter works for Global Security?"

"Yes."

"Because he doesn't. I checked. They've never heard of him. The man is a gambler. He plays cards for a living. Cassie lied to you. What other lies has she told you?" Sarah didn't answer. "Where is she?"

"I told you. I don't know. I left her downstairs. She didn't tell me where she was going."

Murdoch sucked in a breath, studying Sarah. "I'd like to see what's inside that briefcase. You can force me to get a magistrate's search warrant but then I would wonder what you are hiding and why."

"Fine. If that will cause you to leave me alone." She laid the brief-case flat on her desk, turning the front of it toward Murdoch. "Help yourself."

Murdoch opened it and rifled through Sarah's files on an upcoming exhibit of Gutenberg bibles.

"Mrs. St. James, you have a responsible position, one of trust, and a promising career. Be certain of whose side you are on before you throw all of that away."

"I know whose side I'm on, Inspector."

Murdoch buttoned his coat. "That's what troubles me because there's one other thing I know about you."

"What's that?"

"You're a terrible liar," Murdoch said.

FIFTY-EIGHT

After Tresch and Cassie left Tresch's plane, Dekker cuffed Jake and Gabriel to their seats. Twice, he gave them something to eat and let them use the bathroom one at a time. In the early hours of Friday morning, he marched them off the plane and into a panel van, hands cuffed behind their backs and black woolen bags over their heads. After an hour-long drive, he let them out, looped a rope around their waists and tugged them along like reluctant cattle into a creaky elevator that descended in jerky fits and starts before stopping with a thud.

From there, Dekker put them into a windowless, dank room made of concrete. He untied them and removed their hoods but not their handcuffs and left, locking the steel-plated door behind him.

A lone fluorescent tube bracketed onto the ceiling flickered, casting pale light across the floor. Jake blinked, until his eyes adjusted to the near darkness, then paced off the dimensions - ten steps from the door to the far wall and eight steps side to side. Scraps of wire and bits of chipped concrete had collected in the corners. Before Jake could take a closer look, the ceiling light turned off. A faint glow from the adjoining room leaked in through gaps in the seal around the edges of the door.

"Fuck you, Dekker," he said.

Jake was drained, the adrenaline rush from their near escape long past, but he couldn't sleep. It would be daylight in a few hours, though he wouldn't know it. Across the room, Gabriel sat on the floor, back to the wall, head leaning on his shoulder. His wound had continued to leak during the flight, convincing Jake that it wasn't as minor an injury as Cassie had suggested. He asked Gabriel how he was feeling.

Gabriel said he was doing fine but the irritation in his voice told Jake he was lying and not to ask again.

"Where do you think we are?" Jake said.

Gabriel raised his head and struggled to clear his throat. "When Dekker put us on that lift, I counted the seconds until we hit bottom. Based on that, I'd say we're twenty or thirty feet below street level. It had a musty smell and it rode like a bucket dropped into a well. It reminded me of one I rode going down into a mine. Wherever we are, it's someplace that hasn't been used in a long time. No one is going to wander by and offer us a ride home."

"Probably an abandoned tube station like the one you guys used."

"I don't think so. Trains run close to most of those discarded lines. We'd be able to hear them or we'd at least feel the vibrations. There must have been a business on the surface that needed underground storage. It could even have been used as an air raid shelter during World War II."

Jake said, "We have to be close to where Cassie is supposed to bring the Codex to Tresch."

"Why do you think so?"

"Because Cassie will demand to see us before she hands over the Codex to make sure we're still alive."

"She is a formidable woman."

Jake knew this wasn't the best time to try to sort out Gabriel's relationship with Cassie but also knew he might not get another chance.

"She's still in love with you."

Gabriel shook his head. "That's where you're wrong. It's you she loves."

That was the last thing Jake expected Gabriel to say. He wanted to believe him but Cassie hadn't given him any reason he should.

"I don't think so. Not since she found out you were alive."

"Too much time has passed for us and she knows that I'm not the man I was. I've seen how she looks at you when you're not aware. She used to look at me the same way, but no more."

"It won't matter which one of us is right unless we can get out of here. You're the master thief. You must have broken into places more secure than this. Can't you get us out of here?"

Gabriel chuckled. "I may be weak and wounded but I haven't forgotten how to do my job." He leaned over onto his side and began to squirm.

"What are you doing?"

Jaw clenched against the pain in his leg, Gabriel pulled his hands from behind him and under his feet and up to his chest, then, breathing hard, he sat upright, feet stretched out in front of him.

"Okay, your turn."

Jake dropped to the floor and repeated Gabriel's maneuver, then jumped to his feet. "Now how do we get out of these plastic cuffs?"

"Position the locks above your thumbs and center them between your hands, then use your teeth to tighten the cuffs as much as you can."

"Tighten them? I thought you were going to tell me how to get them off," Jake said.

"Just do it."

Jake wiggled his wrists, maneuvering the locks. Then he bit each strap and yanked as hard as he could. The cuffs pinched his wrists but didn't release. "Well that worked great."

Gabriel said, "I should have killed you when I had the chance."

"Hey, don't blame me, Houdini. Your trick didn't work but at least now I can scratch my nose instead of my ass."

"Good for you. Now pay attention. Raise your hands as high above your head as you can, then flare your elbows out and squeeze your shoulder blades together."

Jake followed his instructions. "Okay. And, for my next trick… what?"

"This is the important part. Slam your hands into your stomach, belt high."

"You want me to punch myself in the belly? Why? Because you can't?"

"Stop arguing and just do it if you want to get out of here. As hard and as quick as you can."

Jake shook his head. "Okay." He sucked in a deep breath and

slugged himself. "Ooof!" Bent over, he grunted as air rushed out from his lungs. "Oh, shit. I can't believe I let you talk me into doing that. I'll bet you're enjoying this."

"Immensely. Now do it again," Gabriel said. "Harder and quicker."

Jake straightened, raised his hands over his head and gut-punched himself again. This time, the impact drove his wrists outward, snapping the locks on the cuffs. Laughing, Jake held his hands up.

"Un-fucking believable. That really worked. You're next."

Gabriel shook his head. "I'm too weak. I won't be of much use, but you...you, my friend, are both annoying and resourceful."

"Thanks. I guess that means you're not going to kill me."

"Ah, I would have very much liked to keep that promise, but, to my regret, conditions have changed and we have to adapt if we are to survive. Now let's have a look at that door. Help me up."

FIFTY-NINE

assie saw Murdoch for an instant before the elevator door closed as he studied the Library lobby looking for her and Sarah. She knew he wouldn't find either of them and expected him to head straight to Sarah's office. When he realized that Sarah wouldn't or couldn't tell him where to find her, he'd consider her next move. Would she risk being spotted on the street by a cop or a camera or would she hide somewhere in the Library until she could slip out under cover of darkness. Either way, he'd be waiting for her. There was a third option, one Cassie counted on him to ignore – that she'd do neither.

She had twenty-four hours to steal the Codex Leicester and deliver it to Tresch. Having recovered her share of fine art and rare books, she knew that the Codex would have been shipped in a case like the one Tresch had used for the Magna Cartas. The case would have been shipped to the Library in a custom-designed wooden crate. The crate wouldn't be locked because it would have been shipped in specially designed containers transported by secure vehicles.

If the Codex was still in the crate, it would be easy to steal. All she would need is a pry bar. If it had been unpacked and placed inside a vault, it could just as well be on Mars. Wherever it was, she would have to pull the job off under the watchful eyes of the Library's cameras and under the noses of the guards roaming the grounds.

The Library's computer network would tell her where to find the Codex. She'd have to figure out the rest on the fly. She assumed that the guards had been told to watch for her. If she stayed off the public floors, there was a decent chance that she wouldn't run into any of them.

Using Sarah's keycard, Cassie took the elevator to Basement Level

One where the Facilities and Maintenance departments were located. She kept her head down and away from the surveillance cameras, making it harder for the guards monitoring the video feeds to recognize her.

She passed a cafeteria filled with people having lunch which meant there were empty offices nearby. Turning down another corridor, she slipped into a vacant office and closed and locked the door. The nameplate on the desk said the office belonged to Philip Wiley, Facilities Manager. There was a photograph of a smiling couple on the wall. She had passed the man in the hall before he went into the cafeteria. It was Wiley and the woman was probably his wife. She hoped he took a long lunch.

She logged on to Wiley's computer using the credentials Ian Thorpe had given her. A Google search told her that the Codex was composed of eighteen sheets of paper, about twelve by seventeen inches each, with writing and illustrations on both sides. When Leonardo da Vinci wrote the manuscript in the 16th century, the pages were folded in half and bound to create a 72-page book. More than four hundred years later, the volume had been unbound, returning it to its original eighteen pages. Photographs of Bill Gates' display of the Codex after he bought it for thirty million dollars depicted each page mounted between panes of clear glass. When transported, the pages were sealed in protective covers like those used with the Magna Cartas. Easy enough for Cassie to conceal.

Next, she searched the Acquisitions department's records. The Codex Leicester had arrived the day before at the loading bay at the north end of the Library before being moved to the Centre for Conservation where rare masterpieces were preserved and safeguarded when not on display. The tracking number the Library had assigned to the Codex began with the numerical month, day and year followed by the letters HB and five digits, 87143. She memorized the number.

The Centre was in a separate building connected at ground level to the main Library by a wide public terrace. A quick check of the design schematics revealed a corridor on Basement Level Two running from the loading bay to the Centre.

The schematics didn't include any information regarding security.

Sarah's keycard might open any locked doors but it wouldn't blind cameras, disable motion sensors or open vaults. She searched the Library's network for more information, getting excited when she found a folder labeled *Security* only to discover that it was password protected. She needed to do more digging but was afraid that Wiley would start knocking on his locked door any minute. She logged off his computer and left.

Going back the way she came, Cassie stopped at a door marked *Women's Changing Room*. Ducking inside, she rifled through several lockers until she found a security guard uniform and stuffed it into a canvas tote bag someone had left on the floor. Two doors down, there was a closet with maintenance supplies where she found coveralls and knee-high rubber boots. She added them to her bag and walked to the elevator with the purposeful stride that said she belonged, ignoring the puzzled looks of the few people she passed.

Cassie took the elevator to Basement Level Five, then headed straight to the utility closet where Jake had discovered the thieves' shaft into the sewer. There was an assortment of tools on the closet shelves. She chose a pry bar, several screwdrivers, a flat rasp contoured to a blade-like point, a wrench, a pair of pliers, and a wire cutter. She pulled the coveralls and boots out of the bag and replaced them with her jeans, shirt, jacket, shoes and the tools.

After donning the coveralls and boots, she opened the shaft, slung the bag over her shoulder and clamped a flashlight between her teeth as she began climbing down the rungs bolted to the shaft wall. After a few steps, she reached up and pulled the trapdoor over the opening. She could hear rats scurrying below, waiting to welcome her back to the sewer. An hour later, she surfaced at the abandoned York station and did the only thing she could do. Wait.

And worry about Jake. And Gabriel. But, if she was being honest, more about Jake than Gabriel. Whatever they'd once had was gone.

Her thoughts turned to Prometheus. Sitting alone in the empty, cavernous station, she realized that she could never forgive him. That part was easy. The hard part was deciding what to do about it.

Soon, she'd return to the Library to commit a crime that could send her to prison for years. It was a risk she was willing to take. She had promises to keep and scores to settle.

SIXTY

Cassie climbed out of the sewer shaft and into the utility closet at 11:45 p.m. She'd timed her return to coincide with the midnight shift change for the guards knowing that people would be tired and distracted whether they were coming or going and less likely to notice an unfamiliar face. Her plan was to get to the lower level entrance to the Centre for Conservation before the new crew was in place and had begun making their rounds.

She changed into the guard's uniform, leaving the coveralls and boots on a shelf. Its owner was heavier and shorter than her. The hem of the pants hit just above her ankles. She cinched the belt as tight as it would go to keep the pants around her waist. The blouse ballooned around her middle. She slid the strap for the canvas bag over her shoulder, feeling the weight of the tools against her side. The jacket hung loose, tent-like, across her frame, hiding the bag.

The poor fit was fine with Cassie. Whoever was monitoring the feeds from the video cameras would see a guard and that's all that mattered. She made it to the Centre without incident, acknowledging the only guard she passed with a quick nod.

There were two doors at the entrance to the Centre. One was tall and wide enough to accommodate a fork lift truck making a delivery from the loading bay. The other was for foot traffic. Cassie held her breath when she swiped Sarah's keycard across the lock on the smaller door. The indicator light flashed green. She turned the handle. No alarms sounded when she entered. The lights were off and, best she could tell, no one else was there.

Cameras were mounted opposite the doors watching who came and went but there were no cameras aimed down the dozen rows of shelves, each twelve feet high and fifty feet long, that filled the room. They were lined with unopened crates, sealed containers and other protective cases. Cassie walked out of camera range and into the nearest aisle, breathing easier knowing that she was now invisible and began searching for the Codex.

"Please be in a wooden crate," she said.

After walking down several aisles and shining her flashlight on different tracking numbers, she got the hang of the inventory system. Thirty minutes later, she found the crate containing the Codex Leicester. The Gods were smiling on her, she thought. Her plan, however hastily conceived, had gone off without a hitch. This was the hard part and it was done.

To that moment, she'd remained calm but when she took the crate off the shelf and laid it on the floor, her heart began to race. It was the same thrill she felt every time she laid hands on whatever she was after. The sensation was so visceral, so unlike any other high she'd ever known, that she knew she couldn't give it up. Where that left her with Promethcus and with Jake were questions she'd answer another day.

The case was held together by long screws too deeply anchored to yield to a screwdriver. The wood screeched as she levered the pry bar into the joints and forced the screws to surrender. Every few minutes, she stopped and listened for footsteps, continuing after confirming she was still alone. With a final thrust of the pry bar, the top of the crate came loose. She set it aside. A rectangular case lay in the center surrounded by dark gray foam. There was a latch on one side. She released it and opened the case. The eighteen pages of the Codex were stacked one on top of another, each sealed in a rigid acrylic pouch.

She set the case on the floor and wedged the wooden crate between two other crates to keep it from falling open and scattered the tools across several aisles. Except for the rasp which she slid inside her belt on her left side like a short sword, tightening the belt as much as she could to keep it in place. She walked out of the Centre. The door hadn't closed behind her when she stopped in her tracks.

"Put the case down and raise your hands," Ian Thorpe said, aiming a gun at her.

He was flanked by two beefy guards, arms loose at their sides.

They locked eyes with her, giving her tight-lipped grins that said they were going to enjoy this. The scar tissue around their eyes and their flattened noses told Cassie they'd taken and thrown their share of punches. They were more brawlers than boxers, dangerous all the same.

Cassie shook her head. The Gods were laughing, not smiling at her.

"Isn't it past your bedtime, Ian?" Cassie said, keeping a firm grip on the case.

"The case," Thorpe said, "Put it down."

She ignored his instruction. "Where'd you find this pair? On the street with their hands out and their zippers down?"

One of the men started toward her but Thorpe raised his hand, holding him back.

"You're not half as clever as you think. I never bought that rubbish about a security audit. I figured all along it was a cover for a heist and I was right. You're just a common thief. And, a murderer according to the police."

"Top marks on that one, Ian. My bad luck you decided to work late."

"Luck had nothing to do with it. I've been waiting for you to make your move ever since I gave you those login credentials. Set them up to give me an alert whenever you got online so I could see what it was you were looking at. When you used Wiley's computer to find where we were keeping the Codex, all I had to do was wait for you to come after it. I already called Inspector Murdoch and told him to come pick up his dangerous fugitive. He'll be here any minute. We'll be front page news, you and I." He tipped his head toward one of the guards. "Now, put down that case before I let Derrick take it from you. He's not known for being gentle."

Cassie knew Thorpe was right. She'd relied on luck instead of the careful preparation a job like this required. She could blame that on Tresch for not giving her enough time but underestimating Thorpe was a bigger mistake.

"I'm not going to give you this case, Ian. I've worked too hard for it. If Derrick thinks he can take it from me, he can try."

"You're forgetting about this," he said, waving the gun.

"I don't think you want to explain to Inspector Murdoch why you killed an unarmed woman, especially when you had two strong men who could easily handle a girl like me."

"All right, lads," Thorpe said. "She's all yours."

The men advanced toward her. She did the one thing they didn't expect. Attack. She spun around, wielding the case like a shield, slamming it into Derrick's solar plexus and leaving him doubled over and gasping.

The second man grabbed her from behind, wrapped his arms around her, lifted her off the ground and squeezed the breath out of her. She dropped the case, drew the rasp from her belt and stabbed him in the arm. He howled and let her loose. She turned and kicked him in the side of the head, knocking him flat, then pressed the point of the rasp against his jugular vein. Thorpe took a step toward her, then stopped, his eyes wide, his mouth open.

"Not the same as sitting behind your desk, is it, Ian? Drop the gun or he dies."

"I'll shoot."

"Ever kill anyone, Ian?"

Thorpe said, "Always has to be a first time."

"You can't stop your gun hand from shaking. That's because of all the adrenaline. Means you'll probably miss. Even if you don't, I'll still kill him. And you don't see my hand shaking. Now put the gun down."

Thorpe hesitated, not taking his eyes off Cassie, then slowly lowered the gun to the floor.

"Now kick it over to me and lay face down."

With Thorpe on the ground, Cassie scooped up his gun, slid the rasp back alongside her leg, picked up the case and ran.

"Get her," Thorpe screamed.

Cassie looked over her shoulder. The guards were running toward her. She fired a shot in their direction, making sure it went high and wide. The two men dove for cover and stayed where they were.

She heard sirens wailing, drawing closer, as she turned a corner and banged through a door leading to an internal stairway. There were heavy footsteps overhead. She leaned over the rail, looking up to see who was coming. Murdoch stared back at her, both frozen for a moment.

Cassie took off again, Murdoch racing after her. She reached the utility closet on Basement Level Five ahead of him.

"It's over, Cassie," Murdoch called out. "You're boxed in. You've no way out. It's time to give up."

Cassie knew he was close by but couldn't see him and hoped that meant he couldn't see her. She stepped into the closet and closed the door. After stuffing the coveralls and boots in the canvas bag, she pulled the trapdoor away from the shaft and, holding the case under one arm, lowered herself several rungs down the ladder, then pulled the lid over the shaft.

"It's not over until I say it's over," she said, not caring that Murdoch couldn't hear her.

SIXTY-ONE

U p you go," Jake said.

Knees bent, Jake ducked under Gabriel's arm, supporting him as he helped Gabriel to his feet.

"Let's give this a try," Gabriel said, taking a tentative step with his wounded leg. "Fils de pute!"

"What did you say?" Jake asked.

"That's French for motherfucker. My leg hurts like a fucking motherfucker."

"Oh, it sounded like something you'd order for dinner."

Gabriel stared at him, openmouthed, and shook his head. "Honestly, I don't know what Cassie sees in you."

"Lucky for me, you don't have to. Come on."

They hobbled to the door. The keyhole for the lock was chest high. Gabriel ran his finger across the surface and stuck his pinkie into the opening.

"It's a skeleton key lock. Pretty typical for a building this old. Uses a lever to open and close the bolt. Find me a coat hanger and I'll get us out of here."

"Don't go away," Jake said.

Crawling along the walls in the dark, Jake searched the floor with his hands for the scraps of wire he'd seen before Dekker turned out the lights. He returned to the door with a handful of varying lengths and handed the pieces to Gabriel.

"Best I could do."

Gabriel studied the wires, selecting four that were six to eight inches long and letting the others fall to the floor. "I like these. They're made of baling wire. Soft enough to bend and rigid enough to do the job."

He twisted two lengths together, making a stronger, single piece, then did the same with the other two. He bent the ends of each new piece into an L shape and inserted the short end of the first piece into the keyhole until it snagged the lever. He gave it a slight tug to lift the lever, then inserted the second piece, again by the short end, until it grabbed the bolt. He pulled on the bolt and it gave way, slipping out of the strike plate and unlocking the door.

"Voila," Gabriel said. He lifted the handle and pulled the door back a few inches. A shaft of light brightened their cell. Jake peered thru the opening. "What do you see?"

"No sign of Dekker or Tresch. We're at the end of a hallway, maybe twenty-five feet long, then it goes left."

The hallway, like their cell, was concrete, the walls rough and pock-marked. Single-bulb ceiling lights were spaced ten-feet apart. The air was damp and stale.

Jake took his time getting to the end of the hall, then stopped and listened. He looked back at Gabriel and shook his head, then peeked around the corner. The next corridor ran twice the distance as the first and was empty. There were no doors on either side but there was one at the end of the hall. Jake trotted to the door. It was a solid slab of thick-hewn wood and it was locked. He pressed his ear against the door but couldn't hear anything on the other side. He ran back to their cell.

"There's a door at the end of the next hallway. It's got one of those skeleton locks."

Gabriel threw his arm across Jake's shoulder. Jake wrapped his arm around his waist and they left their cell doing a three-legged walk. When they reached the second door, Gabriel was breathing hard. Dark blood was seeping through his bandage and his face was pale. Jake studied his leg, then looked at Gabriel who shrugged.

Jake patted him on the arm. "You've got this."

Gabriel gave him a weak smile. "Part de gateau. Or as you Americans say, piece of cake."

He picked the lock and Jake pulled back the door. It opened into a dimly lit, brick-walled, domed tunnel. Scraps of paper, empty food cartons, discarded beverage cans and other trash were scattered across the floor.

Jake said, "Looks like an Airbnb for the homeless." Behind them, the tunnel was dark. Ahead of them, they could see a faint glow. "That way."

The tunnel led them into a massive underground expanse of vaulted chambers, all made of brick. Powerful lights hanging from the nearest arches flooded the surrounding area while obscuring whatever lay in the darkness behind them.

Gabriel said. "I know this place. It's a catacombs."

"Where are the dead bodies?"

"It's not that kind of catacombs. It was for stabling horses used to build the underground railway back in the 19th century."

"And you know this because?" Jake asked.

"Because this is where we rehearsed stealing the Magna Cartas. Over there, past that next arch there should be a mockup of the display cases we built."

Jake crossed the chamber. A replica of the display case stood in the shadows just beyond the reach of the lights. He turned toward Gabriel, giving him a thumbs-up until he saw Dekker with his arm locked around Gabriel's throat and a gun pressed against his temple.

"Out for a stroll, are you, lads?"

SIXTY-TWO

Cassie left the York Road station dressed in the clothes Tresch had given her. Carrying the Codex case, she stuck to the sidewalk along York Way, opened the burner phone and pressed 1. Tresch answered.

"Do you have it?"

"Yes."

"Take the Regents Canal towpath to the Camden Lock Market. Dekker will meet you there in thirty minutes. Don't try anything heroic or your friends will die."

Tresch ended the call. Taking the towpath meant she had to walk. Cassie studied the burner phone. It had to have built-in GPS. That was the only way Tresch could have known how long it would take her to get to the market on foot. He'd been tracking her ever since she left his plane.

Afraid that Tresch could also monitor her calls on the burner phone, Cassie opened the phone she'd stolen from Sarah and called Gunnar.

"Are you ready?" she asked.

"If you have what I need."

"I do," she said and gave it to him.

"How much time do I have?" Gunnar asked.

"Half an hour."

"That may not be enough."

"It has to be," she said and hung up.

Cassie pulled Ian Thorpe's gun from her jacket pocket. It was a Glock 17. The magazine was full - seventeen rounds. She put one in the chamber and tucked the gun behind her waist.

Her options were limited. Tresch would know if she ditched the burner phone, took another route or raced to get there early so she could set up an ambush. As much as she hated playing by his rules, she checked the route on Google Maps and started walking.

The winding towpath ran alongside the canal. The slowly moving water was the color of midnight ink. A succession of walls, fences, overgrown shrubs and trees on the other side blotted out light from the streets above. With the cloudy, moonless night, the towpath was enveloped in darkness.

Cassie came around a bend and saw soft lights encircling a sign painted on the side of a building – *Camden Lock Market*. A flight of stairs led from the towpath up to the market. Dekker was waiting for her at the bottom of the stairs. Cassie stopped in front of him, staying out of his reach. He had a gun in his right hand.

"That it?" he asked, pointing to the case she was carrying.

Cassie nodded. "As promised."

"Open it."

"No."

He took a step toward her. "I said open it."

Cassie held her ground. "It's for Lord Tresch, not you. I'll open it for him."

He stuck out his hand, reaching for the case. "I'm to make sure you really have the Codex."

"And if I don't?"

"I'll kill you and throw your body in the canal."

Cassie sighed, dropped the case to the pavement, then shoved it with her foot.

"Have it your way. Do it yourself." Dekker glanced at the case, then at Cassie, his brow furrowed for a moment, hesitating. "C'mon. Let's get this over with. There's a latch on the front. Even someone as stupid as you can open it."

Glaring at her, he dropped to one knee, set his gun in front of him and tilted the case with both hands. In a flash, Cassie had the Glock aimed at Dekker.

"Hands and knees," she told him. He looked up at her and started to make a grab for his gun. "Do it. Please. Do it so I can blow your fucking head off."

"Bloody hell, bitch."

"Bloody right, dumb shit. Hand and knees, then scoot back." Dekker crawled five feet away from her. "That's far enough. Turn around." Cassie pocketed his gun, a Sig Sauer P226 9 mm., and picked up the case. "Take me to Tresch and if you try anything or if anything has happened to Jake or Gabriel or if I just get tired of looking at your fat ass, I'm going to put a bullet in your spine. Now, move."

Dekker led Cassie past a parade of shops, restaurants and bars all closed for the night until they reached a storefront for a tea shop on the outer edge of the shopping district. They continued around to the rear of the building. Dekker entered a code on a keypad and a double garage door opened.

Inside was the black Mercedes sedan Dekker had used when he drove her into the city for the ransom exchange. She touched the hood. The engine was cold. Next to it was a BMW i8, a low-slung power-house sports coupe. The hood was warm, the engine still ticking. The tinted windows prevented her from seeing inside.

"Whose car is that?" Cassie asked.

Dekker shook his head. "The Pope's. Fuck if I know. Over here." He nodded toward an ancient freight elevator with wooden doors that opened top-to-bottom instead of side-to-side. He pushed them apart, stepped in and turned around, facing her. "You wanted to see Tresch. This is how we do it."

Cassie waved her gun at him. "Face in the corner, hands in your back pockets. Turn around before I tell you and…"

"Yeah, yeah, yeah. You're gonna put a bullet in me spine. Don't miss because you won't get a second chance," he said.

Cassie pulled the elevator doors closed and examined the control panel. There were only two buttons, B and G. They were on the ground level. She pushed B. The elevator descended, gears whining, the car swaying like a swing in a breeze until it came to a stop. She opened the doors and backed out into a short, wide corridor that ended at the intersection with another hallway.

"Okay," she told him. "Out you go. Nice and easy. Keep your hands where I can see them." Dekker faced her, hands raised chest high, grinning like he'd won the lottery. "What are you so happy about?"

Cassie felt the barrel of a gun against the back of her neck.

"He's just glad to see me," Lady Liliane Tresch said. "Put your gun and the briefcase on the floor. And do not doubt for one second that I'll pull the trigger if you refuse."

She jammed the barrel of her gun into the base of Cassie's skull. Cassie silently cursed herself for having let Lady Tresch fool her.

"I believe you," she said and set both down.

"Uhh," Dekker said. "She's...ah... got another gun."

"Is that right, Cassie?"

Cassie nodded. "It's Dekker's. I made him give it up."

"Dekker, really now," Lady Tresch said. "How could you?"

He blushed and clenched his jaw. "Won't happen again, m'lady."

"I should think not. Cassie, don't be difficult. You know what to do."

Cassie took the Sig from her jacket pocket, holding it by the barrel, and laid it next to the Glock. As soon as she stood, Dekker smacked her across the face with the back of his hand. The blow staggered her, but she kept her feet. He raised his hand to hit her again.

"That's enough for now," Lady Tresch said. "You'll have another chance soon enough. Come along, Cassie. It's time for our reunion."

They walked side-by-side. Dekker followed, his gun trained on Cassie.

"So, you were in it from the beginning," Cassie said.

"In it," Lady Tresch said with a chuckle, "I was the beginning. It was my idea. I cultivated Malcolm Bridges and provided all the information necessary to steal the Magna Cartas. Then, I made sure the Trustees saw me as the hardliner who'd never pay a dime of ransom because I knew they didn't have the balls to say no. That allowed me to reluctantly go along when they gave in to our demands."

"And your ugly divorce, was that part of the plan?"

"Not at first. I loathe my husband and he returns the favor. But that doesn't mean we can't be useful to one another. When I broached the subject, he jumped at the opportunity. We both needed the money, despite any outward appearances. I came up with the plan and he had the underworld connections to recruit our team. Then we told our lawyers to escalate our war so that no one would suspect that we were working together."

"How does someone in your position suddenly turn to crime?"

"Oh, this wasn't my maiden voyage, dear. I've done many things you wouldn't approve of. That's how I achieved my position. But, ransoming the Magna Cartas has given me enough money to live a quiet, luxurious life away from all these pompous Lords and Ladies."

"As long as your husband doesn't cheat you out of your share."

"I assumed from the start that he would try so I made certain that Dekker would be fiercely loyal to me by paying him twice what he did and by seeing that his appetite for young girls was always satisfied."

Cassie wanted to puke at the thought of Dekker and those poor girls but she held her revulsion and anger in check.

"Except Dekker didn't save you when those men forced you into that car after the costume ball. Your husband called it an unamicable settlement of your divorce."

"I called it a pleasant drive with Dekker's cousins. They took good care of me and told my husband what he wanted to hear."

"Is that your BMW in the garage?"

"Yes. My newest toy. Dekker called me as soon as he knew you were on the way with the Codex and I came right over."

"Lord Tresch will be surprised to see you."

"And that," Lady Tresch said, "is what makes for a good reunion."

Cassie thought for a moment. "Was stealing the Codex always part of the plan?"

"No, but I wasn't surprised when Dekker told me about it. My husband couldn't stand that I was the one who'd put the job together. He always had to prove that he was smarter and bolder than me. I would never have agreed to taking such a foolish risk. And I never would have let you and your friends leave the castle alive."

"Your husband tried to kill us but it didn't work out for him," Cassie said.

Lady Tresch shook her head. "Sometimes I think he'd fail at falling down."

"Was the money worth having Malcolm Bridges and the Library

guards murdered?"

She stopped, put her hand on Cassie's arm and stared at her with cold, steely eyes.

"They're dead, aren't they. I was protecting what was mine."

"Is that what you'll say when Dekker kills us?"

"No, my dear. I'll simply say goodbye."

SIXTY-THREE

ady Tresch led Cassie to the edge of the vaulted catacomb chamber where Lord Tresch was waiting. They were in the shadows beyond the perimeter, able to see without being seen.

The all brick chamber was a hundred feet across, the ceiling surrounded by supporting pillars. Tresch was opposite Cassie, pacing and looking at his watch.

Jake was propped against a pillar on her right, his hands and feet bound with rope. A man with an AR-15 semi-automatic rifle slung across his chest stood close by. She remembered him as the one who'd pulled her from the wrecked limousine thinking she was dead.

Gabriel was to her left, lying on the ground near the far edge of the chamber. Another guard she recognized from Culzean Castle was next to him, his rifle at his side, rubbing the bruised jaw she'd given him.

"You first," Lady Tresch told her. "Have your moment and then I'll have mine."

Followed by Dekker, Cassie stepped into the circle of light. Tresch stopped pacing.

"At last," he said. "Bring the case to me, Dekker."

She ignored Tresch and ran to Gabriel, kneeling at his side. His eyes were closed. His cheeks were grey, his breathing shallow. A small pool of blood had collected beneath his leg and the wound had a pungent, infected odor. She held his hand and whispered.

"Gabriel, it's me."

He opened his eyes. "You came back."

"I told you I would. I'm going to get you out of here."

He took a deep breath and coughed, his chest rattling. "Come closer."

She leaned in, her ear next to his mouth. "Kill the son-of-a-bitch for me."

"Of course."

She kissed his forehead, then stood and watched as Dekker held the Codex case in his arms in front of Tresch like an offering. Tresch released the latch and opened the case. A vein popped in his forehead as he pawed at the foam liner, then ripped it out and knocked the case to the floor. He marched toward Cassie, fists clenched at his side.

"Where is the Codex?"

Cassie said. "You didn't think I was going to give it to you just so you could kill us. Let us go. I'll call you in an hour and tell you where you can find it."

Tresch signaled to the two men who trained their rifles on Gabriel and Jake.

"Tell me or watch them die."

Cassie looked at Jake. "What do you think, partner? Is he bluffing?"

Jake's eyes lit up. "Partner, huh?" Cassie smiled and nodded. "He's bluffing. He knows that if he kills Gabriel and me, there's no way you'll tell him. If he wants the Codex, his only play is to let us go."

"And, if I'd rather kill you than have the Codex," Tresch said, "who holds the winning hand?"

Jake sighed. "You do. A hundred million pounds is a nice pot."

Lady Tresch came into the chamber. "Make that fifty million."

"Liliane!" Tresch gasped, "you're…you're…"

She walked up to him. "I believe the word you're looking for is alive. Yes, I'm alive, thanks to Dekker. My investment in him paid off more than my investment in you. My god, William, you are such a fool. If you'd done what I told you instead of trying to outdo me with the Codex, this would all be over. We'd each have more than enough money. But you had to have it all and then some and now I have to clean up your mess yet again."

Cassie said, "You may not be giving him enough credit. If he was willing to have you killed so he could keep the money, he might have hedged his bets and moved it where you can't find it."

Eyebrows raised, Lady Tresch studied Cassie, then looked at Lord

Tresch. "Is there something you want to tell me about the money, William?"

He crossed his arms over his chest. "No, of course not. It's all there. I make no apologies for what I did. You're an insufferable cunt and the sooner I'm through with you, the better. And, don't tell me you wouldn't have done the same thing if you'd have been smart enough to think of it."

She raised a finger. "Let's hold that last thought for a minute. Show me the money."

Cassie looked at Gabriel who'd turned his head toward her. She tapped her chest and cleared her throat. He nodded and began coughing, softly then building to a hacking spasm. She rushed to his side, putting herself between him and the guard.

He winked, then whispered, "I've got a bit left in the tank when you make your move."

Tresch opened his phone and pulled up the website for the Cayman Island bank where the ransom had been wired. Lady Tresch stood by his side. Color drained from his face as the page for their account opened and showed a zero balance.

"That's impossible...it can't be...it's gone...all of it...gone." He started toward Cassie. "You bitch! You did this! Where's my goddamn money!"

Lady Tresch stepped in front of him. "I should be asking you that question, William."

"Me? Me? I didn't do anything with it?" He pointed at Cassie. "She did it."

Cassie stood, angling her side to the guard. "It wasn't me. I didn't have the account information and, even if I did, I wasn't authorized to access the funds. Weren't the two of you the only ones that could do that?"

Bits of spittle flew from Tresch's mouth as he shook his fist at Lady Tresch. "Then it had to be you. I didn't steal the money. You did it to get even with me for...for..."

"Trying to murder me," Lady Tresch said. "Not my style. I would have just killed you and then all the money would have been mine."

Tresch stiffened his back and stuck his chin out at her. "You don't have the balls."

"Really, William. I guess you don't know me as well as you thought."

She drew her gun and shot him in the throat, hitting his jugular vein. A geyser of blood exploded from his neck, raining down on Lady Tresch, as he collapsed to the floor.

Cassie whirled toward the guard next to her, crushing his windpipe with her elbow. The other guard raised his rifle, ready to open fire from across the chamber. Dekker put two rounds in his head, then spun and aimed at Cassie as Gabriel pulled himself up in front of her, taking Dekker's bullet in his chest. Cassie wrestled the guard's rifle from his grasp, firing a burst that traced an arc from Dekker's belt to his neck. His body fell at Lady Tresch's feet.

Cassie slammed the butt of the rifle against the guard's temple, knocking him unconscious. She held the rifle waist high and pointed it at Lady Tresch.

"Give it up. The money's gone."

Lady Tresch wiped her husband's blood from her eyes and did a slow turn around the chamber. She nudged Lord Tresch's body with her shoe and nodded. Dropping to one knee, she squeezed Dekker's hand and closed his eyes.

"Leave the gun on the floor," Cassie said. "It's over."

Lady Tresch struggled to her feet and looked at her.

"You're wrong, dear. It's almost over," she said.

Then she stuck the gun barrel in her mouth and pulled the trigger.

"Noooo," Cassie cried.

She flinched, turned away and bent over, hands on her knees, stunned. Breathing deeply, she gathered herself and knelt next to Gabriel. He was alive. She pressed her hands against the sucking wound in his chest to stem the bleeding.

"Hang on," she said, "You're going to make it."

He put his hand on hers and shook his head. "It's okay."

Tears ran down her cheeks as she pressed harder. "No. It's not okay."

"Listen to me," he said, his voice feeble and raspy. "I'm sorry for everything. Jake's a good man. Hang on to him."

She nodded, unable to speak. His hand fell away from hers and he died. She held him for a moment, then crossed the chamber to Jake.

"Gabriel?" he said. She shook her head. "I'm so sorry."

She took his face in her hands and kissed him long and deeply, then untied him and kissed him again, their arms wrapped tightly around each other. She pulled away, leaned her head against his for a moment, then helped him up.

"C'mon, partner, we've got a lot to do."

SIXTY-FOUR

Inspector Murdoch surveyed the catacomb chamber. Cassie and Jake stood next to him. She had given Murdoch a quick summary of what had happened when she called him, filling in more details when he arrived.

Forensic technicians were taking measurements and photographs and were marking shell casings and other pieces of evidence with numbered yellow plastic triangles. The surviving guard had been taken to the hospital for evaluation of his head injury. The bodies were covered with sheets.

"It's a slaughterhouse, isn't it?" Murdoch said. "Four dead and one concussed, plus those three unfortunate British Library guards whose bodies we found in another chamber. And I'm left with the two of you to sort it all out."

"We can explain everything," Jake said.

"I don't doubt that," Murdoch said. "The question is whether any of it will be true."

He drove them to Scotland Yard and put them in separate interrogation rooms. After watching them through the one-way mirrors in each room, he decided to begin with Cassie. He joined her and placed a tape recorder on the table.

"You haven't asked for a lawyer," he said.

"I don't need one."

"And you haven't asked to call anyone. Why is that?"

"There's no one to call."

"You're wanted for questioning in the warehouse murders. You ran from me in the British Library last night. Today, you're hip-deep in dead bodies. Are you certain you don't want a lawyer or to call anyone?"

"Positive. Do you want me to tell you everything or not?"

Murdoch turned the recorder on. "Talk to me."

For the next hour, she took him through the last five days except for two details she kept to herself.

"And that's when I called you," she said when she finished.

Murdoch sighed. "By your account, that was half an hour after the shooting ended. What were you doing during that time?"

"Trying to collect ourselves and find our way out of the catacombs so we could get a cell signal. The place is a maze."

"Yes, it runs beneath the entire Camden Lock Market. Used to be for stabling horses, I'm told. The entrance from the garage behind the tea shop doesn't appear on any maps. Turns out that Lady Tresch owned the property." He thought for a moment. "Ian Thorpe claims that you stole the Codex Leicester."

"I stole the case that it was in. I left the Codex behind."

"And used the case to bluff Lord Tresch."

"Yes."

"Then why go to the trouble of stealing the case? Why not buy a briefcase and tell him that it was for the Codex?"

"Because there was a label inside the case that said it was the property of the Gates Foundation and that it contained the Codex. The bluff couldn't have worked if Tresch didn't believe I really stole it, which I didn't. I left it inside the shipping crate. You can check with the Library."

"We did. And it's as you said. The Codex was found in the shipping crate and Ian Thorpe has been asked for his resignation. Tell me again about the ransom money."

"Like I've told you the first three times you asked, it found its way back to the Magna Carta Trustees account. What else is there to know?"

"Someone had to know the wire instructions when the ransom was paid. I take it that was you." She nodded. "You must have memorized it when Mrs. St. James gave it to Sir Robert."

Cassie nodded again. "Anything else you'd like to know?"

"Perhaps the identity of the person who sent the money on its way."

"All I can tell you is that he's not subject to the UK's jurisdiction."

"I suppose I shall have to take your word for it."

"Then I'm free to go?"

Murdoch stood. "Not because I think you're innocent. I'm just not certain what you're guilty of beyond stealing the Codex case. The Crown Prosecutor would throw me out of his office if I brought him that charge. He'll be much happier knowing that we solved Malcolm Bridges' murder as well as the ones at the warehouse and that we avoided a national scandal with the Magna Cartas."

"What about Jake?"

"I've no doubt that he'll vouch for your story but I'll give him a chance anyway."

Cassie waited for Jake on a bench across the street from Scotland Yard. An hour later, he ran to her, dodging honking cars, picked her up and spun her around, both laughing. He set her down.

"Where to, partner?" he asked.

"The Library. Sir Robert is waiting for us."

***

JAKE, CASSIE and Sir Robert sat with Sarah St. James in her office.

"I don't know how to thank you," Sir Robert said. "I regret terribly that I lost confidence in you. Please forgive me. I've expressed my gratitude to Prometheus and told him what a wonderful job the two of you did."

"Thank you," Cassie said. "And you should thank Sarah for retrieving the Codex and putting it back in the shipping container."

"Is that so," he said. "Where was it?"

Sarah said, "Cassie hid the Codex in an abandoned tube station on York Road."

"I didn't give her much time to go get it, either," Cassie said. "I knew that Inspector Murdoch wouldn't believe I'd only stolen the case. Sarah had to return it to the shipping crate to back up my story."

"Tell me," Sir Robert said. "Would you really have turned the Codex over to Lord Tresch?"

"To save Jake and Gabriel's lives? Without a doubt."

"As would I." He turned to Sarah. "You've had quite an adventure this last week."

"I've had my fill of adventure. I'll be glad to return to my boring curating duties."

"I'll see to it that you get a nice raise for all you've done. There is one thing I don't understand, Cassie. Why did your man in Iceland... what's his name?"

"Gunnar," she said.

"Yes, Gunnar. Why did he only return eighty-five million pounds of the ransom. What happened to the other fifteen?"

"We thought the Trustees would want to set up trust accounts for the survivors of the three library guards."

"Five million pounds for each sounded right. You're very generous people," Jake said.

Sir Robert smiled. "Indeed, we are."

***

CASSIE AND JAKE STOOD on the balcony outside their tenth-floor suite at the George V Hotel in Paris. They'd checked in two days ago after leaving London. It was near midnight. They were wearing the hotel's plush bathrobes and nothing else. The breeze was refreshing. The city spread out below sparkled and glowed. Jake poured them each a glass of wine.

"Here's to a weekend in Paris spent making love and ordering room service," he said. Cassie's cellphone was in the bedroom behind them. It rang four times before quieting. "I'll bet that's Prometheus again. He's called you half a dozen times since we got here. Eventually, you're going to have to answer."

"I briefed Gunnar on what happened and he said he would send Prometheus a report. I'm not ready for anything else."

"Why not tell him that so he'll leave you alone."

"Because he won't. He'll insist I come to the island to talk about what he did to Gabriel and me."

"His terms. His territory. I get that but you can say no."

"You're right except that's the only way he does things. He won't apologize. He'll say he did it for my own good and that he'd do it all over again."

"What will you tell him?"

"That he's a cruel old man and that what he did was unforgiveable."

"Will you quit or ask him about the next job?"

She looked at him, hesitating. "I don't know."

Jake put his hands on her waist. "What will you tell him about us?"

"He already knows that you helped recover the Magna Cartas and the ransom money."

"I'm not talking about that. I'm talking about you and me teaming up. Prometheus will never go for that. You can't trust him after what he did to you and Gabriel. He'll do the same to us or worse. So, the hell with him. Let's go out on our own. People who need us will find us."

"Oh, Jake. You make it sound so simple when it's not."

"Don't tell me Prometheus made you sign a non-compete agreement or that he's like the mob where there's only one way out."

"I didn't sign anything and Prometheus would never hurt me."

"You can't be sure. If you're not with him, he could see you as a threat either because you might give away his secrets or use them against him."

Her phone rang again. She recognized the ring tone.

"It's Gunnar." Cassie walked into the bedroom and answered, putting the call on speaker. "Hello."

Gunnar said, "You remember Costin Pretescu, the fence you killed in Bosnia?"

"That was a long time ago."

"Not long enough for his brother, Lucian. Since Costin died, he's been looking for his killer and someone put him on your trail."

"How do you know that?"

"I monitor anyone who might be a problem for us. I've been on Lucian Pretescu since Bosnia. In the last couple of days, he's been bragging on the dark web that he knows who killed his brother and that he's going to even the score. He knows where you're staying and he's coming for you. Get out. Now," Gunnar said and ended the call.

"It's a bluff." Jake said. "You're telling me that after all these years, the brother pops up hot on your trail. C'mon. Prometheus put Gunnar up to it. He wants you to run back to him so he can protect you. Once you do that, he owns you."

"Maybe, but I trust Gunnar." She went to the balcony and looked down at the street in front of the hotel. Two black SUVs pulled up. Eight men got out and headed for the lobby. "Get dressed."

They pulled on their clothes and opened the door. Their suite was at the end of the floor across from the entrance to a stairwell. The hallway was empty.

"What did I tell you," Jake said. "It's a bluff."

The elevator door opened and two black-clad men got off carrying handguns at their sides.

"I don't think so. Quick. Take the stairs."

They pushed through the door. Cassie started to go down but Jake stopped her and motioned her to one side.

"They expect us to run. Let's switch it up."

Jake braced himself against the wall behind the door. Seconds later, when the first man came through, Jake shoved the door back at him, knocking him toward Cassie. She grabbed him by the arm and flipped him over the rail. The second man followed. Jake let him pass, then kicked his legs out from under him, sending him tumbling to the next landing.

Cassie leaned over the rail. The first man had fallen ten flights. They continued down to the second man who was unconscious but alive. Cassie scooped up his gun as the stairwell door one flight below opened and two more of the men looked up at them.

Jake tugged on Cassie's sleeve. "Let's back up."

They returned to the tenth floor and ran for the service elevator in the middle of the floor. They got on but their pursuers were left to pound on the doors as they closed. Cassie hit the button for the lobby.

"I saw eight of them get out of their cars," she said. "They've split up into pairs. If the first two didn't get us in our room, the others would cover the stairwells and the entrances."

Jake stopped the elevator at the fourth floor. "This is where we get out."

She followed him into the corridor. "Why? We're no better off here."

Jake pulled the fire alarm on the wall. "We need company."

They ran up and down the hall, pounding on doors, shouting *fire, fire*. As guests stumbled out of their rooms, they herded them into the stairwell. When the stairs were clogged, Jake and Cassie joined them, emerging into the lobby that was packed with guests making their way outside. Firemen going the other direction pushed through the crowd in search of the fire while hotel staff urged everyone to remain calm.

"Did any of those guys look like he could be Petrescu's brother?" Jake asked when they reached the sidewalk across the street from the hotel.

Cassie shook her head. "All I saw were four guys that could have been Slavs or Romanians or Russians or who knows what."

Jake pointed to four men dressed in black standing together near the hotel entrance. "Did they look like those guys?"

Before Cassie could answer, one of them saw her and took off toward them with the other three close behind.

"Let's get out of here," she said.

"Hold on. What are they going to do? Gun us down in the middle of the street in front of all these cops and firemen?"

"What are you suggesting?"

"That we stop doing what they expect us to do. C'mon."

Jake headed toward the nearest policeman and tapped him on the shoulder.

"Do you speak English?" The cop rocked his hand back and forth, meaning a little bit. "How about this." He pointed toward the advancing men and shook his finger at them, then turned to the cop. "Those guys are going to blow up the Eiffel Tower."

The cop's eyes got wide. He let loose a flurry of French into his radio and ran toward them. The foursome stopped in their tracks and took off in the opposite direction.

"Well done," Cassie said.

"I guess I was wrong about the bluff," Jake said. "But I wasn't wrong about Prometheus. He and Gunnar were the only people that knew where we were staying. We even checked in under fake names to make sure no one bothered us. You said you trust Gunnar. That means Prometheus gave you up."

Cassie looked at Jake. "I guess we just went out on our own."

A NOTE FROM THE AUTHORS

Thanks for adding *All Gone* to your library. Readers depend on readers to recommend good books, and authors depend on readers to generate positive word of mouth for their books. If you liked *All Gone*, please leave a review on Amazon, Goodreads, or any other online platform of your choosing, even if it's only a few words. It will make a big difference, and Joel and Lisa will be very thankful.

ABOUT THE AUTHORS

Photo © 2017 Meghan Doll

Joel Goldman is the bestselling author of the Lou Mason thrillers, the Jack Davis thriller, the Alex Stone thrillers and, with Lisa Klink, the author of the Ireland & Carter thriller series. Together with Lee Goldberg, he founded Brash Books where they publish the best crime novels in existence. He was a trial lawyer for twenty-eight years. He wrote his first novel after one of his partners complained about another partner, prompting him to write his first thriller, kill the son-of-a-bitch off in the first chapter and spend the rest of the book figuring out who did it. And he never looked back.

Photo © 2012 Kat Shadian

Lisa Klink started her career in the world of *Star Trek*, writing for *Deep Space Nine* and *Voyager* before coming back to Earth for shows such as *Martial Law* and *Missing*. In addition to writing for television, she's scripted a theme park attraction and authored graphic novels, short stories, and three novels in The Dead Man series. Klink is also a five-time champion on *Jeopardy*.

www.ingramcontent.com/pod-product-compliance
Lightning Source LLC
Chambersburg PA
CBHW02123325062626
47155CB00008B/2988